HARDCASTLE'S QUARTET

Graham Ison

This first world edition published 2014
in Great Britain and the USA by
SEVERN HOUSE PUBLISHERS LTD of
19 Cedar Road, Sutton, Surrey, England, SM2 5DA.

Trade paperback edition published
in Great Britain and the USA 2015 by
SEVERN HOUSE PUBLISHERS LTD

Copyright © 2014 by Graham Ison.

All rights reserved.
The moral right of the author has been asserted.

British Library Cataloguing in Publication Data

Ison, Graham author.
  Hardcastle's quartet.
  1. Hardcastle, Ernest (Fictitious character)–Fiction.
  2. Police–England–London–Fiction. 3. Murder–
  Investigation–Fiction. 4. Great Britain–History–
  George V, 1910-1936–Fiction. 5. Detective and mystery
  stories.
  I. Title
  823.9'14-dc23

ISBN-13: 978-0-7278-8420-6 (cased)
ISBN-13: 978-1-84751-530-8 (trade paper)

Except where actual historical events and characters are being
described for the storyline of this novel, all situations in this
publication are fictitious and any resemblance to living persons
is purely coincidental.

Typeset by Palimpsest Book Production Ltd.,
Falkirk, Stirlingshire, Scotland.

GLOSSARY

ACK EMMA: signallers' code for a.m. (*cf* PIP EMMA)
APM: assistant provost marshal (a lieutenant colonel of the military police)

BAG CARRIER: an officer, usually a sergeant, deputed to assist the senior investigating officer in a murder or other serious enquiry
BAILEY, the: Central Criminal Court, Old Bailey, London
BAILIWICK: area of responsibility
BEAK: a magistrate
BEF: British Expeditionary Force in France and Flanders
BRIEF, a: a warrant *or* a police warrant card *or* a lawyer *or* a barrister's case papers
BUCK HOUSE: Buckingham Palace

CARNEY: cunning, sly
CHESTNUTS OUT OF THE FIRE, to pull your: to solve your problem
CHINWAG: a talk
CID: Criminal Investigation Department
CLYDE (*as in* D'YOU THINK I CAME UP THE CLYDE ON A BICYCLE?): to suggest that the speaker thinks one is a fool
COMMISSIONER'S OFFICE: official title of New Scotland Yard, headquarters of the Metropolitan Police
CULL(E)Y: alternative to calling a man 'mate'

DAPM: deputy assistant provost marshal
DARTMOOR: a remote prison on Dartmoor in Devon
DDI: Divisional Detective Inspector
DSC: Distinguished Service Cross

FLUFF, a bit of: a girl; an attractive young woman
FOURPENNY CANNON, a: a steak and kidney pie
FRONT, The: theatre of WW1 operations in France and Flanders

GANDER, to cop a: to take a look
GPO: General Post Office
GREAT SCOTLAND YARD: location of an army recruiting office
and a military police detachment. Not to be confused with New
Scotland Yard, half a mile away in Whitehall
GUV *or* **GUV'NOR:** informal alternative to 'sir'

HACK: the driver of a Hackney carriage *or* a taxi *or* the vehicle
itself *or* a newspaper reporter
HALF A CROWN *or* **HALF A DOLLAR:** two shillings and
sixpence (12½p)

JIG-A-JIG: sexual intercourse
JILDI: quickly (*ex* Hindi)

KC: King's Counsel: a senior barrister

MANOR: a police area
MATELOT: a sailor, usually of the Royal Navy
MC: Military Cross
MONIKER: a name or nickname
MONS, to make a: to make a mess of things, as in the disastrous
Battle of Mons in 1914
MUFTI: army officers' term for plain clothes (*ex* Arabic)

NICK: a police station *or* prison *or* to arrest *or* to steal

OLD BAILEY: Central Criminal Court, in Old Bailey, London

PICCADILLY WINDOW: a monocle
PIP EMMA: signallers' code for p.m. (*cf* ACK EMMA)
PLANTING, a: a burial
PROVOST, the: military police

ROYAL A: informal name for the A or Whitehall Division of the Metropolitan Police

ROZZER: a policeman

SAM BROWNE: a military officer's belt with shoulder strap

SAPPERS: the Corps of Royal Engineers (in the singular a member of that corps)

SCREWING: engaging in sexual intercourse *or* committing burglary

SHIFT, to do a: to run away, or escape

SILK, a: a King's Counsel (a senior barrister), named after the silk gowns they wear

SKIP *or* SKIPPER: an informal police alternative to station-sergeant, clerk-sergeant and sergeant

SMOKE, The: London

SOMERSET HOUSE: formerly the records office of births, deaths and marriages for England and Wales

SOV or SOVEREIGN: one pound sterling

STUFF GOWN: a barrister who has not been elevated to King's Counsel status

TOBY: a police area

TOD (SLOAN), on one's: on one's own (rhyming slang)

TOPPED: murdered or hanged

TOPPING: a murder or hanging

WAR HOUSE: army officers' slang for the War Office

WAR OFFICE: Department of State overseeing the army (now a part of the Ministry of Defence)

WHITE-FEATHER JOHNNY: man avoiding military service

YOUNG SHAVER: a youth or young man

ONE

I
t had started to rain. Not very much, but enough to prompt Police Constable Harold Barnes to curse before removing his glazed waterproof cape from its belt hook and fastening it around his shoulders. As the rain increased, he sought some shelter and, making his way to the doorway of 29 Whilber Street, he stopped under the portico. The section sergeant had visited Barnes ten minutes ago outside the Royal Mews and he would not be round again for at least an hour. Barnes decided, therefore, that it was safe to have a smoke and took out his pipe.

It was just as he was filling it with his favourite Country Life smoking mixture that he happened to glance down into the basement area. It was then that he saw the body of a woman.

Shoving his unlit pipe back into his pocket, Barnes pushed open the cast-iron gate and descended the few steps into the basement. The body was face down, head to one side. On closer examination, he saw that it was the body of a young woman with long black hair attired in a bust-bodice corset, black art silk stockings and one black glacé court shoe. And nothing else. Barnes knelt down and felt for a pulse, but the woman was dead.

Returning to pavement level, he withdrew his whistle from beneath his cape and blew three short, sharp blasts.

Minutes later PC Ben Holroyd, who was on the neighbouring beat, rounded the corner at a run. Breathless, he skidded to a halt.

'What's up, Harry?'

'Got a stiff, Ben,' said Barnes, pointing down into the basement area. 'Looks like a suicide.'

'Ain't you the lucky one?' Holroyd laughed. Both he and Barnes knew that it would involve Barnes in a considerable amount of report writing. 'I'll leg it back to the nick and call out the cavalry.'

Barnes returned to the portico and took out his pocketbook. Licking his pencil, he began to write his report. *On Wednesday 12th June 1918 at 6.32 a.m. at 29 Whilber Street, London, S.W., 1*

discovered the body of a woman in the basement area. Descending
to the location, I ascertained that she was dead.

Barnes spent the next twenty minutes recording such details that
he knew would be asked for by the CID officers deputed to investigate
the matter. He noted the position of the body, the fact that one shoe
appeared to be missing, and that the body had been almost dry when
he found it. He paused thoughtfully and licked his pencil again before
adding the time that the rain had started to fall.

The weather in that June of 1918 was cooler than was to be
expected. Although at one point reaching 77 degrees Fahrenheit,
the north-east wind kept temperatures generally lower than usual
and over an inch of rain fell. Of greater concern than the weather,
however, was the fact that 25 million people had died worldwide
as a result of the Spanish influenza pandemic, more than the
combined losses of the war that was grinding slowly to its bloody
close on the Western Front.

But on that Wednesday the twelfth of June it was matters closer
to home that were troubling Divisional Detective Inspector Ernest
Hardcastle of the A or Whitehall Division of the Metropolitan Police.
And he was in a foul mood.

The onset of this ill temper had occurred at breakfast when he
mildly enquired why there was no marmalade, a query that had
caused his wife to launch into a lecture about the shortage of jam
in general and marmalade in particular.

'According to the *Daily Mail*,' explained Alice, 'there's a shortage
of oranges to make the marmalade with. I would've made plum jam
instead, but the heavy rains destroyed a lot of this season's crops.
And plums have shot up from sixpence a pound to half a crown,
so there's no plum jam either. Disgraceful, I call it.'

'It's the war.' Hardcastle wished he had not asked about the
marmalade, and returned his attention to the morning newspaper.

But matters only got worse when Hardcastle reached the tram
stop. Apart from the rain, the tram that usually took him from
Kennington Road to Westminster was stationary and showed no
signs of moving. The conductorette was standing on the step of
the tram. As her small audience of disgruntled passengers
increased, she explained that the tram ahead had been in collision
with an army lorry and that the soldier driver had been slightly

injured; it was an accident that Hardcastle condemned as 'damned carelessness' on the part of the military. Bringing his policeman's mind to bear, he decided that as the tram was on fixed tracks and the lorry was not, the fault must rest with the army driver.

Hardcastle stepped into the road. The first cab to come along was a hansom, numbers of which had increased of late due to petrol shortages and the fact that many motor drivers were at the Front. But Hardcastle had no intention of going to work in a horse-drawn conveyance. He waited for a motor cab.

'Whitehall, cabbie, and don't take all day about it.'

'What's up with you, mister? Get out of the wrong side of the bed this morning?' growled the driver as he yanked down the taxi-meter flag.

On the brighter side, that morning's newspaper carried reports of the fighting on the Western Front. Allied troops – British, Empire, French and American – were now largely out of their trenches and fierce battles were swinging back and forth between Compiègne and Montdidier.

Finally arriving at Cannon Row police station, Hardcastle swept into the front office. The police station was immediately opposite the forbidding structure of New Scotland Yard, constructed to Norman Shaw's plans from Dartmoor granite hewn, fittingly, by convicts from the nearby prison that took its name from its bleak Devon surroundings.

The station officer stood up. 'All correct, sir.'

'I'm glad you think so,' snapped Hardcastle, irritated by the formal report that officers were obliged by the regulations to make, whether all was correct or not. 'Anything I should know about?'

'Yes, sir. PC 107 has found the dead body of a woman in a basement in Whilber Street. Sergeant Marriott is on the scene already, sir.'

'What are the details?'

'According to 107, sir, it looks as though the deceased fell from a first-floor window.'

'It'll be either accident or suicide, I suppose,' said Hardcastle. 'Where's Mr Rhodes?' Rhodes was the detective inspector in charge of the CID for the Cannon Row subdivision. 'Is he up there?'

'No, sir, he's dealing with a break-in at a jeweller's shop in Artillery Row, sir.'

'Dammit!' exclaimed Hardcastle. 'I'd better go up to Whilber Street and take a look, I suppose. And to cap it all, Skipper, I've come out without my tobacco pouch.'

The DDI walked out to Parliament Street and called in at the tobacconist to buy an ounce of St Bruno tobacco before hailing a cab.

When Hardcastle arrived in Whilber Street, he was greeted by Inspector Joplin, the patrolling officer. Standing nearby were Detective Constables Henry Catto and Basil Keeler, and PC Barnes. PC Holroyd was also there, having returned to Whilber Street with Inspector Joplin.

'All correct, sir,' said Joplin, saluting.

'Who found this here body, Mr Joplin?' asked Hardcastle as he raised his umbrella.

'PC 107 Barnes, sir,' said the inspector. 'He's a good officer.'

'Pleased to hear it,' muttered Hardcastle in response to this gratuitous piece of information. He did not think that one had to be a 'good officer' to come across a dead body. Glancing at Catto and Keeler, he frowned. 'What are you two supposed to be doing?'

'Waiting for orders, sir,' said Catto nervously. Although he was a competent detective, Catto was always apprehensive in the DDI's presence.

'Start knocking on doors, then,' snapped Hardcastle. 'Find out if anyone knows anything. You shouldn't have to be told what to do.' And with that inadequate instruction, he walked across to join Marriott.

'Good morning, sir.' Charles Marriott raised his bowler hat. As a detective sergeant (first class) he was the officer Hardcastle always selected to assist him in murder enquiries. Not that there was any evidence of murder in this case. At least, not yet.

'Tell me the tale, Marriott,' said Hardcastle, declining, as always, to return the sergeant's greeting.

Marriott briefly described the circumstances under which PC Barnes had found the body. 'I noticed that a first-floor window was wide open, sir, and called at the house. There's a young maid there by the name of Hannah Clarke. She told me that she works for a Mrs Georgina Cheney, but that Mrs Cheney was not at home, even though she should've been. It looks as though our body is likely to be that of Mrs Cheney. The maid told me that Mrs Cheney's husband is a Commander Robert Cheney, Royal Navy.'

'Is he there?'

'No, sir. Miss Clarke thinks he's at sea.'

'Has she identified the body as being this here Mrs Cheney?'

'No, sir. She was so upset at the thought that it might be her mistress that I deemed it unwise to involve her.'

'Very wise, Marriott. Don't want her crying her bloody eyes out all over our evidence. I'll have a word with her later on. Have you sent for the divisional surgeon?'

'Yes, sir. He's down in the basement now, having a look at the body.'

'Who is it?'

'Doctor Thomas, sir.'

'Well, he's no bloody good. Send for Spilsbury.'

'Already done, sir.' Marriott knew that the DDI would want Dr Bernard Spilsbury to attend this latest suspicious death. 'But can we be sure that it's not an accidental death? Or even suicide?'

'It's murder, Marriott, until someone tells me it ain't,' said Hardcastle, and descended to view the body for himself.

'A nasty one, Inspector,' said Dr Thomas, glancing up as Hardcastle joined him.

'And your opinion, Doctor?' Hardcastle spoke in a detached way, paying more attention to studying the dead woman's face than listening to a medical practitioner in whose findings he placed little faith.

'Undoubtedly died as a result of falling out of the window,' said Thomas, and stood up.

'Well, we'll see about that,' said Hardcastle. 'But Dr Spilsbury's on his way.'

'Oh? Is that really necessary?' asked Thomas, taking the DDI's comment as a slight on his professional judgement.

'Don't hurt to have a second opinion,' rejoined Hardcastle tersely, and left Thomas to put his paraphernalia away in his Gladstone bag.

As Hardcastle returned to street level, a cab drew up and Dr Bernard Spilsbury alighted. Attired as usual in morning dress with a cape and a top hat, he was a tall, austere figure of a man with a commanding presence.

Dr Thomas gave Spilsbury a brief nod and climbed into the cab that the pathologist had just vacated.

Although only forty-one years of age, Spilsbury enjoyed a formidable prestige in the field of forensic pathology. The *cause célèbre* that brought him to the notice of the public had occurred four years previously. His evidence in what became known as the Brides-in-the-Bath case was instrumental in proving categorically that George Joseph Smith had murdered three of his wives, thus negating the defence argument of accidental drowning. It was that notorious series of murders that had established Spilsbury's reputation. Thereafter, whenever defence counsel learned that Spilsbury would be appearing for the Crown, they would spend hours reading learned works on causes of death before subjecting him to cross-examination.

'Ah, good morning, Hardcastle,' said Spilsbury, as the DDI raised his hat. Ignoring the increasing rain, he swept off his hat and handed it, together with his cane, to Police Constable Holroyd. 'I'm told you have a cadaver for me.'

'Indeed, sir,' said Hardcastle, and opened the gate leading to the basement area.

Descending the half-dozen steps, Spilsbury knelt beside the body and conducted a number of tests. Still kneeling, he made a few notes on the back of an envelope. 'When did it start raining?' he enquired of no one in particular.

'Twenty-five past six, sir,' said PC Barnes, who had been leaning over the railings watching Spilsbury at work.

'Splendid,' said Spilsbury. 'You've got a good man there, Inspector. Very observant.'

'So I've been told,' muttered Hardcastle.

'The cadaver's almost dry,' Spilsbury continued, 'and I'd estimate the time of death to be at least eight hours ago, but I may change that view after I've conducted the post-mortem examination. Perhaps you'd be so good as to have it covered.'

'And the cause of death, sir?' asked Hardcastle.

'My first impression is that death was a result of falling from that window,' said Spilsbury cautiously as he pointed up at the open window that had previously attracted Marriott's attention. 'On the other hand, my dear Hardcastle, if it was the fall that had caused this young woman's death I'd've expected there to be some blood surrounding the cadaver. But there's none. However,' he continued, standing up and brushing his knees, 'I'll be able to tell you more when I've had the opportunity to examine the cadaver more closely. Be so good as to have it sent to the usual place.'

'Very good, Doctor.' Hardcastle knew that Spilsbury always carried out his post-mortem examinations at St Mary's Hospital at Paddington.

'I'll examine the unfortunate woman this afternoon,' said Spilsbury as he retrieved his hat and cane from PC Holroyd.

'Call the good doctor a cab, lad,' said Hardcastle.

'Yes, sir,' said Holroyd, and stepped into the roadway as he sighted a taxi.

'Mr Joplin.'

'Sir?'

'Be so good as to arrange for the removal of the body to St Mary's Hospital at Paddington,

'Very good, sir,' said Inspector Joplin.

That matter put in hand, Hardcastle turned to Marriott. 'And now we'll have a word with the housemaid. What was her name again, Marriott?'

'Hannah Clarke, sir.'

'Ah, yes, that's the girl.'

It was some time after Hardcastle had hammered loudly on the knocker of the Cheneys' house that the frightened face of Hannah Clarke appeared round the door.

'I'm Divisional Detective Inspector Hardcastle of the Whitehall Division, lass.'

'Oh, sir, I saw all the policemen outside. What on earth has happened?' asked the housemaid as she bobbed a curtsy. Dressed in standard domestic uniform, she wore a floor-length dress, apron and a lace coronet cap beneath which her blonde hair was swept up into a tight French roll.

'I think we'd better come in,' said Hardcastle.

'Yes, sir, of course,' said Hannah and led the detectives towards the kitchen.

'I think we'll use the drawing room, Hannah.'

'I'm not sure the mistress would like that, sir.'

'I doubt she'd mind in the circumstances, lass.' Hardcastle opened the door to the drawing room and marched in. 'Now, then, you just sit yourself down.'

'Are you sure, sir?' The idea of taking a seat in the drawing room was clearly alien to the young girl.

'It'll be all right, Hannah,' said Marriott. 'How old are you?'

'Er, nineteen, sir,' said Hannah, after a pause, but remained standing.

'Have you worked for Mrs Cheney for long?

'A year come next month, sir.' It was, however, a statement that was subsequently proved to be untrue.

'Now, lass, d'you have a photograph of your mistress anywhere?' Hardcastle asked.

'Yes, sir,' said Hannah. Crossing to the escritoire, she handed a framed studio portrait to Hardcastle. 'I dusts it every day, sir,' she added with a smile.

'I'm sure you do, lass,' said Hardcastle. After studying the image for a few seconds, he passed it to his sergeant. 'What d'you think, Marriott?'

'That's her, sir.' Marriott returned the frame to the housemaid.

'I'm sorry to have to tell you that a body has been found in the basement, Hannah. Judging by this photograph it would appear to be your mistress,' said Hardcastle as gently as he could.

'Oh, the poor woman.' Hannah Clarke emitted a sob that quickly became a flood of tears, and felt in her pocket for a handkerchief.

'Do you live here, lass?' asked Marriott. 'Or do you come in every day?'

'No, I live in, sir,' said Hannah between sobs. 'I've got a very nice room on the top floor, but I don't know what I'll do now. I suppose I'll have to try for another position.'

'And where does Mrs Cheney sleep?' asked Hardcastle.

'She has a bedroom on the first floor, sir. At the front.'

'Perhaps you'd show us, then.'

Hannah stood up, still dabbing at her eyes with her handkerchief, and led the way upstairs.

The bedroom into which the maid showed the two detectives was a large, airy room, and contained a double bed that, although slightly crumpled, showed no sign of having been slept in. The other furniture comprised a large rosewood wardrobe, a matching dressing table adorned with a hairbrush, pots of face cream and other cosmetic items. In front of the dressing table was a satin-covered low-backed chair. A basin and ewer stood on a marble-topped washstand in one corner. A pink satin *peignoir* had been thrown carelessly on a chaise-longue and there was a single black glacé kid shoe on the floor near the bed.

'Did you make this bed this morning, Hannah?' asked Hardcastle.

'No, sir. This is the first time I've been in here since yesterday morning.'

'That's a high window sill, sir,' observed Marriott. 'Bit difficult to fall out of it accidentally, I'd've thought.'

'So would I, Marriott,' said Hardcastle, moving across the room. He had rapidly come to the conclusion that Georgina Cheney had been pushed rather than fallen accidentally. He examined the window sill closely, but found nothing that would assist in his investigation. Nevertheless, he decided against saying anything in the presence of the distraught maid.

They returned to the drawing room on the floor below.

'How about you make us a nice cup of tea, lass,' said Hardcastle. 'I expect you could do with one yourself.'

'Very good, sir,' said Hannah, and disappeared.

'What d'you think, sir?' asked Marriott.

'I don't think she fell accidentally; the window sill's too high,' said Hardcastle, confirming what Marriott had said earlier, 'but I suppose it's possible she committed suicide. There again a woman committing suicide would either take both her shoes off, or leave 'em both on.' For a moment or two he pondered that intriguing enigma. 'But we'll have to wait and see what the good doctor has to say about it.'

'We'll have to do something about getting hold of Mrs Cheney's husband, sir,' said Marriott. 'The maid told me that he's in the Royal Navy and she thinks he's at sea.'

'That'll mean a trip to the Admiralty,' said Hardcastle. 'At least it'll make a change from dealing with the army.'

The maid came back into the room bearing a tray of tea. Marriott moved a small table so that she could set it down.

'That's what we need to cheer us up, lass,' said Hardcastle. 'Ah, I see you've found some ginger nuts. They're my favourite.' He leaned forward and took a biscuit. 'You told my sergeant earlier this morning than Mrs Cheney's husband is in the navy, Hannah.'

'Yes, sir. The commander's in one of them big ships with Admiral Beatty. At least, I think that's what the mistress said.'

'I don't suppose you know where that ship is, do you?' asked Hardcastle, brushing biscuit crumbs from his jacket.

'No, sir. The mistress said as how it's secret and no one had to know.'

'Very wise of her,' said Hardcastle. 'Where's your tea, lass?'

'I thought I'd better have mine in the kitchen, sir. It don't seem proper having it in here.'

'I think we can make an exception in the circumstances, Hannah. You go and fetch your cup and bring it in here.'

'If you're sure, sir,' said Hannah. She returned a few moments later and stood awkwardly in front of the two CID officers.

'Now you sit yourself down,' said Hardcastle, 'and tell us all about your mistress.'

'She was always very good to me, sir.' Hannah finally yielded to Hardcastle's suggestion and perched uncomfortably on the edge of an armchair, giving an impression of embarrassment at being invited to sit down in one of the family's reception rooms. 'She'd often give me sixpence to go to the Bioscope in Vauxhall Bridge Road. As a matter of fact, I was there last night. I saw that Charlie Chaplin in *A Dog's Life*. It was ever so funny.'

'He used to live just down the road from me,' said Hardcastle, biting into another biscuit.

'Gosh!' said Hannah, and stared at Hardcastle in open-mouthed admiration, as though that made him as famous as the little tramp that Chaplin depicted so well.

'But it was a good twenty years before I moved in,' explained the DDI.

'Did your mistress have many visitors, Hannah?' asked Marriott, determined to shift his DDI away from reminiscing.

'I don't know as how I ought to say, sir.'

'Now look, lass,' said Hardcastle. 'Mrs Cheney's dead and no harm'll come to you for speaking out, but it might help me to find out exactly what happened to her.'

'Well, sir, there was one or two gentlemen callers, but the mistress said that they was friends of the commander's and that they was taking her out to the theatre on account of her being lonely what with the commander being at the war.'

'D'you happen to know the names of any of these gentlemen, Hannah?' asked Marriott.

'No, sir, the mistress never let on, but it weren't none of my business anyway. But they was all very nice gents.'

'Were any of them in uniform?' asked Marriott.

'One of them was in the navy and another was in army uniform.

He told me he was a pilot. But there was a couple what was wearing ordinary clothes. Not uniforms, I mean.'

'Did one of these gentlemen happen to call last night, before you went off to see Charlie Chaplin?' asked Hardcastle.

'No, sir. I left here at about six o'clock.'

'And what time did you get back?'

Hannah glanced guiltily at the DDI, but remained silent.

'I'll bet you met a gentleman admirer, Hannah,' said Marriott gently, immediately recognizing the reason for the girl's reticence. 'A pretty girl like you must have lots of admirers.'

Hannah blushed. 'He's a footman from one of the houses down the road, sir,' she said, casting her eyes down. 'After the pictures we went for a walk down Vauxhall Bridge Road and looked in the shops. It must've been about ten o'clock before I got back here.'

'And you have a key, I presume.'

'Yes, sir. The mistress was very good and she always said it was so as I could let myself in without disturbing her. There's no other staff here, you see. On account of the war. Mrs Cheney told me that the butler joined up in 1914 and got hisself killed.'

'And when you got home did you see Mrs Cheney?'

'No, sir. I thought she'd be in bed so I went straight up to my room.'

'Did you hear anything?' asked Hardcastle. 'Any unusual noise, perhaps.'

'No, sir, nothing. To tell the truth I was quite tired out and I went straight to sleep.'

'You said you had a key, Hannah,' said Marriott. 'Which way did you come in?'

'By the front door, sir. The mistress told me always to come in that way. Anyhow, the basement door's locked up and bolted from the inside. The mistress don't like the idea of anyone being able to get in that way, not with the commander being away.'

'And you didn't look down into the basement when you came in, I suppose.'

'No, sir. I never thought to.'

'Have you done any cleaning this morning, Hannah?' asked Marriott suddenly.

'Cleaning, sir?'

'Yes, Hannah. I imagine you have a set routine for doing the housework.'

'Oh, I see, sir. There wasn't much to do. Just an empty bottle and two glasses on the table there.' Hannah pointed at the occasional table on which the tea tray was now resting.

'What did you do with them?'

For a moment the young housemaid looked mystified by the question. 'Well, I threw the bottle in the dustbin, and washed the glasses and put them away, sir,' she said, as though that was the obvious thing to have done.

'Where is the dustbin?'

'It's in a cupboard in the kitchen, sir.'

'How does it get collected, then? You said the basement door is locked and bolted.'

'Yes, it is, sir, but I have to move it out into the basement every Friday. That's the day the dustmen come.'

'Show Sergeant Marriott where you put the bottle, Hannah,' said Hardcastle, realizing why Marriott had posed the question.

'It's all right, sir, I'll get it,' said Hannah, springing to her feet.

'No, let Sergeant Marriott pick it up, lass.'

Moments later, Marriott returned with the bottle in a paper bag. 'I'll get this across to Fingerprint Branch, sir.'

'I think that'll be all for the time being, Hannah,' said Hardcastle, as he stood up. 'But in the meantime, don't do any more cleaning up. A fingerprint officer will be here later.'

'If you say so, sir, but what am I to do now, now that the mistress is . . .?' Hannah could not bring herself to complete the sentence, and gave a convulsive sob.

'The best thing is for you to stay here. I'll get in touch with Commander Cheney and I've no doubt that he'll be able to come home straight away.' A thought occurred to Hardcastle as he reached the door of the drawing room. 'Did Commander and Mrs Cheney have any children, Hannah?'

'Yes, sir. There's Roland, he's twelve and away at Dartmouth training for the navy, and young Tom is at Eton. He's ten.'

TWO

D r Bernard Spilsbury was standing in the centre of the white-walled examination room at St Mary's Hospital in Praed Street, Paddington.

'I've had occasion to revise my original view of the cause of death, my dear Hardcastle. The woman was strangled.'

'I knew that that Doctor Thomas didn't know what he was talking about,' muttered Hardcastle.

'Who?' Spilsbury raised his eyebrows.

'He's the divisional surgeon who reckoned death was a result of falling from the window. He was leaving as you arrived.'

'I'm sure he came to that conclusion with such evidence as was available to him at the time,' said Spilsbury, unwilling to criticize a fellow member of his profession, whatever his private thoughts might have been. 'But as I said this morning it was the lack of blood surrounding the cadaver that caused me to revise my opinion. The woman was already dead when she fell from the window. Or should I perhaps say when she was *pushed* from the window? But that, of course, is your preserve rather than mine, Hardcastle.'

'You see, Marriott, I said it was murder.' Hardcastle glanced at his sergeant with a satisfied smile. 'Your estimate of the time of death, sir?' he asked, turning back to Spilsbury.

'As I implied at the scene, my dear Hardcastle, about ten last night, or to be on the safe side shall we say between ten and midnight,' said Spilsbury. 'Death was due to strangulation by firm application of the assailant's thumbs to the carotid arteries, and the thyroid cornu was fractured. I would suggest that the killer was a man, confirmed by the fact that sexual intercourse had recently taken place. Now the rest is up to you.'

'Thank you, Doctor,' said Hardcastle. 'We'd better go and find the bugger now, I suppose.'

The cab set down the two detectives outside the Admiralty in Whitehall.

'Pay the cabbie, Marriott, and don't forget to take the plate number.'

'Yes, sir.' It was a requirement that a claim for the cost of using a licensed motor Hackney carriage had to be accompanied by the plate number. But Marriott knew that; it was something of which the DDI had reminded him every time they hired a cab.

'I want to see someone in the records department,' Hardcastle announced to the uniformed custodian at the entrance to the Admiralty.

'If it's about your pension you're in the wrong place,' said the custodian. He glanced at Hardcastle's moustache. 'Royal Marines, was you? That's in Stamford Street, Lambeth.'

'I'm a police officer,' snapped Hardcastle, thrusting his warrant card in the man's face. 'And you can direct me to an officer who can deal with my enquiry. Now!'

'Oh, I do beg your pardon, sir,' said the custodian, immediately adopting a craven attitude and revolving his hands around each other in a washing motion. 'Fred, show these gents up to Lieutenant-Commander de Courcy's office,' he shouted, turning his head.

A messenger emerged from a small cubbyhole. 'This way, gents.' He led Hardcastle and Marriott through a number of labyrinthine passages and up a flight of stairs. He knocked on the door of de Courcy's office and opened it. 'Two gents from the police to see you, sir,' he said.

The tall figure of Hugo de Courcy limped across his office with hand outstretched. 'It's Inspector Hardcastle unless I'm much mistaken, and Sergeant Marriott.'

'Indeed, Commander,' said Hardcastle as he shook hands. 'It must be all of two years since we last spoke. You've got a good memory.'

'I see you've acquired another half stripe since we were here last, Commander,' said Marriott. 'And a Distinguished Service Cross,' he added, nodding at the blue and white ribbon on de Courcy's jacket.

'And much good it's done me,' said de Courcy bitterly. 'I eventually got a seagoing appointment in the old *Cornwallis* and lost a leg when she was torpedoed off Malta in January last year. Consequently I was sent straight back here to my old job. Fortunes of war, I suppose,' he added as he returned to his desk and sat down awkwardly. 'However, enough of my grousing. Take a seat and tell me how I can help you.'

'I'm investigating the murder of a Mrs Georgina Cheney, Commander. She's the wife of Commander Robert Cheney who—'

'Good God!' exclaimed de Courcy, cutting across what Hardcastle was saying, 'but I know Bob Cheney. What happened, Inspector?'

Hardcastle explained the circumstances under which Cheney's wife had been murdered. 'It's necessary for the commander to be contacted as quickly as possible,' he continued. 'And there's the added complication of his two sons: one is at Dartmouth and the other is at Eton, so I'm told by the Cheneys' housemaid. They'll have to be told, but it'd be better if their father was to do it.'

'Yes, yes, of course,' said de Courcy, rapidly making notes on a pad. 'I'll get a signal off to his ship straight away.'

'Is he serving far away, Commander?' asked Marriott.

'I shan't know which ship he's in until I make some enquiries, but I couldn't tell you even if I did know. Official secrets and all that.'

'You've no idea how long it'll be before he gets back to London, then?' said Hardcastle.

'I'm afraid not,' said de Courcy. 'We might be in luck if he's serving in home waters or he's at a stone frigate in the UK.'

'What in hell's name is a stone frigate?' asked the DDI.

De Courcy laughed. 'It's what the navy calls its shore establishments, Inspector. Usually a naval barracks.'

'Damn funny business,' muttered Hardcastle.

'I'm afraid the navy's a bit like that,' said de Courcy. 'I've no doubt you have some esoteric practices in the police.'

'That's a fact, Commander,' muttered Hardcastle with feeling. 'It would be helpful if you could ask Commander Cheney to call at Cannon Row police station before he goes home to Whilber Street, and then I can explain what's what.'

'Yes, of course. I'll keep you informed, especially if there seems to be a problem.'

It seemed that Lieutenant-Commander de Courcy had not met with any problems in contacting Commander Cheney, and neither had he wasted any time. At half past eight the following morning an elderly constable appeared in the doorway of Hardcastle's office just as the DDI was filling his first pipe of the day.

'There's a Commander Cheney downstairs, sir. He says as how you want to see him.'

'Show him up, lad.' Hardcastle always addressed constables as 'lad' regardless of their age. 'And ask Sergeant Marriott to step in.'

A minute later, the somewhat dishevelled figure of a naval officer arrived in the DDI's office, his cap tucked beneath his left arm. His uniform was worn and appeared not to have been pressed for some time. The three gold-lace rings on each sleeve were tarnished, as was his cap badge, and his medal ribbons, including those of the Boer War, were faded.

'Robert Cheney, Inspector. You'll have to excuse my rig, but I've come straight from Scapa Flow. Hell of a journey, starting with a crossing from the Orkneys to Inverness and then the night train to Euston.' He dumped a small suitcase on the floor.

'You'd better sit down before you fall down, Commander,' said Hardcastle. 'I dare say you could do with a cup of tea.'

'That would be most welcome.' Cheney took out a cigarette case. 'D'you mind?' he asked.

'Not at all,' said Hardcastle, at last lighting his pipe.

'I'll arrange for the tea, sir,' said Marriott, and left the office in search of the police station matron.

'I'm sorry that you've come home to bad news, Commander,' said Hardcastle, never very polished when it came to offering condolences.

'Strange business, war,' said Cheney reflectively. 'One usually expects that one's wife would be the recipient of bad news, not the other way round. Incidentally, the Admiralty didn't tell me exactly what happened. Was it an air raid?'

For a moment or two, Hardcastle was taken aback. 'I'm afraid your wife was murdered, Commander,' he said.

Slack-jawed, Cheney stared at the DDI. 'Murdered!' he eventually managed to utter.

'There's no doubt of it. Dr Spilsbury, the leading pathologist, is adamant that she was strangled,' said Hardcastle, and went on to relate the circumstances under which Georgina Cheney's body had been found in the basement area of 29 Whilber Street.

'My God! But who would have done such a thing?'

'That's what I'm endeavouring to find out.'

Marriott reappeared in the office followed by the police station matron.

'I've brought your tea, sir,' said the matron, 'and I managed to get you some ginger biscuits.'

'That's very kind of you, Mrs Cartwright,' said Hardcastle as he dropped a few pennies on the matron's tray. 'How's your boy?'

'Doing very well, sir, thank you. He's a battery quartermaster sergeant now. I was going to talk to you about his future when you've got a moment.'

'I'll be happy to do so, Mrs Cartwright, but I'm a little busy right now. Perhaps later today.'

'Of course, sir.' Bertha Cartwright picked up her tray, nodded to Commander Cheney and left the office.

'I'm sorry about that, Commander,' said Hardcastle as he handed Cheney a cup of tea. 'Bertha Cartwright's an absolute gem, but she doesn't always know when to pick the right time for a chat.'

'I've got a coxswain like that,' said Cheney absently, and stared out of the window.

'If I'm to find out who murdered your wife, Commander, I'm going to have to ask you some personal questions.'

'Carry on, Inspector.' Cheney turned his gaze back to the DDI and spooned sugar into his tea.

'I've been told that your wife was seeing other men.' Hardcastle saw no point in evading the issue. Being a naval officer, Cheney was presumably accustomed to straight talking, even about his private life.

'Who the hell told you that?' demanded Cheney angrily, but immediately apologized. 'I'm sorry, Inspector. I know you're only doing your job.' For a moment or two he paused pensively. 'Our marriage wasn't always harmonious after the present conflict began; I suppose you could call it one of the casualties of war,' he said, without elaborating. 'I'm a career sailor and during the thirteen years of peace between the South African wars and the outbreak of this one I was stationed in Malta. At least, for ten of them. And that's where I met and married Georgina. She was the daughter of a senior diplomat.'

'Must have been an enjoyable time,' said Hardcastle, intent on getting the naval officer to reveal more of his personal life.

'Oh, it was, but in a sense it was unrealistic too. The nights were hot and our social circle comprised a charming group of people: navy, army and the civil service, and one or two businessmen. There were society balls where the champagne flowed and we danced into

the small hours. It was an idyllic time and I suppose Georgina
imagined that that sort of life was the way it would always be for
a naval officer's wife. And then the bloody war started,' he added
bitterly.

'Is that when your wife returned to London, Commander?' asked
Marriott.

Cheney turned, as though seeing the sergeant for the first time.
'She didn't return; she arrived here for the first time. She was born
in Malta, d'you see. It was in November 1913 actually, after I was
ordered to join HMS *Dreadnought* with the Grand Fleet. Of course
the boys, Roland and Thomas, were both born in Malta, and it was
a bit of a shock for the three of them to move to a cold England.
I'm afraid it was a particularly sobering experience for Georgina,
coming to a London that she didn't know at all, and where she had
no friends.'

'I understand that your two sons are away from home,' said
Marriott.

'Yes. Roland's at Dartmouth and Thomas is at Eton. I suppose
that that, and my own absence, left Georgina with time on her
hands. But I didn't know of any other men in her life. What made
you think that, Inspector?' Cheney turned back to Hardcastle.

'Policemen have this habit of picking up gossip,' said Hardcastle,
unwilling to identify Hannah Clarke, the Cheneys' maid, as his
source. Neither did he intend to tell Cheney that Spilsbury had
discovered that Georgina had indulged in sexual intercourse just
before her death.

'Well, if that's all I can help you with, Inspector, I'd better see
about telling the boys what's happened to their mother. Not something I look forward to doing. The thing I most need now is a hot
bath and a change of clothes. I've been granted compassionate leave
and I'll be at Whilber Street for the next few days if there's anything
else I can assist you with.'

'I've spoken to your maid, Commander, and she did mention
seeking another position,' said Hardcastle, 'but I suggested that
she remain there until you got home.'

'Thank you,' said Cheney, and nodded vaguely. 'I've not met the
girl.' He picked up his suitcase and left the room, a much saddened
man – as much from the death of his wife as the prospect that she
might have been unfaithful.

'Have Catto and Keeler come up with anything from the Cheneys' neighbours, Marriott?' asked Hardcastle.

'They're in the office waiting to see you, sir.'

'Fetch 'em in, then,' said the DDI, relighting his pipe. 'Well?' he barked, when the two detective constables entered.

For once Henry Catto was more confident than usual in the DDI's presence, probably because he had something worthwhile to report. But that feeling did not last long.

'Basil and I—' Catto began, but got no further.

'Who the hell's Basil?' demanded Hardcastle.

Catto immediately regressed to the nervous state that the DDI usually brought on. 'Er, I mean DC Keeler, sir.'

'Well say so, Catto. I can't be expected to know the Christian names of my detectives. You're damned lucky I know you're called Catto.'

'Yes, sir,' said Catto, now in a state of complete nervous flux. 'DC Keeler and I called at several houses on either side of 29 Whilber Street, sir, and one or two opposite. The occupant of number twenty-eight, immediately across the road from the Cheneys' house, a very nice lady called Mrs Winifred Curtis, was quite informative.'

'I hope you're about to be as well, Catto. For God's sake get on with it.'

'Yes, sir. She told me that she has seen gentlemen callers at the Cheneys' house on several occasions.'

'Times?'

'Usually in the late evening, sir. Sometimes at about seven, more often quite a bit later.'

'What sort of men were they?'

'One was in army uniform, one in the navy, and one in civilian clothes, sir.'

And that was exactly what Hannah Clarke had told him when he had interviewed her. Hardcastle leaned back in his chair. 'It seems that Georgina Cheney had a busy social life after all, Marriott. So much for the commander's claim that she had very few friends. She certainly seems to have made up for lost time since her husband went to sea.'

'This Mrs Curtis seems to spend a lot of time gazing out of her window, sir.'

'She's the sort of neighbour I like, Marriott,' said Hardcastle, 'so long as she doesn't live anywhere near me. I think we'll pay her a visit.'

Winifred Curtis primped her upswept hair as she opened the door and smiled at the two detectives. She was an elegant woman, probably in her late forties, early fifties even, and was attired in a peach silk afternoon gown despite it being only half past ten in the morning. But in the DDI's experience the war had slowly brought about the abandonment of dress conventions and people had started wearing whatever they liked whenever they liked.

'Good morning, madam.' Hardcastle raised his hat. 'We're police officers, but there's nothing for you to worry about.' Since 1914, he had learned that the arrival of the police at the door of someone who may have relatives in the armed forces usually heralded bad news.

'I suppose you've come about that poor Georgina Cheney,' said Mrs Curtis, as she showed the detectives into the drawing room. 'Two very nice young policemen came here yesterday. Henry and Basil they were called. We had a cosy little chat about all sorts of things over a cup of tea.'

'I see.' Hardcastle preferred not to know that his detectives had wasted their time taking tea and indulging in 'a cosy little chat'. 'I'm Divisional Detective Inspector Hardcastle of the Whitehall Division, madam, and this is Detective Sergeant Marriott.'

'How very nice,' murmured Mrs Curtis. 'I dare say you could do with a nice cup of tea too. Please sit down.'

'Thank you, Mrs Curtis, tea would be most welcome.'

Mrs Curtis leaned across and rang a small brass tea bell. Moments later a maid appeared in the doorway and bobbed.

'Perhaps you'd bring us some tea, Lottie, my dear. And the biscuits.'

'Yes, ma'am,' said Lottie and disappeared.

'I'm lucky to have that girl,' said Mrs Curtis. 'It's so difficult to get decent staff since the war began, you know. Most of them go off to make munitions and get paid twice as much as I could afford to pay them.'

'I'm sure you're right, madam,' said Hardcastle.

'My last maid left to become a wine waitress at Liverpool Street

Station of all places. I never realized that they had wine waitresses at railway stations. It's quite remarkable what the women of this country are doing these days. D'you know, Inspector, I had a young lady come here the other day to sweep the chimneys, and she was quite well-spoken too.' Winifred Curtis prattled on unabated. 'I really can't see that Mr Lloyd George will be able to avoid giving women the vote after this dreadful war's over. Not that I agree with what that Mrs Pankhurst was doing. Throwing bricks through windows isn't going to achieve anything.'

'I'm sure you're right, Mrs Curtis, but we were talking about Mrs Cheney,' said Hardcastle, intent on stemming the flow of the woman's incessant twittering. 'I'm told by my detectives that she entertained gentlemen friends.'

'I suppose that's what some would call it,' said Mrs Curtis, with a toss of her head, but paused as the maid returned. 'Ah, the tea. Put it down over there, Lottie my dear.'

'I've brought some ginger snaps like you said, ma'am,' said Lottie.

'That nice young Henry of yours told me that you'd probably pop in, Inspector, and he said that you were partial to ginger snaps.' Mrs Curtis smiled at Hardcastle.

'Indeed I am,' said Hardcastle. 'I must remember to give him a pat on the back.'

'He told me he was only a constable,' Mrs Curtis continued. 'I'm sure you ought to make him a sergeant.'

'It's not in my hands, madam.' If Hardcastle had his way Catto would never be a sergeant. 'You were going to tell me about Mrs Cheney's visitors.'

'Was I?' Winifred Curtis looked vague. 'Oh yes, of course.' She leaned forward in the manner of a conspirator. 'There was one young man wearing army uniform, and another time there was a sailor. I'm not sure about the man in ordinary clothes; he might have been one of the others who'd changed out of uniform.'

'How old were these men, Mrs Curtis?' asked Marriott, looking up from his pocketbook.

'Ah, now that I think about it, perhaps the civilian man was a bit older. Yes, I'm sure it couldn't have been one of the others in mufti. That is what the soldiers call civilian clothes, isn't it?'

'I believe so,' said Marriott, somewhat impatiently. 'But what were their ages?'

'The soldier and the sailor couldn't have been more than thirty, I suppose, if that; probably younger. Yes, now I think about it, they were definitely younger. It was difficult to see without my binoculars.'

'Your binoculars?' queried Hardcastle. 'Why would you need binoculars?'

'To spot enemy aeroplanes, of course. We usually keep them here, but my husband sometimes takes them with him when he goes on duty.'

'Is your husband in one of the forces, madam?'

'Sort of. He's a major in the army, but he's very busy recruiting.'

Hardcastle failed to see why a recruiting officer should need binoculars, but decided to let it drop; it was difficult enough extracting some useful information from Winifred Curtis.

'Did you see any of these men calling at Mrs Cheney's house last night, madam?' asked Marriott.

'Last night . . .' Mrs Curtis adopted a thoughtful expression. 'Yes, I believe I saw the civilian man call there at about nine o'clock. I remember thinking to myself that it was rather late. Not socially acceptable really, not for a gentleman caller. Particularly when the lady of the house is there alone. And she is alone, you know. I didn't know whether to feel sorry for her or despise her. Consorting with men while her husband was away. I mean it's not the sort of thing one expects of a—'

'Did you see this man leave?' Hardcastle, becoming increasingly irritated by the woman's vacillation, cut across what she was saying.

'No, I didn't. You see Cuthbert came in at about half past nine and we sat chatting. Cuthbert's my husband, Inspector. I went up to bed at about a quarter past ten, but Cuthbert stayed down here reading the paper. I don't know what time he came to bed. I was fast asleep, which makes a change. I sometimes have a terrible job sleeping, you know. I'm always worried in case there's another of those dreadful air raids.'

'Can you describe this man you saw last night, Mrs Curtis?' asked Marriott.

'Ordinary,' said Winifred Curtis, after giving the matter some thought.

'Could you be a little more specific?'

'He was wearing a suit, a dark suit. Oh and he had a hat. But he didn't have an umbrella. I particularly noticed that he didn't have an umbrella.'

'And his age, Mrs Curtis?' asked Marriott.

'Oh, I've no idea. I couldn't see him that clearly, not without my binoculars.'

'Did he arrive in a cab, Mrs Curtis?' asked Hardcastle.

'In a cab?' Mrs Curtis looked vague. 'I don't think so, but he might've done, I suppose. I mean he could have got out at the end of the street and walked the rest of the way, couldn't he?'

'Which recruiting office does your husband work at?' Marriott finally gave up his attempt to obtain a description of Mrs Cheney's caller. Unfortunately, it was probably her murderer.

'You'll find the major at the one in Whitehall,' said Mrs Curtis proudly, as though he could not possibly be anywhere less prestigious.

'Did you ever speak to Mrs Cheney?' asked Marriott.

'No. At least only occasionally. We'd sometimes exchange a few words if we happened to meet in the street.'

'Did she ever mention these callers of hers?'

'No, she didn't, and I didn't think it my place to ask. I'm not a busybody, you know.'

'Thank you, Mrs Curtis,' said Hardcastle, rising to his feet. 'And thank you for the tea. You've been most helpful.'

'It was my pleasure. And if there's anything else, I'm always here, and I enjoy a chat.' Winifred Curtis smiled, and rang for the maid. 'The gentlemen are just leaving, Lottie.'

'Ye gods!' exclaimed Hardcastle, once he and Marriott were in the street. 'That woman's barking mad.'

'I thought I'd ask where Mrs Curtis's husband worked, sir. If we can get him on his own, he might be able tell us more.'

'Quite likely, unless he's as scatterbrained as his wife,' said Hardcastle as he hailed a taxi. 'The recruiting office in Great Scotland Yard, cabbie. That's the turning by the Clarence pub, not the police headquarters.'

'I know where it is, guv'nor,' said the cabbie irritably, as he yanked down the taximeter. 'I've been doing this job for twenty years.'

Ignoring the cab driver's waspish riposte, the DDI settled himself in his seat. 'We'll see what the galloping major has to say about all this, Marriott.'

THREE

The complete absence of volunteers at the recruiting office at Great Scotland Yard, just off Whitehall, was an indication of the extent to which enthusiasm for the war had abated. In 1914, the British public thought that it would 'all be over by Christmas', and young men had flocked to the Colours for fear that they would miss the 'fun', as they had called it. But now they were wondering *which* Christmas would see an end to the conflict.

Countless millions of British, Empire, American and Allied troops had died in and around the blood-soaked killing ground that was no-man's-land. And as many Germans and Austro-Hungarians had perished too. But the reality was that little had been achieved by their sacrifice save the potential for field upon field of gravestones in a peace that had yet to come.

An elderly sergeant-major, his tunic bearing Boer War medal ribbons, was seated at a desk just inside the door. Possibly approaching sixty years of age, he was clean-shaven and had a rubicund countenance that seemed to betray a liking for gin. Glancing up as Hardcastle and Marriott entered the recruiting office, he spent a moment or two studying Hardcastle.

'If you'll forgive me for saying so, sir, I think you might be a touch too old to join up,' he said, before switching his gaze to Marriott. 'Although you might just qualify.'

'We're not here to enlist,' said Hardcastle sharply. 'We're police officers.' And he introduced himself and Marriott.

'I do beg your pardon, gentlemen. How can I help you?'

'I'm looking for Major Cuthbert Curtis.'

A tired smile crossed the man's face. 'Ah, you've been talking to my wife,' he said. 'I'm *Sergeant*-Major Cuthbert Curtis, at your service, gentlemen. I suppose you've come to talk to me about the unfortunate death of Georgina Cheney.'

'Indeed we have, Mr Curtis,' said Hardcastle, who long ago had learned that warrant officers should be addressed as 'mister'.

'My wife gets confused by military ranks, apart from which I think she believes there is some sort of social stigma attached to me not being an officer,' said Curtis, waving a deprecating hand. 'And I'm not really a sergeant-major anyway. I'm in the Territorial Force, but I'm a bit too old for active service now, although I did do my bit in South Africa. So this is the best I could offer to help the war effort. Not that there's much doing here nowadays; the country is war weary and the death toll is a deterrent.' He stood up and tugged at the bottom of his tunic. 'I'm a barrister in the real world,' he continued, 'but I give a day or two here when I can be spared from the demands of the Old Bailey. You'd better come into the office and we can have a chat in private.' He nodded to a corporal seated at another desk. 'Keep an eye on things, Fred, not that I think you'll have much to do.'

'Right you are, Cutty,' said the elderly corporal, another Territorial Force volunteer.

Curtis showed the two detectives into a cubbyhole of an office and offered them a couple of bentwood chairs. 'A very sad business, Georgina being killed like that.'

'What can you tell me about her, Mr Curtis?' asked Hardcastle.

'Not a great deal, I'm afraid, Inspector, even though we lived opposite her. Georgina was a real beauty, but I got the impression that she was rather lonely. I believe that she was born and brought up in Malta and came to London for the first time in 1913. Her husband is a commander in the navy and away at the war. And their two boys are away as well; at school, I suppose.'

'I spoke to Commander Cheney this morning,' said Hardcastle. 'He's been granted compassionate leave.'

'What a wretched homecoming for the poor man. He must be terribly cut up about it. How did it happen, Inspector?'

'She was murdered, Mr Curtis,' said Marriott.

'Murdered? But I thought it was a dreadful accident. I understood that she fell from the window.'

'We believe she was pushed out after being strangled,' said Hardcastle, deciding that he could be more open with a criminal barrister.

'You've got a tricky case on your hands, then, Inspector,' said Curtis thoughtfully.

'We spoke to your wife about an hour ago, sir,' said Marriott, 'and she mentioned having seen men calling at Mrs Cheney's house.

Apparently Mrs Curtis occasionally used binoculars to keep an eye on things, so she said. But she also said that you were in the habit of taking them with you when you went on duty and consequently she didn't have them with her last night.' The question of the binoculars was an irrelevancy, but he was interested to hear what Curtis would say about them.

Curtis slowly shook his head. 'We don't have any binoculars now, Sergeant Marriott. The Defence of the Realm Act forbids the purchase of them, and although the law didn't require it, I brought ours here at the beginning of the war and handed them over to the recruiting officer for safe keeping.' He paused. 'To be frank with you, I'm afraid my wife's mental health has been affected by the loss of our son Gregory. He was a pilot in the Royal Naval Air Service, but he was shot down and killed not far from his base in France early in 1915. She's not really been the same since.'

'I'm sorry to hear that, Mr Curtis,' said Hardcastle. 'Does that mean that your wife's information is unlikely to be of much value?'

'Not necessarily. I think Winifred probably did see what she said she saw. She spends a lot of her time gazing out of the window. The problem is that she refuses to accept that Gregory is dead, and I think she half expects to see him come marching up the road one day.'

'Your wife mentioned seeing a man calling at Mrs Cheney's house at about nine o'clock last night, but she didn't see him leave.'

'I don't doubt that she did, Inspector. I got in at about half past nine and Winifred went up to bed at just after ten. I spent an hour or so reading the evening paper and going over a brief for a rather complicated fraud case I'm due to appear in.'

'Did she mention having seen this man, Mr Curtis?'

'No, she didn't. Not that I'd've paid much attention even if she had.'

'Did you by any chance see the man leave, sir?' asked Marriott.

'I'm afraid not. I don't have much time for looking out of windows.'

'How well do you know Mrs Cheney?' asked Hardcastle.

'Not all that well, Inspector. I've called on her a few times in case there's anything I could do. I suppose you'd call it being neighbourly. It's not a happy state of affairs for a woman to be on her own, especially if she's suddenly faced with a domestic crisis,

like a fuse having blown or a tap washer needing to be replaced.
I'm sure you know the sort of thing I mean. And you can never get
people in to deal with minor repairs like that these days.'

'One other thing, Mr Curtis. If your wife should see any callers
at the Cheneys' house, perhaps you'd let me know.'

'Of course, but isn't that unlikely now that Georgina's dead?'

'Only if the caller doesn't know she's dead, and whoever they
are, they might be able to fill in a few gaps for me.' But Hardcastle
was really hoping that the murderer would call again, and profess
ignorance of the tragedy in an attempt to allay suspicion. He was
even more familiar with the habits of criminals than was the barrister.

'Yes, I understand.'

'What's more it might be necessary for me to mount an observation on the Cheneys' house. I wonder if you'd have any objection
to one or two of my officers doing so from your house.'

'None at all, Inspector. We'd be only too happy to help, and I'm
sure Winifred would welcome the company.'

'Well, thank you for your assistance, Mr Curtis,' said Hardcastle,
determined that if he were to select officers for an observation they
would not be Catto and Keeler. 'If you should think of anything
else, perhaps you'd contact me at Cannon Row police station.'

'Certainly, Inspector. Of course there's always a chance that we
might bump into each other at the Bailey.'

'Are you going to set up an observation, sir?' asked Marriott, as he
and Hardcastle entered the downstairs bar of the Red Lion public
house just outside New Scotland Yard.

'I'm thinking about it, Marriott, but I'll be able to think better
when I've had a couple of pints.'

'Morning, Mr Hardcastle.' The landlord wiped the top of the bar.
'Usual?'

'Yes, please, Albert. And a couple of fourpenny cannons while
you're about it.'

The next ten minutes were spent in silence as the two CID officers
sank their much needed pints, and consumed their steak and kidney
pies.

'D'you think an observation will turn up anything, sir?' asked
Marriott, brushing pie crumbs from his waistcoat.

'Two more pints, Albert, when you've a moment,' said Hardcastle, and turned to his sergeant. 'Wouldn't do any harm, Marriott. On the other hand it might be a good idea if Commander Cheney would agree to my putting a man inside his house rather than in the Curtises' house.'

'Mrs Curtis will be disappointed, sir. I think she's taken a shine to Catto.'

'More than I have,' muttered Hardcastle. He downed his second pint of bitter and wiped his moustache. 'In fact, I think we'll have a chat with the commander later this evening. There's no point in going now. If we turn up at about eight o'clock we might kill two birds with one stone, so to speak.'

When Hannah Clarke opened the door of the Cheneys' house in Whilber Street, she had replaced her maid's uniform with a rather fashionable maroon dress. And she made no attempt at a curtsy.

'Hello, Inspector. Please come in,' said Hannah, and led them into the drawing room.

'We've come to see the commander, Hannah,' said Hardcastle.

'He's gone, sir.' Hannah sat down opposite the detectives and arranged her skirt, making it clear that she had abandoned her inhibitions about sitting down in one of her employers' reception rooms.

'Gone?' Hardcastle raised his eyebrows.

'Yes, sir. He's returned to his ship. He had a telegram, you see. He just stayed long enough to have a bath and a change of clothing, and then he went off to see his sons the very next morning. I think he went to Windsor first to see Tom at Eton, and then to Dartmouth to break the news to his other son, Roland. He told me that he was going straight back to his ship from there.'

'But what about the funeral?' Hardcastle was amazed that the commander had returned to duty without waiting to bury his wife.

'The commander's been in touch with Harrods, sir. They're taking care of all the arrangements.'

'Is he coming back for the funeral?' Hardcastle found it hard to accept that a widower would absent himself from the interment of his late wife. It was something he failed to understand.

'No, sir. He said that his ship is about to sail – that was what the telegram was about – and he never wanted to miss the possibility of going into action.'

'What about the two boys?'

'He said that they wouldn't be going because it would interfere with their education. And he didn't reckon that a funeral was a place for young men anyway.'

'And when is the funeral to be, Hannah?'

'Thursday, the twentieth, sir. Ten o'clock down Brompton Cemetery.'

'Ten o'clock?' exclaimed Hardcastle. 'That's early for a funeral.'

'It was the only time that Harrods could fit it in,' said Hannah. 'The commander did say, though,' she continued, dismissing the matter of the funeral, 'that I was to let you have another look around if you wanted to, or help you in any other way. The master's promoted me to housekeeper, you see, and given me an extra twenty pounds a year.' Hannah smiled at her unexpected good fortune.

'You're a lucky girl, lass, being made housekeeper at your age.'

'Yes, I am, sir. The master's left me in charge of everything while he's away.'

'Well, Hannah, Sergeant Marriott and me would like to have another look round the house. There might just be something we missed when we were here yesterday morning.'

'If there's anything else I can do, sir, just let me know. In the meantime I dare say you could do with a cup of tea.'

'Thank you, Hannah, that would be most welcome.'

'I'll bring it in here when it's made, then,' said Hannah, and walked confidently from the room.

'I think young Hannah's promotion's gone to her head, Marriott,' said Hardcastle as he crossed the room and opened the escritoire. 'She's certainly become more confident of herself since we were here yesterday.'

Hardcastle spent a few minutes sorting through the contents of the escritoire. There was a collection of letters from Georgina's husband, one or two from her sons in a crabbed schoolboy hand, a household accounts book and several bills marked 'paid'.

Hardcastle replaced the letters in their respective pigeonholes and withdrew a leather-bound blotting book from beneath them.

'Ah! I think we have something interesting here, Marriott, and I'm sure it wasn't here yesterday when I looked. Listen to this: *"You might think that you can just abandon me, casting me aside like a toy what you've grown tired of. Well, I can assure you that I shan't let you go that easy. You're not in no position to dictate, not with a career what would be damaged if our little arrangement was to come out. And your wife would have something to say about it. So, unless . . ."* And that's it, Marriott; that's as far as she got. It looks very much as though she was murdered before she could finish it.'

'It seems as though Georgina Cheney was a blackmailer, then, sir, but a bit naive, putting her threats in writing.'

'That don't matter so much, Marriott, but it would've been useful to know who she was going to send this letter to. She was obviously interrupted, either by a caller or because young Hannah came into the room. But it gives us a motive to work on.'

'Perhaps she was interrupted by the arrival of the man she was writing to, sir, and that he then—'

'I'm not sure it was Mrs Cheney who wrote it, Marriott,' said Hardcastle, butting in sharply. 'It's not what you'd call an educated hand and the grammar ain't all that good. But let's not get ahead of ourselves.'

'No, sir.' Marriott knew that the DDI often jumped to a conclusion of that sort himself, but was rarely willing to accept a similar suggestion from others.

'There was an address book somewhere in the desk. I wonder if that'll shed any light on who she was writing to.' Hardcastle ferreted about in the escritoire once more. 'Ah, here we are.' He thumbed through the small book and let out a sigh of exasperation. 'Dammit! The pages A to C have been torn out.'

'That narrows the field a bit, sir,' said Marriott.

'I don't see how, Marriott.' Hardcastle stared at his sergeant. 'Bring that book with you; it might shed some light on Mrs Cheney's other beaus. In the meantime, I think we'll have another look upstairs.'

'Before we do that, sir, a man in army uniform has just approached the front door,' said Marriott, having glanced out of the window.

'Has he, by Jove! Looks like we're in luck.' Hardcastle moved swiftly across the room and dashed into the hall. 'Hannah!' he bellowed, as there was a loud rat-a-tat on the knocker. 'Quickly!'

'Whatever's happened, sir?' asked the newly appointed housekeeper, running upstairs from the kitchen.

'There's a man in army uniform at the door, Hannah. Show him in, but don't say anything about us being here.' And with that, Hardcastle retreated to the drawing room and closed the door.

When the young army officer was shown into the drawing room, Hardcastle and Marriott were standing in front of the fireplace.

'Good evening, Captain,' said Hardcastle affably.

'Oh my God!' The officer's tunic bore wings on his left shoulder identifying him as a pilot and he had several medal ribbons led by the purple and white of the Military Cross. There were three Bath stars on each of his cuffs, and on his collar the distinctive Fleur-de-Lys badges of the Manchester Regiment.

'I take it you were expecting to see Mrs Cheney, Captain,' said Hardcastle, still maintaining the level tones with which he had greeted the airman.

'I, um, oh hell and damnation!' spluttered the embarrassed officer. 'I'd arranged to take her to the theatre.' He paused. 'Oh God! Are you *Mister* Cheney?'

'I'm Divisional Detective Inspector Hardcastle of the Metropolitan Police. Who are you?'

'Guy Slater. But what are the police doing here?'

'Investigating the murder of Georgina Cheney, Captain Slater.'

'Murdered!' Slater sank into a chair. 'Hell's bells! When did this happen?'

'Yesterday. Well, the night before last to be exact,' said Marriott. 'When did you last visit Mrs Cheney, Captain Slater?'

'I saw Georgina on Saturday evening. I took her to see the new musical at the Gaiety Theatre. It was called *Going Up* and was all about this American aviator called Robert who's fallen in love with a girl called Grace and—'

'I'm sure it was a very entertaining play, Captain Slater.' Hardcastle held up a hand. 'But to get back to the point, I presume you brought Mrs Cheney home after the theatre.'

'Of course I bally well did.' Slater contrived to look offended, as though he had been accused of behaving like a cad. 'I wouldn't have left her to find her own way home.'

'And I understand you stayed the night,' said Hardcastle blithely, as though he already knew this to be the case.

'Well, I, um—'

'No need to be shy about being invited into the bed of a good-looking girl like Georgina, Captain Slater. You'd've been a fool to refuse.'

'Oh, what the hell!' exclaimed Slater. 'I wasn't the only one.'

'Perhaps you'd care to explain.' Hardcastle took a seat opposite the young pilot and lit his pipe.

'I'm stationed at Sutton's Farm near Hornchurch.' Slater was now more relaxed. 'And I know of at least one other chap from there who regularly visited Georgina.'

'What was his name, Captain Slater?' asked Marriott.

'I don't think I could possibly betray a confidence of that nature.' Slater smiled diffidently and brushed at his moustache.

'I would remind you that I'm dealing with the murder of Georgina Cheney, Captain Slater,' said Hardcastle sharply, 'and I won't tolerate that sort of misplaced loyalty interfering in my investigation. Now who is this man?'

Slater appeared shocked at the DDI's brusque manner. 'I, um, well, it's actually Flight Sub-Lieutenant Leo Etherington. He's a naval chap. Well, actually, he's in the Royal Air Force now, as am I.'

'But you're wearing army uniform and captain's pips on your cuffs.' Hardcastle, never one too conversant with military uniform, was now totally confused.

'I'm still getting used to it myself, but they haven't decided what sort of uniform we're to have,' said Slater. 'There's some talk of sky-blue with gold stripes on the cuffs like the navy. But in the meantime, we're hanging on to our army kit. They're calling it a "wearing-out" period. Frankly, I don't think the brass hats can make up their minds.'

'So where does Etherington fit into this? Is he in the navy or in this new air force?'

'Yes, he's in the RAF too. When the RAF was formed chaps from the Royal Flying Corps and the Royal Naval Air Service were combined into the new air force. Leo came from the navy, you see. It's all rather complicated, Inspector, and there are some old cavalrymen in the army and a few diehards at the Admiralty who say that the RAF won't last. But aeroplanes are here to stay; I can assure you of that. And as for the cavalry, well, that's a dead duck, despite what Sir Douglas Haig thinks.'

'Maybe,' said Hardcastle, who knew of quite a few innovations that had been imposed upon the Metropolitan Police and were doomed to have but a short life. 'And do you know of anyone else who regularly visited Mrs Cheney?'

'No, but it wouldn't surprise me if there were others. Georgina was quite a fast sort of girl. She enjoyed going to the theatre and dining in good restaurants. And in return she was quite happy to . . .' Slater broke off, embarrassed at his own candour. 'Well, I'm sure you know what I mean, Inspector.'

'Only too well.' Hardcastle had frequently encountered stories of unfaithful wives whose husbands were prosecuting the war at sea, in the field or in the air. 'Perhaps you'd tell this man Etherington that I'd like to see him at Cannon Row police station as soon as possible.'

'I'm not sure that he'd be able to get away, Inspector. You see—'

'Perhaps if I was to get in touch with Major General Sir Hugh Trenchard, Captain Slater, and tell him why I want to see Etherington, he would arrange for him to be released. Apart from anything else, I gather from what you've just said that he comes to London quite frequently.'

Even though he was currently serving as commander of the Independent Air Force in France, the mere mention of the feared 'Boom' Trenchard was sufficient for Slater. 'I'll pass on your request, Inspector.'

The door of the drawing room opened and Hannah appeared with a tray. 'I've brought your tea, sir.'

'Captain Slater isn't staying for tea, Hannah,' said Hardcastle.

Slater stood up. 'Hell, I've got two tickets for *The Bing Boys on Broadway* at the Alhambra tonight. What am I to do with those?' he enquired plaintively.

'You could take Hannah,' suggested Hardcastle.

Slater cast an appraising glance at the young housekeeper. 'I say, what a smashing wheeze!' he exclaimed.

'I couldn't possibly, sir,' Hannah said to Hardcastle. 'I have duties here.'

'Why not, lass? An evening at the theatre would do you good, and the commander's not here.'

'The commander?' queried Slater.

'Georgina's widower is a commander in the Royal Navy, but he's not here to object,' said Hardcastle.

'A *commander*?' This news appeared to depress Slater even more.

'But no hanky-panky, Captain Slater,' cautioned Hardcastle, 'or you'll have me to answer to.'

'Certainly not, Inspector,' said Slater, and escorted Hannah from the room.

Hardcastle heard the housekeeper giggling in the hall and wondered whether she had met Slater before. On a social footing.

FOUR

Hardcastle had never spoken to Major General Sir Hugh Trenchard, and had no idea where he would have found him if he needed to. But the threat of doing so had obviously had the required effect on Flight Sub-Lieutenant Leo Etherington. On the morning following the DDI's questioning of Guy Slater, Etherington appeared at the police station at nine o'clock and was shown up to the DDI's office.

'I'm told you wish to see me.' Etherington, a rather foppish young man, probably in his early twenties, was attired in naval uniform. He wore a single gold lace ring on each of his cuffs, above which, on the left sleeve, was the golden eagle of the Royal Naval Air Service.

'Sit down, Lieutenant,' said Hardcastle, and shouted for Marriott. 'Are you in the Royal Navy or the Royal Air Force?' He was not prepared to take Slater's word for Etherington's status.

'I'm actually in the Royal Air Force now,' drawled Etherington, as Marriott silently entered the office and took a seat behind Etherington. 'But we're having to make do with our naval rig until the powers that be have worked out what we're supposed to be wearing and what ranks we're to be known by. It's all rather a bore.'

'How often did you sleep with Georgina Cheney, Etherington?' Hardcastle had no intention of entering into a discussion about the uniform of the Royal Air Force or its rank structure; neither did he intend to equivocate when it came to interrogating this bumptious young blade.

'Oh, I say, what sort of question's that?'

'One I want an answer to.'

'I don't really think that my private life is anything to do with you,' said Etherington languidly, a supercilious expression on his face, and withdrew a cigarette case from the pocket of his reefer jacket.

Hardcastle slapped a hand on his desk so loudly that the young airman jumped in alarm. 'Mrs Cheney was murdered last Tuesday night, lad, and I'm trying to find out who killed her. Now, answer my bloody question before I'm tempted to lock you up for obstructing me in the execution of my duty.'

'Christ!' exclaimed Etherington, sitting bolt upright. 'I say!' His jaw dropped and he put away his cigarette case. He suddenly realized that this policeman was to be taken seriously. 'It was only a bit of fun. Gina was up for it, don't you know.'

'Where did you meet her?' asked Marriott.

Etherington turned in his seat to face the sergeant. 'As a matter of fact it was at a rather swish affair at the Langham Hotel about five weeks ago. It was some charity ball, I think.'

'D'you have the exact date, Mr Etherington?' asked Marriott.

Etherington took out a pocket diary and thumbed through its pages. 'Saturday, the eleventh of May,' he said, glancing up.

'What was a naval officer doing—?' Hardcastle began.

'I'm a Royal Air Force officer,' Etherington reminded Hardcastle.

'I don't give a damn what you are, lad, and don't bloody well interrupt me again. What were you doing at an expensive function like that on a junior officer's pay?'

'I do have private means.' Etherington almost sneered, but decided that it would be unwise to alienate this rough diamond of a policeman. 'Being in uniform, no one asks any questions, don't you know. Consequently they just let me in free of charge.'

'I'll ask you again. How exactly did you meet up with Mrs Cheney at this charity affair? Or did you take her there as your partner?'

'Good Lord no! I first spotted her at the buffet table. She was a damn good-looking girl and I decided I must get to know her. We got chatting and I danced with her a few times, and then took her for supper.'

'Wasn't she there with someone?'

'Probably, but she didn't seem to care about leaving the poor fellow high and dry, whoever he was. Probably some white-feather scrimshanker, what? Anyway we had a quiet dinner at a restaurant in Covent Garden and I escorted her home to Whilber Street.'

'You didn't leave her at her front door, I suppose,' commented Hardcastle acidly.

'A nod's as good as a wink,' said Etherington. 'I stayed the night.'

'And presumably you saw her several times after that?' suggested Marriott.

'Too bloody true. She used to hold parties at her place. Jolly good they were too.'

'Parties?' exclaimed Hardcastle. 'What sort of parties?'

'You know the sort of thing. A few girls, plenty to drink.' Etherington chuckled at the recollection.

'Was the maid there?' asked Marriott.

'Who, young Hannah? Rather. She joined in. She was good fun, too.'

'The carney little bitch!' exclaimed Hardcastle, furious that Hannah Clarke had been deceiving him.

'Seems that young Hannah was spinning us a yarn, sir.' It was with some difficulty that Marriott prevented himself from smiling as he realized that his chief had been caught out, a rare occurrence for the DDI. And by a nineteen-year-old housemaid-cum-housekeeper at that.

'Where were you last Tuesday evening, Mr Etherington?' asked Hardcastle irritably.

'I was flying. Defence of London and all that, don't you know. You can ask my squadron commander.'

'Who is he?'

'Major Montague Lawford.'

'Did he ever attend these parties?' asked Hardcastle, still fuming at Hannah Clarke's deception.

'Not that I know of. Mind you, I couldn't always go to these get-togethers. Call of duty and all that.'

'You can go.' Hardcastle waved a hand of dismissal. 'But I shall be speaking to your squadron commander.'

'Give my regards to young Hannah if you see her again, old boy.' Etherington picked up his cap and sauntered out of the office.

'That bloody girl's got a lot to answer for, Marriott,' said Hardcastle angrily, 'and she's about to do so.'

Once Etherington had departed, Hardcastle stood up and took his hat and umbrella from the hatstand. But his departure was delayed by the arrival of Detective Inspector Charles Stockley Collins, head of Fingerprint Bureau.

'Ah, Ernie, I'm glad I caught you,' said Collins, as he stepped into the office.

Collins was an expert in the developing science of fingerprint identification, and had given evidence in the case of the Stratton brothers in 1905. The Deptford oil shop murders became a landmark in criminal history. The two Strattons were convicted on the evidence of their fingerprints having been found on a cash box at the scene of the brutal murders of Thomas Farrow and his wife. It was the first time that such evidence had secured a conviction for murder. Many were to follow.

'I hope you've got good news for me, Charlie,' said Hardcastle.

'Yes and no,' said Collins, taking a seat in one of the hard-backed chairs in the DDI's office and opening a file. 'There were fingerprints galore, but I couldn't match any of them in my collection. And that included those on the champagne bottle. One set on the bottle was Georgina Cheney's – I took a set of hers at the mortuary – but there was another set on there too, which so far I've been unable to identify.'

'Somehow I didn't expect that any of her visitors would have previous convictions, Charlie,' said Hardcastle resignedly.

'Once you catch the bugger, Ernie, I'll be able to do some matching.'

'Thanks a lot,' said Hardcastle acidly. 'That's a great comfort.'

'Oh, it's you, Inspector.' After some considerable delay, during which time Hardcastle had hammered on the knocker several times, Hannah Clarke opened the door to admit the two detectives. She was wearing a floor-length pink satin dressing gown and silk slippers – *all of which were probably Georgina Cheney's*, Hardcastle thought – and her blonde hair was loose around her shoulders. She looked as though she had just tumbled out of bed.

'Yes, it's me, young lady, and I want a word with you,' snapped Hardcastle, pushing his way through the door.

'Whatever's wrong?' asked Hannah nervously, as she showed the two police officers into the sitting room.

'For a start, you can tell me about these parties that Mrs Cheney held every week, parties that you somehow forgot to tell me about last time I was here. And, I'm told, it seems you took an active part in 'em.'

'Whoever told you such a thing?' Hannah was clearly alarmed at Hardcastle's aggressive attitude.

'Flight Sub-Lieutenant Leo Etherington for one, and Captain Guy Slater for another,' said Hardcastle, sitting down and taking out his pipe.

Hannah perched on the edge of an armchair. She might have been unnerved by Hardcastle's aggressiveness, but was seemingly not embarrassed to be seen in a state of undress. 'The mistress told me that I wasn't to mention it to anyone, sir, seeing as how the master was away at sea and might not approve.'

'I dare say your mistress was quite right,' said Hardcastle, blowing tobacco smoke towards the ceiling. 'I can't imagine the commander approving of shenanigans of that sort. How often did these parties take place?'

'About once a week, sir,' said Hannah, confirming what Etherington had said.

'What time did they start, Hannah?' asked Marriott gently, realizing that Hardcastle's hostile manner was unlikely to elicit truthful answers from the young housekeeper.

'Usually about ten o'clock of an evening, sir. Being mostly flyers they wasn't able to get here earlier,' said Hannah. 'The mistress said she felt sorry for these young men on account of they was fighting and likely to be shot down and killed any day. But it was just for a few drinks.'

'Not what I heard,' growled Hardcastle.

'I believe there were other young ladies here,' continued Marriott. 'Who were they?'

'I don't rightly know. Some of the young men brought the young ladies with them.'

'What were the names of the men who came?'

'Well,' began Hannah thoughtfully, 'there was Guy and Leo, like you said, and there was another soldier called Jonno.'

'Jonno? Is that his real name?'

'I don't know, sir, but that's what he was called. He came from the same regiment, or whatever they call it, as Guy and Leo.'

'Is that all?'

'There was others, sir, but I don't rightly remember their names.'

'And I suppose that one of them finished up in Mrs Cheney's bed, eh, Hannah?' Marriott paused and smiled. 'Or in yours?'

Hannah Clarke looked away and fussed at her blonde hair, and tears began to well up. 'It was the mistress's idea,' she said, dabbing at her eyes with a handkerchief. 'She said as how these poor young men might—'

'Yes, I know. They might get shot down and killed any day.'

'How often did Mr Curtis call on Mrs Cheney, Hannah?' asked Hardcastle, his ugly mood softening, despite thinking that Hannah's tears were contrived.

'Not very often, sir.' Hannah was surprised at the sudden change in questions, and turned to face Hardcastle. 'He usually come in the mornings about once a week, just to see if the mistress was all right, and if she needed anything done.'

'Did he ever come to these parties?'

'Oh no, sir, never.'

'Did you ever post any letters for your mistress?' Hardcastle was now thinking about the unfinished blackmail letter.

'Oh yes, all the time, sir,' said Hannah.

'D'you know who they were written to?'

'Usually to the master, sir. I remember them particular because they was addressed to Commander R. Cheney, DSC, care of HM Ships. And she wrote to the boys as well.'

'Anyone else? Any gentlemen, for example?'

'Not that I recall, sir. There used to be a post book what was kept by the butler, but like I said before, he was killed soon after he joined up, and nothing's been put in it since. The mistress said not to bother any more. In fact she threw it away.'

'I'll bet she did,' said Hardcastle, half to himself. Furthermore, he did not believe that Hannah could not remember the names on the letters she posted. He stood up and knocked the ash from his pipe on the blackleaded fire basket. 'If I have to come here asking questions again, lass, I'll want the truth. Is that understood?'

'Oh, yes, sir. I'm very sorry, sir, but the mistress—'

'I know,' said Hardcastle, holding up a hand. 'The mistress said you weren't to mention it to anyone. Come, Marriott,' he added, picking up his hat and umbrella.

'Did you and Captain Slater enjoy the show at the Alhambra last night, Hannah?' asked Marriott, as he and the DDI were leaving.

'Oh, yes, sir. It was ever so good.'

Once the two detectives were in the street, Hardcastle stopped and turned. 'Well, I'll go to the foot of our stairs, Marriott. What a carney little bitch. Coming over the innocent and all the time she's giving her favours to any airman who happens by.'

'I wouldn't be surprised if the bold Captain Slater was upstairs in bed while we were talking to her, either, sir.'

'Nor me,' said Hardcastle, sighting a cab. 'Scotland Yard, cabbie.' Turning to his sergeant, he added, 'Tell 'em Cannon Row and half the time you'll end up at Cannon Street in the City, Marriott.'

'So I believe, sir,' said Marriott wearily. He had received this advice on almost every occasion that he and Hardcastle had shared a cab to the police station.

Back at Cannon Row, Hardcastle called Marriott into his office.

'I've been wondering, Marriott,' the DDI began, puffing content-edly at his pipe.

'You have, sir?' Marriott was always disconcerted when Hardcastle announced that he had been 'wondering'. It usually meant that the DDI was about to steer the enquiry in a direction unrelated to anything he had learned so far.

'Yes, I'm wondering whether someone Mrs Cheney knew in Malta was the one what she was putting the black on. If it was her who wrote that letter. If so, he might've been the one what topped her.'

'But how on earth are we to find that out, sir?' Marriott was aghast, fearing that the DDI might be on the point of suggesting a trip to the Mediterranean island fortress with its concomitant risk of meeting a German submarine on the way. But that apart, he did not know what had prompted Hardcastle to think that the subject of the blackmail might be in Malta. In his view he was much more likely to be closer to home.

'Ways and means, Marriott, ways and means,' said Hardcastle mysteriously. 'The Maltese have got an office in London somewhere, haven't they?'

'Probably, sir. I'll find out. We've got a list of embassies in the main office.'

'It won't be an embassy, Marriott. Malta's part of the Empire. You should know that. It'll likely be a high commission. Find out.'

Marriott returned five minutes later. 'The Commissioner-General for Malta is Sir Sebastian Fulljames and he has his office at 39 St James's Street, sir.'

'Good. It's time we had a chat with him. He might just know of someone who knew Mrs Cheney out there, and is now back here.' Hardcastle donned his hat and picked up his umbrella. 'But this is proving to be thirsty work, Marriott. We'll have a pie and a pint first.'

'Sebastian Fulljames, gentlemen. You're from the police, you say.' The frock-coated man who greeted the two detectives was at least seventy years of age. Although balding, he had full grey sideburns that met his equally grey moustache. 'I'm the Commissioner-General for Malta.' Crossing the office towards Hardcastle and Marriott he allowed his monocle to drop from his eye, adroitly catching it and placing it in his waistcoat pocket. 'And what may I do to assist the police?' he asked, shaking hands with each of the CID officers. 'Please do take a seat.' He waved vaguely at a couple of leather-backed chairs before sitting down behind his desk.

'I'm investigating the murder of a Mrs Georgina Cheney, Sir Sebastian,' Hardcastle began, finding it awkward to link Fulljames's title with his Christian name. 'She was found dead at her house in Whilber Street last Wednesday morning.'

'Mmm, yes!' murmured Fulljames, absent-mindedly taking a pinch of snuff. 'Read somethin' about it in *The Times*. Very sad. Great tragedy. Husband at sea, too. Great tragedy. But how can I possibly assist? Never knew the girl.'

Hardcastle glanced at his sergeant. 'You've got all the facts at your fingertips, Marriott. Tell the Commissioner-General.'

'We understand that Mrs Cheney was born and brought up in Malta, sir,' said Marriott. 'We have evidence leading us to believe that she might've been a blackmailer and we're exploring the possibility that the subject of her blackmail was someone she knew in Malta.' Personally he didn't think so, but was obliged to go along with the DDI's theory, however bizarre.

'And you think this person might've murdered the poor girl.' Despite his apparent absent-mindedness, Fulljames got to the nub of the matter very quickly.

'It's a possibility, Sir Sebastian,' said Hardcastle cautiously.

'Mmm!' Fulljames took another pinch of snuff. 'I don't really see how I can help you, Inspector. You see I've never been to Malta.'

'Really, sir?' Hardcastle was surprised that a man who held the appointment of Commissioner-General for Malta was apparently unfamiliar with all that went on there. He glanced around the opulent office, taking in the pictures of the island and the various Maltese artefacts that adorned the walls and Fulljames's desk.

'This job is very much a sinecure, Inspector. I'm really only a sort of agent. If I get any queries that I'm unable to answer, I usually send a wire to Lord Methuen, the Governor, and let his people sort it out. However . . .' Fulljames paused again. 'There is a chap at the Foreign Office who served in Malta before the war started. He may be able to assist you. I've often sent people to see him. Seems to know a lot about the social scene there. His name's Dudley ffrench. I'll jot it down for you.' He scribbled the name on a slip of paper and handed it to Hardcastle.

'Is that how you spell it, sir?' queried Hardcastle, glancing up from the note Fulljames had given him. 'And without a capital letter at the beginning?'

'Yes, that's right, but one pronounces it French apparently,' said Fulljames. 'Strange business,' he added, taking yet another pinch of snuff.

Being familiar with all the government offices that lay within his bailiwick, Hardcastle obviously knew where the Foreign Office was located. But, once there, finding the curiously named Dudley ffrench proved to be a more difficult matter.

An ageing messenger took several minutes thumbing through three or four directories before he established exactly where the diplomat had his office.

'Ah! Got 'im, sir. I knew he was 'ere somewhere.' Closing the directory, the messenger, impaired by a club foot, led them slowly across Durbar Court, up a flight of ornate stairs and along several corridors. Finally he knocked deferentially at a large oaken door.

'Two gentlemen from the police to see you, sir.'

'Ah, you're just in time for tea.' Dudley ffrench was a portly man of medium height who must have been approaching sixty. He closed the file on which he had been working and removed his pince-nez before skirting his desk.

'I'm Divisional Detective Inspector Hardcastle of the Whitehall Division, sir, and this is Detective Sergeant Marriott.'

'How d'you do,' said ffrench, as he shook hands with the two detectives. 'Do take a seat, gentlemen, and tell me how I may be of service,' he added, perching on the front edge of his desk.

'We're investigating the murder of Georgina Cheney, Mr ffrench,' Hardcastle began.

'Good God! I knew a girl called Georgina who married Bob Cheney, a naval officer, in Malta back in oh-five. Could that be the same girl, I wonder?'

'She was certainly married to a Commander Robert Cheney, Mr ffrench,' said Hardcastle.

'Well, I'll be damned,' exclaimed ffrench. 'Who murdered her?'

'We don't know at present, sir,' said Marriott, 'but we were wondering if you could help us with our enquiries. We found a half-finished letter at her house that appeared to be a threat of some sort. It would seem that she was blackmailing someone, but as the letter wasn't completed or addressed, we don't know who it was meant for.'

'And you think that whoever she was writing to might've killed her, is that it?'

'That's a theory we're working on at the moment,' said Hardcastle, even though he was sceptical about the letter's authorship.

'Can't say I'm surprised,' said ffrench. 'Ah, the tea.' He paused as a woman in a blue overall entered with a tray. 'Perhaps you'd be so good as to rustle up two more cups, Martha, there's a dear.'

'Yes, sir.' The woman disappeared to return moments later with two bone china cups and saucers that matched the one already on ffrench's desk.

'You were saying that you weren't surprised, Mr ffrench,' said Marriott.

'Georgina Heath she was called back then, and a flighty little baggage to boot.' The diplomat poured the tea and handed round the cups. 'Whenever there was a dance or a ball – and there were plenty of them before the war – Georgina was always there. I suppose she must've been about seventeen when my wife and I first met her. Her parents were acquaintances of ours; her father was actually a work colleague. Dead now, of course; he was posted to Africa somewhere and died of malaria. Georgina had just finished her schooling at St Edward's College, and was clearly set on trapping a man into wedlock as quickly as possible. In fact, she had quite a reputation, and not a very creditable one at that.'

'What exactly d'you mean by that, sir?' asked Hardcastle.

'Do I have to spell it out, Inspector?' Dudley ffrench raised a quizzical eyebrow. 'How shall I put it? She had a reputation for being a young lady of easy virtue.'

'And presumably Commander Cheney succumbed to her charms,' said Hardcastle.

'Head over heels, old boy. As I recall, he was a lieutenant at the time, holding some vague sort of appointment on the Governor's staff. I think Bob first met Georgina at a ball at Admiralty House. I was there with my wife, and Georgina unashamedly set her cap at Bob. They were married in about . . .' He paused in thought. 'Yes, I was right; it was 1905. She'd've been nineteen then, and Bob was about eight years her senior. The wedding was at St Paul's Anglican Cathedral in Valletta, and was quite a swish affair, I can tell you. An archway of naval officers with drawn swords – all the sort of palaver the navy loves – and whisked off in a carriage drawn by a team of sweating matelots. The honeymoon was spent at a hotel in Pembroke on the east of the island where, one supposes, the marriage was consummated.' Dudley ffrench emitted a cynical laugh. 'But local scuttlebutt suggested that they'd had quite a few practice runs, if you take my meaning.'

'Was there anyone you know of who might've been having an affair with her, perhaps after her marriage?' asked Marriott.

'Possibly,' said ffrench pensively. 'Bob returned to England at the end of 1912 and sent for Georgina some time the following year. If I remember correctly, she must've been without her husband for a good six months before he sent for her. Mind you, she'd got two children by then, but that wouldn't have stopped her. Everyone had servants galore, of course. Butlers, housemaids, nursemaids and all that sort of thing. You didn't have to lift a finger for yourself.'

'I suppose you wouldn't happen to remember the names of any of the people she was close to, would you, sir?'

'There was one young fellow. A barrister by the name of Rollo Henson. Only a year or two older than Georgina, I'd've thought. They were often seen dancing at the various balls. But there could well have been others.'

'Thank you, Mr ffrench,' said Hardcastle. 'You've been most helpful.'

'If there's anything else I can help with, you know where to find me,' said ffrench as he shook hands.

'Most kind, sir,' murmured Hardcastle. 'Should you think of anything else, I'm only across the road at Cannon Row police station.'

FIVE

'At least we have a name to go on now, Marriott,' said Hardcastle when the two detectives were back at Cannon Row. 'This here Rollo Henson that Mr ffrench mentioned.'

'Henson doesn't come between A and C, sir,' observed Marriott.

'What on earth are you talking about, Marriott?' snapped Hardcastle, staring at his sergeant. 'I do know how to spell.'

'The pages A to C were torn out of Mrs Cheney's address book, sir.'

'Well, I know that, Marriott. It was me what found they had been.'

'What I mean is that Henson is unlikely to be the person Mrs Cheney was in the act of writing to, sir. Otherwise she'd've torn out the page with H on it.'

'We don't know she wrote it,' said Hardcastle sternly, 'and it's very dangerous to jump to conclusions of that sort in a murder investigation.'

'Yes, sir.' It was an observation that so contradicted the DDI's own methods that Marriott could think of no other reply.

'But is Henson's name in the book?' persisted Hardcastle. 'It'll be under H,' he added wryly.

Ignoring the DDI's jibe, Marriott flipped quickly through the pages of the address book. 'It's not here, sir.'

'Are you sure?'

'Yes, sir.' Marriott proffered the book.

'All right, all right.' Hardcastle waved it away. 'Ain't there a list of barristers kept somewhere?'

'Yes, sir. It's called the *Law List*.'

'Best get hold of that there *Law List*, then, and see if our Mr Henson's name is in it.'

'It'll be across at the Yard, sir. They've got a library over there.'

'Good, and while you're there see if Mr Collins has got any more results for us.'

It was half an hour before Marriott returned.

'First of all, sir, Mr Collins said that he has nothing to add to what he told you earlier today. He was at a loss to understand why you thought he might have.'

'Never mind that.' Hardcastle dismissed Collins' mild rebuke with a wave of his hand. 'What about Henson?'

'Rollo Henson was born in Tavistock, Devon, in 1883, sir, and was called to the bar of Inner Temple in 1904.' Marriott glanced up from his notes. 'He has chambers in Fountain Court.'

'Does he indeed? Time we had a word with him, then.'

'There's always a chance that he might be at the Old Bailey, sir.'

Hardcastle seized his hat and umbrella. 'Well, at least we know where that is,' he said.

'Ah, this looks like it, Marriott.' Hardcastle paused on the steps of a set of chambers in Fountain Court, examined the board at the side of the door and ran his finger down the list of names. 'Yes, this is the place. Several KCs, Marriott, but Henson ain't one of them. Still wears a stuff gown, I suppose.' He pushed open the door and made his way to the clerks' office.

'Yes?' A middle-aged man wearing a black jacket, pinstriped trousers and a wing collar turned to face the two detectives. For a moment or two he appraised them with a lugubrious expression and then tweaked his waxed moustache.

'I'm here to see Mr Rollo Henson,' said Hardcastle.

'Are you a solicitor, sir?' asked the clerk, crossing from the filing cabinet.

'No, a police officer.'

'Which case?'

'What d'you mean, which case?'

'Which case are you involved in?' asked the clerk, enunciating each word as though Hardcastle was hard of hearing, and peering at him over half-moon spectacles. 'I have to get the brief out, you see. Otherwise Mr Henson won't know what you've come to see him about.'

'I haven't got a case yet,' said Hardcastle. 'I'm still collecting evidence in a murder enquiry, and Mr Henson may have some to give me.'

'That's putting the cart before the horse if you ask me,' muttered the clerk and shook his head. 'All very irregular,' he added. 'Wait here.'

'Queer sort of cove, ain't he, Marriott?' said Hardcastle, as he gazed around the cluttered office in which two, more junior, clerks were at work.

'Come this way, gentlemen,' said the clerk, reappearing in the doorway. He led them up two flights of stairs to a small office in which a solitary figure was poring over a pile of papers. Although cramped, the garret room was furnished to accommodate at least three people, the two vacant desks piled high with briefs and other documents. There were four buckets of sand grouped in the fireplace as a precaution against incendiary bombs. 'The police officers, sir.'

'I'm Rollo Henson. The clerk said you have something to ask me.' Henson was a tall man with handsome features, and longer than fashionable hair that was showing the first signs of greying around the temples, despite his being only thirty-five years old. His suit was of excellent quality and gold links adorned his shirt cuffs. A gold albert linked his two waistcoat pockets, passing through a specially cut hole between two buttons. Hardcastle had little doubt that there was an expensive gold watch at the end of it.

'I'm Divisional Detective Inspector Hardcastle of the Whitehall Division, sir, and this is Detective Sergeant Marriott.'

'Have a seat, gentlemen.' Henson removed piles of briefs from a couple of chairs and dropped them on the floor, vaguely waving away the small cloud of dust that the careless act had created. 'The clerk tells me you think I might have some evidence. I hope you're not here to accuse me of withholding it,' he added with a chuckle. 'Not the done thing for a member of the bar,' he said, settling himself behind his desk and turning sideways to face the detectives.

'I'm investigating the murder of Mrs Georgina Cheney, Mrs Henson.'

'Georgina's been murdered?' exclaimed Henson, his face registering shock at the news. 'When was this?'

'It was in all the newspapers, sir,' said Hardcastle, as though the barrister should have known.

'I've not had much time to read the papers, Inspector. We're a bit shorthanded, what with the war and all.'

'She was murdered at her home in Whilber Street, Westminster, last Tuesday evening.'

'In Westminster, you say? I didn't even know she was in England. The last time I saw Georgina was in Malta, a couple of years before the war started.'

'She moved to this country in 1913, sir,' said Marriott. 'Shortly after her husband was posted back to the United Kingdom.'

'I didn't know that,' said Henson. 'I left Malta at the end of 1912. I'd been practising at the Maltese bar, but decided that there was more to offer back here.'

'I understand that you had an affair with Mrs Cheney in Malta, Mr Henson.' Hardcastle put the accusation bluntly.

'It's no secret, Inspector, but I didn't know she was married at the time otherwise I wouldn't have got involved with her.' Henson reached for a packet of cigarettes and offered one to Hardcastle.

'No thank you, sir. I'm a pipe smoker.'

'Please carry on, Inspector.' Henson offered the packet to Marriott.

'No thank you, sir,' said Marriott, shaking his head.

'You didn't know that Mrs Cheney was married to a naval officer, then.' Hardcastle filled his pipe and spent a moment or two lighting it.

'No, I certainly didn't, at least not immediately. I suppose she must've been in her mid-twenties when I met her.' Henson gazed across the room, collecting his thoughts. 'It was at a ball at Admiralty House, but I assumed that she was a widow. Then a friend of mine who knew the family told me she was married to a naval chap, but that he'd gone back to England. I must say it came as a surprise. One doesn't expect married women to behave like that, especially in a closed social community like Valletta where everyone knows everyone else's business.'

'And you've not seen her since, sir?' queried Marriott.

'Certainly not. I didn't want to finish up fighting a duel with her husband,' said Henson, with a wry smile, 'and I had my own career to consider. As I said just now, I came back to England in December 1912. I was married to Lydia in 1914 – on the Saturday before war broke out as a matter of fact.'

'Weren't you tempted to enlist, sir?' asked Hardcastle.

'That was certainly my intention, and I joined the Inns of Court

Officer Training Corps. But almost immediately I was briefed to appear for the Crown in a sensitive case connected with the war and I've been appearing in similar cases ever since. I can't give you any details, Inspector, but you wouldn't expect me to, would you?' said Henson. 'And before you ask, because I know it's the sort of question policemen do ask, I was at a bar mess dinner last Tuesday evening. And, God help us, it went on until one o'clock in the morning. There were two High Court judges and about thirty other barristers there, which is a pretty good alibi,' he said with a smile.

'I think that'd stand up to cross-examination at the Bailey, sir.' Hardcastle laughed. 'Do you happen to know of anyone else that Mrs Cheney might've been particularly friendly with?'

'Someone with whom she had an affair, you mean?'

'Exactly so.'

'Yes, there was one young army officer.' Henson stubbed out his cigarette in a brass ashtray. 'It was after I'd parted company with her that I heard that this chap was paying a lot of attention to her.'

'D'you remember his name, sir?'

'Ah, now you're asking.' Henson paused in thought. 'I know he was in the Royal Engineers. Yes, got it. Leighton Garside was his name. Single fellow, about Georgina's age I'd've thought. But he was still squiring her when I left for home. They were both quite open about it by all accounts. Very foolish of both of them, and likely to have got a young subaltern into hot water, I imagine. Not that I know much about how the army views these things.'

'Are you sure it was Leighton Garside, sir?' queried Marriott, glancing up from his pocketbook. 'Sounds a strange sort of Christian name.

'I believe so,' said Henson. 'He was always known as Leighton.'

'I think that'll be all for the time being, sir,' said Hardcastle, as he and Marriott stood up. 'And thank you for being so frank. I'll have to see whether this Garside fellow can shed any light on my enquiry.'

'I hope you find whoever killed her, Inspector,' said Henson as he shook hands. 'Young Georgina was a wayward girl, but she didn't deserve to be murdered. I hope you find the fellow who did it.'

'Oh, I'll find the bugger, sir, you can rest assured of that. It won't be long before he's standing on the hangman's trap.'

'Yes, quite so, Inspector, but perhaps you'd let me know when you arrest him. I wouldn't want to finish up defending him; it would be a conflict of interests apart from anything else.'

'All we have to do now is find this Garside chap, Marriott,' said Hardcastle, when they returned to the police station.

'But it was six years ago that he was in Malta, sir. For all we know he might be dead and buried in Flanders by now.' Marriott could not understand why Hardcastle was so insistent on pursuing Georgina Cheney's Maltese affairs.

'You're a pessimistic bugger at times, Marriott. Look on the bright side.'

'On the other hand, sir, he might've been thrown out of the army if his affair with a married woman became known. Conduct unbecoming an officer and a gentleman I think they call it.'

'Well, there's one way of finding out, Marriott. We'll have a word with the APM first thing tomorrow.' Hardcastle shook his head wearily. 'I thought for once that we wouldn't need to involve the army.'

The Assistant Provost Marshal of London District was Lieutenant Colonel Ralph Frobisher of the Sherwood Foresters whose office was in Horse Guards Arch.

As the two detectives walked into the gloomy archway from Whitehall, the dismounted sentry came to attention and raised his sword to the salute. Hardcastle was not entitled to such a compliment, but sentries in central London tended to err on the side of caution whenever they sighted a smartly dressed man in a bowler hat. Hardcastle hooked his umbrella over his left arm and solemnly raised his hat in acknowledgement as he and Marriott entered Frobisher's office.

'Good morning, Inspector,' said Sergeant Glover, the APM's chief clerk. 'The colonel's free if you'd like to go through.'

'Thank you, Sergeant Glover,' said Hardcastle, as he and Marriott entered the inner office.

'Good morning, Inspector.' Frobisher rose from behind his desk when the two detectives entered and shook hands with each of them. 'And what difficult questions do you have for me today?' The APM was accustomed to Hardcastle's frequent visits and the sometimes tortuous problems that he wanted solving.

Hardcastle furnished Frobisher with the details of Georgina Cheney's murder before getting to the point of his visit. 'We have learned that she was born and brought up in Malta, Colonel. We have also learned that after her husband was posted back to England, Mrs Cheney was left alone in Malta for almost a year before moving to London. During the time she was separated from her husband she had several affairs.'

'It happens, Inspector,' replied Frobisher sagely.

'I've been told that one of her paramours was a young army officer named Leighton Garside of the Royal Engineers who was stationed in Malta before the war.'

'And I suppose you want me to find him for you,' suggested Frobisher with a smile.

'That would be most helpful to my enquiries, Colonel,' said Hardcastle. 'Particularly if Garside is now in England.'

'Well, we'd better begin at the beginning,' said Frobisher, and shouted for Sergeant Glover.

'Sir?' Glover appeared in the open doorway.

'Fetch me the 1912 order of battle, Sarn't Glover. It's in the safe.'

When Glover reappeared, he placed a large leatherbound volume on the colonel's desk.

Frobisher spent a few minutes turning the pages and running his forefinger up and down its columns. Eventually he looked up. 'It looks likely that he was attached to one of the two fortress companies based in Malta at that time, Mr Hardcastle. It would have been either 24 Company or 28 Company.'

'I see,' said Hardcastle, who was not greatly interested in the particular unit to which Garside had been attached. 'Is there going to be a problem finding out where he is now?'

'That rather depends,' said Frobisher. 'For all I know he might be languishing in a grave somewhere in Flanders or Egypt or Gallipoli or even Mesopotamia. The trouble with the Sappers,' he continued, closing the large book, 'is that they serve all over the place. If he'd belonged to an infantry regiment of the line it would have been easier to track him down. However, I'll do what I can, but it may take some considerable time.'

'Thank you, Colonel.' Hardcastle was always irritated that the army appeared to approach such matters in what he perceived to be a leisurely fashion. But he failed to appreciate the difficulties the military authorities faced in tracing a man when there were over three million troops under arms in different parts of the globe.

'There is another possibility, Colonel,' suggested Marriott.

'What might that be, Sergeant Marriott?'

'Apparently Garside was quite open about his affair with Mrs Cheney and I gather that the army tends to frown on that sort of behaviour. We've been told that he frequently escorted Georgina Cheney to balls at Admiralty House. It's been suggested to us that this wasn't too clever a thing to do in a place like Valletta where such affairs tend to be open secrets.'

'Are you suggesting that he might've been invited to resign his commission?'

'You'll know better than me how the army deals with such behaviour, Colonel,' said Hardcastle.

'If his conduct became too obvious, I've no doubt that his colonel would've had a few sharp words to say to him. However, I'll start by sending for his record of service from the War House. I'll let you know when I have anything, Inspector, but I must warn you that it could take some time,' Frobisher said again.

In the event, Frobisher achieved a result far more quickly than even he had anticipated. That afternoon Hardcastle received a telephone call from Sergeant Glover asking him to call at the APM's office.

'It was easier than I thought, Inspector,' said Frobisher, once Hardcastle and Marriott were seated in the APM's office. 'Leighton Garside is now a lieutenant colonel currently commanding one of the Royal Engineers' depot battalions and is based at Aldershot.'

'A lieutenant colonel?' exclaimed Hardcastle. 'His little dalliance in Malta don't seem to have done him any harm, then, Colonel.'

'It would have been different if he'd been cited in a divorce, Inspector, but in fact I think it was the prospect of war that saved Garside's career.'

'D'you mean that otherwise he'd've got the sack, Colonel?' asked Marriott.

'It's doubtful. But even as long ago as 1912 the army foresaw problems in the Balkans and it's likely he was let off with a dressing down.' Frobisher gave a wry smile. 'And the wisdom of that has been proved since the war began. The terrible drain on officers since 1914 means that the army is now commissioning just about anyone. Consequently, a trained regular officer is worth his weight in gold. I heard the other day of a greengrocer who'd been commissioned, but at least they had the sense to gazette him to the Army Service Corps. Still specializing in greengrocery, but in uniform, as it were.'

'Do you know the outcome of Garside's affair with Mrs Cheney, then, Colonel?' asked Hardcastle.

'There's a brief note on his record. It would appear that when the liaison came to light, his commanding officer read him the Riot Act. He also warned him that he was within a whisker of getting cashiered if he didn't straighten himself out.' Frobisher glanced up from the file he was reading. 'The CO's view was that Garside's offence was exacerbated because Mrs Cheney was the wife of a serving naval officer.'

'Does that mean it would've been all right if she'd been married to an army officer?' asked Hardcastle mischievously.

'Garside's colonel would probably have thought that to be even worse, Inspector,' said Frobisher, mistaking the DDI's comment for a serious observation. 'Mind you, a hell of a lot of that sort of thing went on in India, particularly in the foothills in summer,' he added with a sigh. 'However, the upshot was that the CO arranged for what could best be described as a punishment posting back to England. Garside was sent to a training regiment, and believe me that's nearly as bad for the staff as it is for the recruits.'

'I'd like to interview Colonel Garside,' said Hardcastle.

Frobisher raised his eyebrows. 'D'you think he might've had something to with this dreadful business, Inspector?'

'It's a possibility that has to be considered, Colonel. I'm afraid that Georgina Cheney's need for male company appears to have continued even after she came to London,' said Hardcastle. 'And more so since her husband went to sea. I've been told that she regularly held parties for young officers at her house in Whilber Street. It seems that they started quite late and one favoured officer was apparently invited at random to share her bed for the night. The officer who got second prize, so to speak, spent the night with the housemaid,' he added impishly.

'Ye gods!' exclaimed Frobisher. 'Have you any idea who these officers were? I shall speak to their commanding officer.'

'They're stationed at Sutton's Farm near Hornchurch, Colonel,' said Hardcastle. 'They're in this newfangled Royal Air Force, and I intend to go down there because it's likely that I'll find some more of their officers who might assist me in my enquiries.'

'In that case I'll speak to the DAPM who's stationed there, Inspector, and ask him to arrange an appointment for you. I hope it will prove fruitful.' But Frobisher was already feeling sorry for the officers concerned; the A Division DDI was not the most gentle of interrogators.

'Doesn't this here RAF have a police force of its own, then, Colonel?' asked Hardcastle.

'Not yet,' said Frobisher. 'Apparently the new RAF is still in the act of establishing itself. They are rather busy fighting the war, and until it's over, the army has undertaken to provide provost and other services on their behalf.'

'I see,' said Hardcastle, not really seeing at all. 'However, I'll go first to Aldershot to interview Colonel Garside.'

'If you speak to Captain McIntyre of the Gordon Highlanders, Inspector, he's one of my provost officers, and he'll be able to point you in the right direction. Aldershot's a bit of a minefield.'

'A minefield?' exclaimed Hardcastle, with a straight face. 'Things haven't got that bad, surely, Colonel.'

'Not quite, Inspector,' said Frobisher, not realizing that Hardcastle was joking. 'Merely a turn of phrase. Let me know when you intend to go down there and I'll alert McIntyre.'

'Thank you, Colonel, and I'll advise you when I intend to go to Sutton's Farm.'

SIX

As it was a Sunday, Hardcastle knew that he had no chance of asking Colonel Frobisher to arrange a visit to the Royal Air Force at Sutton's Farm until Monday. As a consequence, his interview with the RAF officers who knew Georgina Cheney would have to wait, and he reluctantly decided to spend the day at home.

After breakfast he took his usual stroll down to Horace Boxall's corner shop in Kennington Road to buy his tobacco and the *News of the World*.

'I see the French put a stop to Ludendorff's attack near Soissons,

Mr Hardcastle.' Without waiting for the DDI to place his order, Boxall put the newspaper, an ounce of St Bruno and a box of matches on the counter. 'It says here,' he continued, pointing to the front-page article, 'that Foch's lot had two hundred tanks *and* they used mustard gas. I'll bet that made old Fritz stop and think.'

'It looks as though the tide is turning at last, Horace,' said Hardcastle. 'And about time too. I just thank God that the Americans joined in last year.' He placed a half-crown on the counter and pocketed the change that Boxall counted out into the small tray.

'Talking of which,' Boxall went on, 'I see that President Wilson has got all hot under the collar about some film in America. According to a piece in one of the papers, the film had scenes in it of German atrocities against the Belgians, and the audiences lapped it up. But it turned out that it had all been filmed in New Jersey. Blew up in their faces as you might say.'

'I sometimes think that propaganda does more harm than good, Horace.' Hardcastle picked up his newspaper, tobacco and matches, and made his way home.

For once all the Hardcastle family was together. Kitty, the eldest, had at last been obliged to relinquish her temporary position as a conductorette with the London General Omnibus Company, much to Hardcastle's relief. Men discharged from the Colours as no longer fit for active service were nonetheless capable of resuming their former jobs as omnibus conductors. Kitty, never wanting to be idle, was wondering what to do next.

Maud, now a very mature twenty-year-old, was an auxiliary nurse at one of the big houses in Park Lane given over to the care of wounded officers and would not begin night duty until five o'clock that afternoon.

'Well, Wally, are you looking forward to your new career as a postman?' asked Hardcastle, relaxing in his armchair and replete after one of Alice's Sunday roast lunches.

'Not really, Pa. Taking them telegrams was doing something useful.' Walter, the Hardcastles' eighteen-year-old son, was now too old to continue his job as a telegram messenger, and would be starting his new career as a fully fledged postman at five the following morning. He was still fretting at being unable to enlist, but the recruiting sergeant at the local town hall had told him that the war was nearly over and they had enough men. Although thankful to hear that news, Hardcastle was still unsure that the sergeant had been right to be so optimistic.

'It's *those* telegrams, Wally, not *them* telegrams,' said Hardcastle. 'Anyway I could never see that you got much satisfaction from delivering telegrams to people telling them that their loved one had been killed or badly wounded.'

'It was the ones that told them that their man was safe, Pa. That was the good news. Anyway, there's not much future in being a postman.'

'You don't have to stay a postman for the rest of your life. There will always be the chance of promotion if you work hard enough. You could finish up in management.'

'Not for me,' exclaimed Walter firmly. He paused, wondering how best once again to put his ambition to his father, and knowing what his reaction would be. 'I want to join the police.'

'Ah!' Hardcastle knew that his son would renew his oft-expressed desire to follow in his footsteps. He spent a few silent moments filling his pipe and lighting it while considering how best to dissuade the boy. 'You'd have to start at the bottom,' he said, waving out his match and dropping it into the ashtray. 'Ten weeks training for a start, learning the law and your powers of arrest; and that's followed by two more exams before you complete probation. It's hard work, believe me.' He spoke as though familiar with the format, but his own training, twenty-seven years ago, had been far more rudimentary.

'Yes, I know all that, Pa.'

'And promotion's hard to come by,' continued Hardcastle. 'It took me twenty-three years to get to my present rank and I'm now forty-seven. I've got to wait another three years before I can retire on a full pension. And another thing: you'll have a lot to live up to because they'll soon find out your old man's a DDI.'

To Hardcastle's surprise, Walter threw back his head and laughed. 'I do believe you're trying to talk me out of it, Pa.'

'Well, I just want you to know what you'll be up against, son. And when you get married, you'll have to find a woman who'll put up with being a copper's wife. And there aren't many about like your mother.'

'Amen to that,' murmured Alice, seated in the other armchair and busily knitting.

'It's no good, Pa; my mind's set on it.'

'Well, you've another eighteen months to think it over carefully because you can't join until you're twenty. What's more you've got to remember that there'll be a lot of men who'll be coming back after this war's over, and many of them will make good policemen. They'll probably tell you to enlist in the Brigade of Guards for three years and then try again.'

'Well,' said Walter, with an air of finality, 'they can only turn me down, but I'm going to try.'

'Charles has suggested that we get married next year,' said Maud, coming to her brother's aid by changing the subject.

'What?' Hardcastle turned to face his youngest daughter, surprise etched large on his face. 'But how d'you know that the war will be over by then, Maud? You and Charles both said you'd wait until the end of hostilities. And anyway it's only three months since you got engaged.'

Charles Spencer, then a lieutenant in the Loyal Regiment, had been nursed back to health by Maud following a war wound. He had proposed to her in March and, with her parents' blessing, she had accepted.

'Charles is a captain now and has been told that he's been accepted for a regular commission,' said Maud, 'so I can look forward to being an officer's wife.'

'Yes, and you might finish up in India, my lass. I've heard that the climate there is dreadful.'

'It is,' said Alice, who had been born in Peshawar, where her father had been serving as a sergeant with the Royal Garrison Artillery at the time of her birth. 'And your husband will be away on patrol a lot of the time.'

'I suppose Charles hasn't got any eligible friends, has he?' enquired Kitty wistfully, interrupting this talk of marriage. Unfortunately, her self-confidence and strong-willed temperament managed to dissuade most men from thoughts of matrimony.

'It looks as though we'll be losing all our family soon,' said Alice gloomily. She put down her knitting and stood up. 'I think I'll make a cup of tea.'

Monday morning saw Hardcastle relieved to get away from the travails of family life, but at once wondering how he was to pay for a wedding that now looked as though it would take place next year. He knew that he could not economize; undoubtedly Charles Spencer's brother officers would be there in force and they would expect Hardcastle to put on a good show.

But his preoccupation with his mounting financial problems was interrupted by the entry of Sergeant Marriott.

'Good morning, sir.'

'How old is your daughter, Marriott?' asked Hardcastle bluntly.

'My daughter, sir?' Marriott was taken aback to be greeted by such a question. 'She's, um, seven, I think, sir. Yes,' he said, after some thought, 'she's seven, but why d'you ask?'

'Take a word of advice, Marriott. Start saving for the wedding now.'

Marriott laughed. 'I think I've got plenty of time before I start worrying about that, sir.'

'That's what I thought, Marriott,' muttered the DDI, 'but now Maud tells me she proposes to marry next year.'

'Please offer her my congratulations, sir. Well, mine and Lorna's.'

'Thank you, Marriott.' Hardcastle placed his pipe in his pocket. 'But right now we've got a murder to worry about.' He glanced at his watch. 'I think this would be as good a time as any to go to Aldershot and speak to this here Colonel Garside. Give Sergeant Glover at the APM's office a call on that telephone thing and ask him if Colonel Frobisher would be kind enough to alert Captain McIntyre.' Although a telephone had recently been installed in Hardcastle's office, he had no intention of using it, regarding it as a newfangled invention that would not last.

'We met Captain McIntyre last year, sir, when we were investigating the murder at the bureau de change at Victoria station.'

'So we did, Marriott, so we did. I thought I recognized the name.'

A Vauxhall staff car bearing military police insignia was parked immediately outside Aldershot railway station. As Hardcastle and Marriott approached, its military police corporal snapped to attention and saluted. 'Inspector Hardcastle, sir?'

'That's me, Corporal.'

'I'm to take you to Captain McIntyre's office, sir.'

Within ten minutes the car had arrived between the forbidding lines of the three-storey blocks of Salamanca Barracks, and the corporal pointed out Captain McIntyre's office.

Hardcastle and Marriott alighted, and the DDI pushed open a door marked MILITARY POLICE.

'Ah, there you are, Inspector, Hector McIntyre.' The tall Gordon Highlanders officer crossed the room and shook hands with the DDI and Marriott. He was wearing a kilt of the Gordon tartan, a sporran that came to his knees, and a khaki tunic with a cutaway skirt and a brassard bearing the letters MP. 'Good to see you again. Colonel Frobisher told me that you've another murder to deal with.'

'Indeed, Captain McIntyre.'

'Another soldier is it?' McIntyre asked with a laugh. 'That's the trouble with soldiers: we teach 'em to kill people and they go about doing it.'

'It's not necessarily a soldier who did the deed this time, Captain McIntyre, but there is an officer here in Aldershot who might be able to give me some information.'

'Aye, the APM mentioned that you wanted to see a Colonel Garside of the Sappers. He's in command of a Royal Engineers' depot battalion. I took the liberty of making an appointment for you to see him this afternoon.' McIntyre glanced at his watch. 'In the meantime, I dare say you could down a dram or two and see off a spot of lunch in the mess, eh?'

'That would be most welcome, Captain.'

After lunch, McIntyre and the two CID officers were driven from the officers' mess to Barossa Barracks at South Camp. McIntyre then escorted Hardcastle and Marriott to the headquarters block where Lieutenant Colonel Leighton Garside had his office.

Hardcastle had always believed that colonels in home stations would be quite old men, usually with a bushy moustache, a monocle and some physical impairment. But that was probably because most of the officers of that rank that he had met in the past were what the army called 'dugouts': retired officers unfit for active duty who had been recalled to the Colours to replace their fitter colleagues.

Hardcastle knew from Dudley ffrench's description, however, that Leighton Garside was a young man, and he could see that this officer was probably in his early thirties and was clean-shaven. His tunic bore the ribbons of the Military Cross and the 1914–15 Star.

'The two police officers I mentioned, Colonel,' said McIntyre, saluting as he showed the two detectives into Garside's office. He turned to Hardcastle. 'I've arranged for the car to be outside to take you back to the railway station when you're finished here, Inspector.' He faced the colonel and saluted again. 'Colonel.'

'Leighton Garside, gentlemen.' Once McIntyre had departed, the colonel crossed the office and shook hands with Hardcastle and Marriott.

'I'm Divisional Detective Inspector Hardcastle of Scotland Yard, Colonel.' When out of London, Hardcastle often claimed to be from Commissioner's Office, imagining it gave him a status that he did not need. 'And this is Detective Sergeant Marriott.'

'Please take a seat,' said Garside, as he sat down behind his desk. 'I have to admit to being somewhat mystified as to why you should wish to see me.'

'I'm investigating a murder that took place in Whilber Street, Westminster, a week ago, Colonel.'

'I still don't understand . . .' Garside began.

'The victim's name was Georgina Cheney, formerly Heath,' said Hardcastle.

'Good God!' exclaimed Garside. 'Somebody's murdered Gina?'

'You obviously remember her,' said Hardcastle.

'Indeed I do. A sweet girl. We had a fling in Malta back in, what, 1912? Yes, that would be right.' Garside grinned boyishly. 'Damn near cost me my commission, but it was worth it.'

'You did know, I suppose, that she was married to a naval officer at the time.'

'Yes, I did, but what the hell. I was about twenty-seven at the time and still a lieutenant and to be honest I was thinking of quitting the army. I got a hell of a roasting from my colonel when he found out about the affair and he sent me back to Blighty with a black mark against my name. To this very unit as a matter of fact. But then the war started and suddenly there were more important things to think about than casual affairs.'

'Did you ever visit Mrs Cheney in England, Colonel?' asked Marriott.

'No. The last time I saw Gina was when she came down to the port at Valletta to wave me off when I went home in disgrace. I wasn't aware that she was in England. Not a very wise move, considering the Zeppelin and Gotha raids. How did she die, as a matter of interest?'

'She was strangled and thrown out of her bedroom window,' said Hardcastle.

'Bloody hell! Well that lets me out.' Using his right hand, Garside lifted his left arm and dropped it on the desk with a thump 'It's made of tin.' The detectives noticed for the first time that the colonel wore a black glove on his left hand. 'I can manage a lot of things since I lost most of my arm, but strangling someone ain't one of them.'

'Oh, I'm sorry, I didn't realize,' said Hardcastle, furious with himself for failing to notice Garside's disability.

'I was with a tunnelling company sapping under the Messines Ridge. You must've heard about the mines that were set off a year ago.'

'A magnificent effort, Colonel,' murmured Hardcastle.

'I was commanding a company at the time, but we had a fall in the shaft and my left arm was trapped. There was nothing the medics could do but cut it off.' Garside shrugged as he thought back to that day and with it the agonizing belief that he was destined to die trapped beneath the German lines. But then a brave medical officer, himself in great danger from a further fall, crawled along the tunnel and carried out a primitive and immediate amputation. 'By the time the mines were set off, I was in the base hospital at Boulogne, but I felt the tremors even there. They were kind enough to give me a medal for my pains, made me a half colonel and sent me back here again,' he added, speaking with a measure of cynicism. 'It doesn't really look as though I can help you any further, gentlemen.'

'Not necessarily,' said Hardcastle. 'I understand from other people I've spoken to that Mrs Cheney had quite a reputation for being a good-time girl.'

'I don't think there's much doubt about that, Inspector.' Garside took a pipe from an ashtray, and using one hand adroitly filled it from a tobacco jar. 'I thought she might get herself into trouble one day. Not being murdered so much as finishing up with an unwanted pregnancy,' he added, lighting his pipe.

'D'you mind if I smoke, Colonel?' asked Hardcastle, taking out his pipe.

'Good heavens no. My apologies. Here, help yourself.' Garside pushed his tobacco jar across the desk.

'Was there anyone else you knew of that she might've been having

an affair with, Colonel?' asked Hardcastle, once his pipe was alight
with Garside's tobacco.

Garside laughed at Hardcastle's query. 'Quite a few, I imagine.
She was hardly what you'd call the soul of discretion. I seem to
recall that I took her over from a lawyer fellow, name of Henson,
but I've no idea what happened to him.'

'No one else, Colonel?' queried Marriott. Neither he nor
Hardcastle had any intention of telling Garside that Henson had
already been interviewed.

Garside shook his head. 'As I said, there were probably quite a
few, but I don't remember any other names.'

'God damn it, Marriott!' exclaimed Hardcastle, once he and his
sergeant were seated on the train back to London. 'We're getting
nowhere with this damned murder.'

'The Air Force people at Hornchurch might be able to shed some
light on it, sir.'

'Maybe, although I've got me doubts. Nevertheless we'll have
to try.'

But when Hardcastle arrived back at his office at Cannon Row police
station, a message was awaiting him, the outcome of which would
make his task even more difficult than it was at present.

'Sir,' said Detective Inspector Rhodes, appearing on the threshold
of the DDI's office.

'What is it, Mr Rhodes?'

'While you were at Aldershot, sir, a message came across from
the Yard. You're to see Detective Chief Inspector Wensley as soon
as possible.'

'What does the Elephant want, I wonder?' said Hardcastle, using
the name by which the head of the CID was known throughout the
Metropolitan Police because of the size of his nose. It was a sobri-
quet less complimentary than the one used by the press, to whom
he was known as 'Ace' Wensley on account of his detective prowess.

SEVEN

Pausing only to pick up his bowler hat and umbrella, Hardcastle crossed the courtyard and ascended the steps of Commissioner's Office. Raising his hat in acknowledgement of the salute afforded him by the constable on duty at the entrance, he walked along the main corridor and tapped on the door that bore Wensley's name.

'DDI Hardcastle of A, sir. You wished to see me?'

The fifty-three-year-old Detective Chief Inspector Frederick Wensley was in every sense a big man. He was soberly dressed in a dark suit and a wing collar, and sported a pearl pin in his grey tie. His impressive record as a detective, spanning some twenty-three years, had included the solving of numerous murders and robberies, and in 1911 he had stood beside Winston Churchill at the Sidney Street Siege, characteristically armed with only an umbrella. Furthermore, he was one of those rare officers with a modernistic approach to police work and was always on the lookout for improving methods of detection rather than relying on old techniques. Originally a teetotaller, he had begun to drink when he found that informants did not trust a detective who refused to drink with them.

'Sit down, Ernie, and tell me how you're getting on with the murder of Georgina Cheney.'

'Not making much progress, I'm afraid, sir.' Hardcastle gave Wensley the unvarnished details of what little he had learned so far. He knew that any attempt to delude the head of the CID was pointless and admitted that he was not close to making an arrest. 'I've still to see the Royal Air Force officers at Sutton's Farm, sir, but I'm tending towards the killer being someone who knew the woman in Malta.'

'Well, Ernie, I'm about to add to your troubles. I would have given this job to an officer based here at the Yard, but as you've already got the Cheney murder you can have the others.'

'The others, sir?' Hardcastle did not like the sound of that.

'There have been two other similar murders in the last six months.' Wensley drew a docket across his desk and opened it. 'A

Mrs Blanche Hardy was murdered on W Division on the tenth of January. Her body was discovered by her husband, Major Andrew Hardy, at their house in Kings Avenue, Clapham. Major Hardy had returned unexpectedly from France having been granted leave. He didn't advise his wife that he was on his way, believing that his homecoming would be a nice surprise. In the event, the surprise turned out to be his.'

'And the other one, sir?'

'The other one was on the twenty-seventh of March. Mrs Hazel Lacey, the wife of Lieutenant Colonel Gerard Lacey, was found at the Wardour Hotel in Wardour Street on C Division. Her body was discovered by a chambermaid. Colonel Lacey was in Ypres when he got the news.'

'And both are unsolved, of course, sir?'

'So far, Ernie. Both victims had been killed by manual strangulation, and each was a well-to-do young woman whose husband was a regular officer serving overseas. So you can see that there is a similarity between those two and your Cheney murder. It looks as though we might have a multiple murderer on our hands.'

'Did Dr Spilsbury examine those two, sir?'

'Yes, he did. And I suggest that you make him your first port of call. I want you to put all three toppings together and see if you can find a common factor, other than those I've outlined. If you want more manpower just say the word and you can have whatever you need.'

'But won't the DDIs on those divisions resent me taking their cases off of them, sir?'

'I doubt it, Ernie. You wouldn't have minded if I'd given the Cheney murder to someone else, would you? You Royal A chaps are always telling me how much you have to do,' said Wensley with a smile. 'Anyway, Fowler and Sullivan will do as they're told, and if you have any trouble from them let me know. I'll soon put them right.'

'Very good, sir.'

'Keep me informed from time to time, Ernie. I know that Basil Thomson is tied up with Special Branch these days, but he has taken an interest in these toppings and it doesn't do to get on the wrong side of the assistant commissioner for crime.'

Hardcastle seated himself behind his desk and reached for his pipe. He was aghast at having been presented with two more murders to solve, but it was a compliment that 'Ace' Wensley had shown sufficient confidence in him to give him the task. He shouted for Marriott.

'Sir?' said Marriott, buttoning his jacket as he entered the DDI's office.

'You know I've always been a fair man, don't you, m'boy,' said Hardcastle jocularly.

'Yes, sir.' Marriott had no alternative but to agree, whatever his inner thoughts may have been.

'And I've always believed in sharing things.'

'Yes, sir,' said Marriott apprehensively.

'Well, m'boy, this is what I'm going to share with you.' Hardcastle went on to explain about the monumental task with which he had just been saddled by Detective Chief Inspector Wensley. 'So I've decided to let you share in the undoubted glory that will result from three successful prosecutions.'

'Thank you very much, guv'nor,' said Marriott with a hint of sarcasm. He knew that the investigation of three murders would afford him very little time for any sort of social life over the next few weeks, if not months. He knew also that his wife Lorna would not be pleased and that she would question, yet again, why he had not stayed in the Uniform Branch instead of becoming a detective.

'I wondered how long it would be before the powers-that-be at Scotland Yard would put two and two together, my dear Hardcastle.' Dr Bernard Spilsbury turned from the cadaver he was exploring and invited the DDI and Marriott to take a seat.

'Mr Wensley suggested that there were similarities between the murders of Blanche Hardy, Hazel Lacey and Georgina Cheney, sir,' said Hardcastle.

'I can only speak from a pathologist's point of view, of course, but I would tentatively postulate that the pattern of strangulation indicates quite strongly that the same person was responsible for all three murders. The positioning of the thumb marks and fingermarks on the throats of all three victims seems to suggest it. And in each case there was a fracturing of the thyroid cornu. In both the Hardy and Lacey murders, sexual intercourse had taken place recently. It had also taken place in the case of Mrs Cheney, but I told you that when I did her post-mortem.'

'Is there any way in which the semen can be identified as

belonging to the same person, sir? So that it can, for example, be compared with the other cases,' asked Marriott.

'Oh, if only there were, my dear Marriott,' said Spilsbury, 'forensic science would have made a great advance.'

'Where are we going to start, sir?' asked Marriott, once he and the DDI were back at Cannon Row police station.

'We'll take the first one first, Marriott,' said Hardcastle, as though that were obvious. 'We go down to Brixton nick and have a word with Mr Cornelius Fowler.'

'Yes, sir.' Marriott glanced at the clock behind Hardcastle and sensed that an early night was out of the question.

'Come, Marriott, there's work to be done.' Hardcastle picked up his hat and umbrella and made for the door.

Once in Whitehall, the DDI stared impatiently up and down the street in search of a cab. Although the murder of Blanche Hardy had occurred six months ago, the DDI gave the impression that there was not a moment to lose.

Mounting the steps of the three-storey building in Brixton Road, Hardcastle pushed open the inner door and approached the counter.

Deliberately ignoring the callers, the elderly station officer, his four-bar chevron indicating that he was a station sergeant, continued to write in the large Occurrence Book.

But Hardcastle was accustomed to dealing with such malcontents whose churlish behaviour was most likely the result of being passed over for promotion to inspector rank. He rapped sharply on the counter with the hook of his umbrella, causing the sergeant to look up with a frown. Rising ponderously from his desk the sergeant ambled across the room and peered at the callers.

'In a bit of a hurry are we?' he enquired sarcastically.

'DDI Hardcastle of A. When you can spare the time, *Sergeant*, perhaps you'd be so good as to direct me to Mr Fowler's office.'

'Oh, I'm sorry, sir. I didn't realize who you was, sir,' said the station officer, becoming immediately obsequious. He lifted the flap in the counter and pointed to a door. 'Through there and up the stairs, sir, and it's the first door on the right. I can get a PC to show you, sir,' he added unwisely.

'I'm quite capable of climbing a flight of stairs and finding the

DDI's office without assistance,' snapped Hardcastle, further adding to the sergeant's discomfort.

He pushed open the W Division DDI's door. 'Well, Connie, old son, I've come to pull your chestnuts out of the fire.'

'Yes, I heard that the Elephant had given you this job, Ernie. And I'm very pleased to get shot of it. I don't like having unsolved cases on my books. But of course you don't have much to do on A Division so I suppose you can fit it in.'

'*Not much to do!*' exclaimed Hardcastle, still irritated by the station officer's curmudgeonly attitude. 'I've got the seat of government on my patch, along with Parliament, Buck House, Clarence House, Marlborough House and Westminster Abbey, to say nothing of Windsor Castle and the Palace of Holyrood House in Edinburgh.'

'Bloody hell, Ernie, you'd better have a drink.' Without further ado, Fowler withdrew a bottle of Scotch and three glasses from his bottom drawer.

'This is Marriott, my bag carrier, Connie.'

'I suppose your guv'nor's roped you in for this job, has he, Skipper?' Fowler busied himself pouring the whisky and handing it round.

'So, tell me the tale,' said Hardcastle, having taken a goodly sip of Fowler's Scotch.

'Major Andrew Hardy is with the Tank Corps somewhere in France,' Fowler began. 'He came home on leave on the tenth of January to his house in Kings Avenue – that's the smart end of my manor – and found his wife Blanche dead in the bedroom. She'd been strangled. There was no sign of forced entry, so I'm presuming that the murderer was known to her.'

'Didn't Mrs Hardy have any staff, sir?' asked Marriott. 'A housemaid or something of the sort?'

'Unusually no, Skip. According to Major Hardy there used to be a housemaid, but it seems Mrs Hardy got rid of her, although the major didn't know who the girl was or why his missus got shot of her. By all accounts there was a woman who came in twice a week to do the cleaning, but apparently Mrs Hardy did her own cooking. When she wasn't out to lunch or dinner, that is. Local enquiries suggested that she went out quite often and usually in the company of a man not her husband. And before you ask, there were several different men, but we've not been able to trace any of them.'

'D'you reckon she was a bit of a good-time girl, then, Connie?' suggested Hardcastle.

'Looks that way. Incidentally, she wasn't short of cash. According to the woman who came in to clean, Mrs Hardy had quite a fortune of her own.'

'How would a charwoman know that, sir?' asked Marriott.

'The charwoman, a Mrs Beatrice Groves, said that she and Mrs Hardy often sat in the kitchen having a bit of a chinwag over a cup of tea, and Mrs Hardy told her all sorts of things. I got the impression that Blanche Hardy was a bit lonely and sometimes poured out her heart about things not usually discussed with household staff.'

'D'you have an address for Mrs Groves, sir?' Marriott was busily taking notes.

'There you are, Skip.' Fowler handed a docket to Marriott. 'It's all in there: statements, names and addresses, post-mortem report. Take it with you. I shan't be needing it any more,' he added with a laugh.

The following morning Hardcastle spent an hour studying DDI Fowler's docket on the Blanche Hardy murder and making himself fully conversant with the details.

'Time we got ourselves up to Vine Street nick, Marriott,' he said, opening the door of the detectives' office. 'We'll take a cab.'

'Yes, sir,' said Marriott, as he raced down the stairs after the DDI. He was not quite sure why Hardcastle had mentioned taking a cab; he always took a cab when he went about his enquiries knowing that his expenses claims would never be queried.

Vine Street police station was hidden in a small turning between Piccadilly and Regent Street. As the two detectives alighted from their taxi, Hardcastle paused to look up at the four-storey building.

'The Marquess of Queensberry was brought here to Vine Street twenty-three years ago, Marriott, after he'd been arrested for criminal libel against Oscar Wilde.'

'Really, sir?' Marriott was surprised, yet again, at the rare flashes of historical knowledge that his DDI revealed from time to time.

'Can I help you, sir?' The policeman standing on the doorstep moved to block the entrance.

'I'm DDI Hardcastle from A, lad. I've come to see Mr Sullivan.'

'Very good, sir.' The PC sketched a salute. 'I take it you know the way,' he said, pulling open the heavy door.

DDI William Sullivan was a sharp dresser. Always immaculately attired, he wore a well-cut suit with a double-breasted waistcoat and sported a monocle. He invariably carried a Malacca cane, substituting an umbrella for it only when rain threatened. It was a style of dress that caused him to be known, to villains and policeman alike, as 'Posh Bill with the Piccadilly window.' Furthermore, it was rumoured that he had a small mirror fixed inside his curly brimmed bowler hat in order to ensure that his hair was tidy whenever he entered a building. None of which endeared him to Hardcastle; in fact, the two DDIs disliked each other, but masked that enmity with a false bonhomie.

'Good morning, Ernie old boy,' exclaimed Sullivan effusively, when Hardcastle and Marriott entered his office. 'The Elephant warned me you'd be turning up on my doorstep.'

'Yes, Bill, I've come to clear up one of your toppings for you. Mr Wensley reckoned it was too difficult for you C Division people.'

'It's not that I couldn't solve it, old boy, it's just that we don't have the time on a busy working division like St James's. We'd've got around to it eventually.'

'Not what I heard,' muttered Hardcastle, as he and Marriott sat down uninvited.

'It's all there, Ernie.' Sullivan handed Marriott a thick docket. 'I'll give it to your skipper because I suspect he'll be doing most of the work. But in short, Hazel Lacey was found by an hysterical chambermaid called Rose Miller in her room at the Wardour Hotel in Wardour Street on the twenty-seventh of March. She'd been strangled. It's presumed that Mrs Lacey was having an affair with the man who booked the room.'

'Do you know who that man was, sir?' asked Marriott.

'According to the manager, Skip, a man calling himself Kenneth Reeves made the booking by telephone the day before. None of the hotel staff remember seeing Reeves and exhaustive enquiries have failed to find any trace of him.'

'That's a great help,' said Hardcastle acidly. 'It means I'll have to start from scratch. Wensley said that her husband's in the army. Is that true?'

'He's a lieutenant colonel in The Buffs. He came home for the funeral, but he's now back in France.'

'Well, I'm not bloody well going over there to talk to him,' said Hardcastle grimly.

It was a somewhat disgruntled Hardcastle who returned to his police station at Cannon Row. He sat down behind his desk and filled his pipe, once again to contemplate the enormity of the task that the head of the CID had given him.

His reverie was interrupted by the arrival of Marriott clutching the two dockets containing details of the investigations that the police on W and C Divisions had carried out.

'I've been through the papers, sir. Mr Collins' men examined both scenes for fingerprints, but found nothing that matched anything in their records.'

'Comes as no surprise,' said Hardcastle moodily.

'But it seems that Mrs Groves was not interviewed in depth, sir.'

'Who the hell's Mrs Groves, Marriott?'

'Beatrice Groves is the charwoman who was employed by Blanche Hardy, sir. If you remember, Mr Fowler at Brixton said that Mrs Hardy confided in her. Might be worth having a talk with her.'

'I was just going to suggest that, Marriott. Where does she live?'

Marriott turned to the page in the docket that contained Mrs Groves' brief statement. 'Saxby Road, sir. It's only a short walk from the Kings Avenue address where Mrs Hardy was found.'

'And what does Mrs Groves' statement say, Marriott?'

'Just that she was employed by Mrs Blanche Hardy as a cleaner, sir, and the dates.'

'Is that it?'

'Yes, sir.'

'That's bloody sloppy police work, Marriott, and what's more—' But Hardcastle prevented himself from making an adverse comment about DDI Fowler's supervision of his detectives. He would never criticize a senior officer to a sergeant, whatever his personal opinion might have been. He pulled out his hunter and flicked open the cover. 'That's a job for this afternoon, I think. But first we'll sink a pint or two at the Red Lion, Marriott. Then we'll be properly equipped to go about police business.'

The detectives' arrival in the downstairs bar of the pub was somewhat marred when Hardcastle caught sight of Charlie Simpson, a reporter from the *London Daily Chronicle*, perched on a bar stool.

'Morning, Mr Hardcastle. Can I buy you a pint?'

'Provided it's without prejudice, Simpson,' said Hardcastle, coining a useful legal phrase that, in his mind, precluded him from being under any obligation. Although the CID officers from Cannon Row rarely paid for their beer in the Red Lion, the DDI saw no reason why a Fleet Street hack should not put his hand in his pocket.

'I hear you've got two more murders on your plate now, Mr Hardcastle,' said Simpson, once he had ordered a round of drinks.

'Now who would have planted a little seed like that in your mind?' scoffed Hardcastle.

'A little bird at the Yard, guv'nor.'

'Take a word from one who knows, Simpson. Get yourself some *reliable* informants.'

Simpson laughed. 'Yeah, all right, guv'nor, but have you got a titbit for me? Like when you're going to make an arrest.'

'Don't worry,' said Hardcastle. 'You'll be the last to know. Now, if you don't mind, I'd like to get on with my beer.'

'Well, if you'll excuse me, Mr Hardcastle, I've got a deadline to meet.'

'Don't let me detain you,' said Hardcastle, as Simpson picked up his hat and made his way upstairs.

'Someone's been talking to the press, sir,' said Marriott.

'You have a happy knack of getting to the nub of the matter, Marriott,' said Hardcastle sarcastically. 'And it could've been anyone. Somebody on W or C Divisions, or even at Commissioner's Office. It's surprising what a detective will do for the price of a couple of Scotches.'

EIGHT

The dwellings in Saxby Road were terraced and had probably been built early in Queen Victoria's reign. The house in which Beatrice Groves lived was well maintained, its windows sparklingly clean and the doorstep freshly whitened.

The door was answered by a plump, jolly woman probably around forty years of age. At the sight of the two detectives, she whipped off her apron and secreted it behind her back.

'Mrs Groves, is it? We're police officers, madam,' said
Hardcastle. 'But there's nothing to concern yourself about,' he
added hurriedly.

'Yes, I'm Beatrice Groves. I suppose you've come about poor
Blanche.'

'We have indeed, madam. I'm Divisional Detective Inspector
Hardcastle of the Whitehall Division and this is Detective Sergeant
Marriott.'

'You'd better come in.' Mrs Groves showed them into the parlour
at the front of the house and invited them to sit down. 'From
Whitehall, you say? I thought the Brixton police were dealing with
this terrible business.'

'They were originally,' said Hardcastle, 'but the head of the
Criminal Investigation Department has asked me to look into it.'
He thought it unwise to mention that the thinking at Scotland Yard
was that Blanche Hardy had fallen victim to a killer who went on
to murder two other women.

'Those other detectives didn't seem too interested in what I had
to tell them,' said Beatrice Groves, 'but I don't know how you
detectives do your work.'

'I understand that you worked for Mrs Hardy, Mrs Groves.'
Hardcastle was not going to be drawn into a discussion about the
shortcomings of the Brixton police.

'For about eighteen months. I had to do something when my
Billy was killed on the Somme in 1916. He put his age down and
volunteered for the London Regiment. I told him not to go; that
there were younger single men who still had to do their bit, but he
wouldn't listen. He'd never listen, my Billy.'

'You were going to tell us about Mrs Hardy,' said Hardcastle,
gently steering Mrs Groves back to the purpose of his visit.

'So I was. Now, where was I? Oh yes, I saw this advertisement
in the newsagent's asking for a cleaner. Well, I'd never done anything
like that before; I'm a toffee maker by trade. The pension don't
amount to much, but I don't suppose Billy thought it'd come to that.
They was all convinced it'd be the other chap what got killed. But
needs must when the devil drives, and Blanche took me on. I used
to go round for a couple of hours three mornings a week to do for
her. There wasn't much to it; she was a tidy soul and seemed to be
out more than she was in.'

'We've been told that you got to know her well, Mrs Groves,' said Marriott.

'Yes, dear, we was more like friends than mistress and servant. I'd not been going round there more than a week when she told me to call her Blanche. I mean it didn't seem right not to call her madam, but she wasn't having any of it. Sometimes we'd sit in the kitchen and she'd pour her heart out, the poor dear.'

'I'm told that she once had a housemaid. Do you know what happened to her?'

'I don't know who she was. She was never there when I was; she was only part time, you see. Blanche said as how she didn't have much need for a maid because there was nothing for the girl to do now I was going in, so she let her go.'

'When would that have been, Mrs Groves?' asked Marriott.

'About a year ago, I suppose, but I'm not sure.' Beatrice Groves spent a few seconds staring at the empty fireplace before looking at Marriott again. 'I rather got the impression that Blanche was a lonely soul, Sergeant, what with her husband being at the Front. A major he is, by all accounts. And I know what it is to worry about a man what's mixed up in the fighting. Not that I have to worry about that any more.' Her face took on a sad expression.

'We've heard that Mrs Hardy had a number of gentlemen friends, Mrs Groves,' said Hardcastle. 'D'you know anything about that?'

'She did mention that there was one or two gents, friends of her husband she said, what'd come round occasionally and take her out to supper or the theatre. But who'd blame her? I s'pose it stopped her worrying about her man and I know what that's like. Reading the newspapers every day to see if your hubby was in the casualty lists.'

'But surely you'd've been notified immediately if your husband had become a casualty,' suggested Hardcastle.

'Not always. Sometimes it took the War Office ages to tell you when someone had been killed or taken prisoner. It was them poor souls whose man was posted missing that was the worst. Not that it happened to me. My Billy was killed outright on the first day of the Somme. First of July 1916 that was. That General Haig sent our men out to be bloody well slaughtered by all accounts, if you'll excuse my French.'

'D'you happen to know the names of any of these gentlemen friends of Mrs Hardy?' asked Marriott.

'No, Blanche never mentioned who they was, and it wasn't my place to ask.'

'I've been told that Mrs Hardy was quite well off,' said Hardcastle, changing the subject slightly.

'Yes, she was. She mentioned once that her father had left her a tidy sum when he died. She told me that he'd owned a factory in Middlesbrough and that he'd made a lot of money out of making jam and biscuits and that sort of thing. She was certainly always dressed in beautiful clothes. As a matter of fact, she gave me one or two frocks that she said she didn't need any more. Not that they fitted me,' said Beatrice Groves, with a laugh. 'But I was able to sell 'em.'

'Did she happen to mention which plays she'd seen?' asked Marriott.

'Plays?' For a moment or two, Mrs Groves gazed pensively out of the window. 'There was only one she told me about. It was called *Zig-Zag* and it was on at the Hippodrome,' she said eventually. 'Blanche really enjoyed it because it made her laugh. Well, it would with that George Robey in it. I told her that having a good laugh would take her out of herself.'

'Do you remember which night it was that she went?'

'I was a Saturday. I only remember that particular time because it was the Saturday before Christmas, so that would have been—'

'The twenty-second of December last,' said Marriott, as he checked the date in his pocket diary.

'Well, thank you for your assistance, Mrs Groves,' said Hardcastle, rising to his feet. 'You've been most helpful, but we might need to see you again.'

'That's all right, Inspector. I'm always here.'

The two detectives walked down Saxby Road towards Lyham Road in search of a cab.

'Why did you ask that question about any of the plays that Mrs Hardy might've seen, Marriott?'

'Having got the date and the theatre, sir, we might be able to find out who bought the tickets.'

'You're coming on a treat, Marriott.' Hardcastle laughed. 'But there are about thirteen hundred seats in the Hippodrome,' he said, having made it his business to gather odd scraps of information like that. 'Are you suggesting we interview everyone who bought tickets?'

'It might come to that, sir,' said Marriott, mildly irritated that the DDI had made fun of his initiative.

'Perhaps so,' said Hardcastle thoughtfully. 'We certainly didn't get much to help us from Mrs Groves, but at least she told us as much as she knew. Tomorrow we'll see what these daredevil flyers at Sutton's Farm have to say for themselves. Remind me to arrange it with Colonel Frobisher when we get back to the nick.' He paused. 'How do we get to Hornchurch, Marriott?'

Marriott knew that the question would be asked sooner or later. 'Underground train from Westminster to Hornchurch, sir. It's about an hour's journey.'

'Bugger that!' exclaimed Hardcastle crossly. 'I'm not travelling on an Underground train to carry out a murder enquiry. We'll take a cab.'

'That'll cost a pretty penny, sir.'

'We're conducting three murder enquiries, Marriott,' said Hardcastle, 'and I'm not wasting time sitting on a bloody train for an hour when we can get there in half the time by taxi. If the Commissioner don't like it, he can lump it.'

Wednesday morning was a dull and overcast day with intermittent showers. And to make matters worse, Hardcastle and Marriott had to stand in Bridge Street for at least ten minutes before the DDI sighted a cab.

'D'you know where Sutton's Farm is, cabbie?' demanded Hardcastle.

'What, the flying corps airfield near Hornchurch?'

'That's the place.'

'Course I do, guv'nor, but it'll cost yer.'

'That's all right,' said Hardcastle, 'because the Commissioner of Police is paying. And that means you don't take us by the scenic route. Understood?'

'Would I do such a thing, guv'nor?' asked the cabbie plaintively, as he wrenched down the flag.

A sentry, wearing the distinctive wrap-over tunic of the Royal Flying Corps and holding a rifle with a fixed bayonet, stood motionless at the entrance to Royal Air Force, Sutton's Farm. Behind him was a sign bearing the legend: 78 Squadron Royal Flying Corps.

'I see they haven't got around to changing that sign yet, Marriott,' said Hardcastle, and then addressed himself to the sentry. 'We're police officers,' he announced.

'There's some military police officer waiting for you in the guard-room, mate,' said the sentry, moving only his mouth.

'It's "inspector" to you, *mate!*' snapped Hardcastle, and pushed open the door of the single-storey wooden hut behind the sentry.

'Ah, you must be Inspector Hardcastle.' The speaker was an army officer with crowns on his cuffs and a brassard bearing the letters DAPM on his right arm. 'James Corrigan, Welsh Guards.'

'I'm grateful for your assistance, Major Corrigan,' said Hardcastle. 'This is Detective Sergeant Marriott.'

'Perhaps if we adjourn to the mess for a cup of coffee, you would explain how you want to play this,' said Corrigan.

The officers' mess was on the far side of the airfield and as they walked around the perimeter a Sopwith Camel took off towards them. Hardcastle and Marriott ducked involuntarily.

'They don't fly that low, Inspector,' said Corrigan, who had not even flinched. 'They've lost too many pilots in combat for them to risk doing low-level aerobatics.'

There were six or seven officers seated in the mess. Most were reading newspapers or magazines such as *The Field* or the *Illustrated London News*, but one or two were writing letters. Neither Captain Slater nor Sub-Lieutenant Etherington was among them.

Once the coffee had been served, Corrigan asked, 'What exactly do you want to do here, Inspector? Colonel Frobisher said you were investigating a murder, but he didn't elaborate.'

Hardcastle explained about the murder of Georgina Cheney and told him of the parties at her house in Whilber Street that had been attended by officers from this squadron. He did not, however, mention the other two murders that he was now investigating. At least, not yet.

'Sub-Lieutenant Etherington suggested that Major Lawford could vouch for his whereabouts on the night of the murder, and presumably he can also tell me where Captain Guy Slater was that night. There was also an officer known only as Jonno who also attended these parties and I'd like to have a word with him.'

'In that case, we'll start with Major Lawford,' said Corrigan, only pausing to pick up his cap and don his Sam Browne as they left the mess.

It was a short walk to the squadron's headquarters block where Major Lawford had his office.

'Good morning, Monty.' Corrigan led the way in and saluted.

'Good day to you, James.' Lawford, wearing Royal Flying Corps uniform, stood up and glanced enquiringly at the two detectives.

'This is Divisional Detective Inspector Hardcastle of the Metropolitan Police, Monty,' said Corrigan, 'and his assistant, Detective Sergeant Marriott.'

'How d'you do, gentlemen. Montague Lawford.' The squadron commander crossed the office and shook hands. 'What can I do for the police? Not these young fools racing around the countryside in their motor cars again, surely.' He paused and stroked his moustache. 'No, I suppose not.'

'It's a little more serious than that, Major,' said Hardcastle, as the four of them sat down. 'I'm investigating a murder.'

'If it was a German, it's allowed,' said Lawford jocularly, but seeing that his comment had not amused Hardcastle, he apologized. 'Sorry, not a good joke. How d'you think I can help you?'

Once more, Hardcastle explained about the murder of Georgina Cheney and the parties she had held.

'Good God!' exclaimed Lawford. 'D'you think that one of my officers might've murdered the woman, Inspector?'

'It's a possibility I'm bound to consider, Major. I've established that both Captain Slater and Sub-Lieutenant Etherington were present at these parties, but both those officers deny being there on the night of Tuesday the eleventh of June. Etherington assured me that you would be in a position to confirm that, as far as he was concerned.'

Lawford picked up his walking stick and rapped loudly on the wall. A sergeant appeared immediately.

'Sergeant Devlin, be so good as to get me the duty log for . . .' Lawford paused and glanced at Hardcastle. 'The eleventh of June, you said?'

'That's correct,' said Hardcastle.

'You better bring the log for the twelfth as well, Sergeant Devlin.'

'Won't be a moment, sir.'

A minute later, Devlin returned with the two logs and placed them on Lawford's desk.

'Slater and Etherington,' said Lawford, running his finger down the entries. 'Captain Slater was on night patrol and took off at nine pip emma. He returned at two ack emma.' He looked up. 'That seems to let him off the hook, but according to the log Etherington was off duty until he reported for morning patrol on the twelfth at nine that morning.'

'Have you any idea where Etherington might've been, Major?' asked Marriott.

'No. I don't recall seeing him in the mess that evening, but he might've been in his quarters.'

'Is there any way of checking that?' Marriott had begun making a few notes.

'I could ask around. Some of the other officers might have seen him, or he might've gone down to the local pub, the Dog and Duck, for a drink. It's a great favourite.'

'That would be helpful, Major,' said Hardcastle. 'There is one other officer that I was told attended these parties, but the only name I have is Jonno.'

'Jonno?' Lawford leaned back in his chair and surveyed the ceiling. 'We've two or three officers here called John,' he said, looking at Hardcastle again, 'but the only one who's known as Jonno is Lieutenant John Cavanaugh.' He glanced at the log again. 'But Cavanaugh was flying on the night in which you are interested, Inspector.'

'Nevertheless, perhaps I could speak to him if he's here, Major.'

Lawford glanced at a blackboard on the wall of his office on which was chalked names and times. 'Yes, he should be. I'll send for him. It might be better if you were to speak to him somewhere else, Inspector. If you question him with me here, he might be a bit reticent in telling the truth, if you know what I mean.'

'I think that would be for the best. Would it be possible for me to speak to Etherington again?'

'Certainly, I'll arrange that for you.' Once again, Lawford rapped on the wall with his walking stick.

'Sergeant Devlin, see if you can find an empty office where Inspector Hardcastle could talk to an officer.'

'Yes, sir.'

'And then find Sub-Lieutenant Etherington and Lieutenant Cavanaugh and tell them to report to me.'

'Very good, sir.'

'Shouldn't take long, Inspector,' said Lawford, once Devlin had departed to make the necessary arrangements.

'Would you prefer it if I stayed out of this, Inspector?' asked Major Corrigan

'On the contrary, Major,' said Hardcastle. 'Your presence might just make young Etherington take this enquiry seriously. Last time I spoke to him, he didn't seem too impressed by the gravity of the matter.'

Sergeant Devlin returned five minutes later. 'Mr Etherington and Mr Cavanaugh are both on patrol, sir. They'll be returning at one o'clock. I've found a spare room just along the corridor, sir.'

'Thank you, Sergeant Devlin.' Lawford stood up. 'That settles it, then. Perhaps you gentlemen would care to join me in the mess for lunch. I'll arrange for the two officers to be available from two o'clock onwards. Who would you like to see first, Inspector?'

'Sub-Lieutenant Etherington, if you'd be so kind, Major,' said Hardcastle.

'Very good. Arrange that, Sergeant Devlin, would you?'

NINE

The lunch in the Sutton's Farm officers' mess had been a particularly good one. The three courses with wine, followed by port, caused Hardcastle later to observe that, war or no war, the Royal Air Force seemed to know how to take care of the important things in life.

At a quarter past two, Hardcastle, Marriott and Major Corrigan made their way to the room that Sergeant Devlin had set aside for them.

'I took the liberty of asking Sergeant Devlin to arrange the room the way I thought you'd want it, Inspector,' said Corrigan. 'It's the way the military police do things.' Devlin had placed a table in the centre of the room with three chairs behind it and one in front, nearest the door. A shaft of sunlight shone through the window, illuminating the otherwise dull room. Corrigan moved one of three chairs back against the wall beneath the window, the reason for which became apparent later.

'Admirable, Major, thank you,' said Hardcastle, as he, Corrigan and Marriott sat down.

Outside, a number of aircraft engines burst into life, the revolutions increasing and then diminishing as the tiny Sopwith Camels climbed into the clearing sky.

The languid figure of Flight Sub-Lieutenant Etherington appeared immediately.

'I've been told you want to see me again, Inspector.' It was then that Etherington noticed the DAPM sitting in a corner of the room. 'Oh, this looks serious,' he said.

'Sit down,' said Hardcastle sharply.

'I do not intend to involve myself in this interview, Mr Etherington,' said Corrigan, 'other than to advise you to answer the inspector's questions truthfully. It's a very serious matter he's dealing with.'

'I've told you everything I know about Gina Cheney, Inspector, if that's what this is about,' protested Etherington mildly, but nonetheless he appeared somewhat apprehensive.

'When we spoke to you last Friday, Mr Etherington, you told us that on the night of Tuesday the eleventh of June you were flying.' Marriott was looking at his notes as he spoke, as though he was quite happy with what Etherington had said previously.

'Yes, I was.'

'But you weren't, were you?' Marriott looked up and concentrated his gaze on Etherington. 'My inspector has spoken to Major Lawford and he informed him that you were off duty that evening. So, where were you?'

'I think there must be some mistake. I'm sure I was flying. Sergeant Devlin keeps the logs and he sometimes gets the entries wrong, don't you know.'

Major Corrigan frowned, but remained silent. By his code of conduct it was bad form for an officer to lay blame on a subordinate for anything.

Hardcastle took out his pipe and began slowly to fill it. 'Right now, Etherington, I'm sorely tempted to arrest you on suspicion of murdering Georgina Cheney,' he said mildly. It was a statement that surprised even Major Corrigan, to say nothing of Etherington's shock at the accusation.

'Oh God!' Beads of sweat appeared on the young officer's brow. 'I was at her house that night, but I had nothing to do with her murder. I didn't even go inside.'

'Ah, now we're getting there,' said Hardcastle. 'What were you doing at Mrs Cheney's house?'

'I called for Hannah Clarke, the maid, and took her to see Charlie Chaplin in *A Dog's Life* at the Bioscope in Vauxhall Bridge Road. Not my sort of movie, I have to say, but that's where she wanted to go so I took her.'

'You have seriously obstructed me in a case of murder, Etherington,' said Hardcastle, 'and if you weren't engaged in defending London in that flying machine of yours, I'd nick you right now and charge you with that offence.' But the DDI's fury was more with Hannah Clarke who had deceived him yet again. Flight Sub-Lieutenant Etherington certainly did not fit the description of 'a footman from one of the houses down the road' with whom Hannah claimed to have spent the evening. He determined that he would have another serious word with Commander Cheney's newly appointed housekeeper.

'I'm sorry, Inspector,' said the now thoroughly contrite Etherington, 'but I didn't want to get Hannah into trouble.'

'You'd better tell us exactly what happened,' said Marriott, turning to a fresh page in his pocketbook.

'I called for Hannah at about six o'clock. I knocked at the front door and she answered it. I asked her if she wanted to come out with me and she said that she'd like to see Charlie Chaplin in some film that was showing locally. She wouldn't let me in, but told me to wait in the street while she changed and got her hat and coat. We took a cab to Vauxhall Bridge Road and after the movie I treated her to supper and brought her back home. Again in a cab.'

'Did you go into the house when you returned to Whilber Street?' asked Marriott.

'No, unfortunately. Hannah said that her mistress was probably asleep and she didn't want to disturb her.'

'So,' said Hardcastle, 'despite spending money on two cab fares, the cost of getting into the picture house and the price of a couple of suppers, you didn't get the bit of jig-a-jig you was expecting.'

'It wasn't like that,' protested Etherington.

'I didn't come up the Clyde on a bicycle, Etherington, and don't take me for a fool,' said Hardcastle. 'You'd slept with her once before and you fully expected to do so again.' He stated that as a matter of fact, rather than one of speculation.

'Yes,' said Etherington, with obvious reluctance, 'but that was after one of Gina's parties.'

'How well did you know Blanche Hardy?' Hardcastle asked suddenly.

Etherington's face assumed a blank expression. 'I don't know anyone of that name.'

'Or Hazel Lacey?'

'No. Were they at Gina's parties? There were a few girls there who I didn't know.'

'Get out before I change my mind about arresting you,' snapped Hardcastle crossly, 'and send in Cavanaugh.'

'I'm sorry, Inspector,' said Etherington again, and stood up, still visibly shaking after his bruising encounter with the DDI.

'I've got to hand it to you, Inspector,' said Corrigan, once Etherington had left the room. 'You certainly know how to get the truth out of people.'

'I've had plenty of experience,' said Hardcastle tersely. Although Major Corrigan was a likeable fellow, it was obvious to the DDI that a Welsh Guards officer recently seconded to the Military Foot Police had a lot to learn about the art of interrogation.

The door opened and Lieutenant John Cavanaugh, attired in the uniform of the Royal Flying Corps, appeared in the room.

'I understand that you wanted to see me, Inspector.'

'You understood correctly. Sit down.'

Cavanaugh glanced at Major Corrigan, saluted, removed his cap and took the seat vacated by Etherington. 'Do you mind if I smoke?' he asked.

'Not at all,' said Hardcastle, taking the opportunity to relight his pipe.

'Thank you.' Cavanaugh withdrew a gold case and spent a brief moment selecting a cigarette. He appeared perfectly composed and gave the impression of wondering why the police should want to talk to him. But he did not have long to wait.

'How often did you have sexual intercourse with Mrs Georgina Cheney, Mr Cavanaugh?' Hardcastle posed the question in an almost conversational tone.

'What?' Cavanaugh's cigarette case fell from his hand and dropped noisily to the table as the young lieutenant's face assumed an expression of shock.

'The question was quite clear,' said Hardcastle.

'But why are you interested in that, Inspector? There was nothing underhand about it. The lady was a willing partner.'

'She's been murdered,' said Hardcastle bluntly.

'Yes, I know. Guy Slater told me, but surely you can't think I had anything to do with that.'

'How often did you attend Mrs Cheney's little parties, Mr Cavanaugh?'

'Three or four times, I suppose.'

'And how often did you finish up in her bed?'

Cavanaugh blushed scarlet. 'Only the once.' He almost whispered the reply, and glanced nervously at Major Corrigan. 'But I'm not married.'

'No, but Mrs Cheney was,' said Marriott. 'To a naval commander, and I doubt he'd've been too happy about it.'

'Oh my God! But she told me she was a war widow.'

'More like a grass widow,' commented Hardcastle drily. 'When was the last time you were at her house?'

'I must've been two or three weeks ago.'

'And where were you on the night of Tuesday the eleventh of June?' Hardcastle knew what Major Lawford had told him, but as usual he was checking the facts.

Cavanaugh took out a pocket diary and flicked through the pages. 'I was on patrol from nine o'clock that evening, returning here at two in the morning.'

'Did Major Lawford ever attend these parties, Mr Cavanaugh?' asked Marriott suddenly, a question that surprised even Major Corrigan.

'Good Lord, no! And I don't think he'd've approved if he knew that any of us did, either.'

'Well, he does now,' said Hardcastle, a comment that did little to ease Cavanaugh's discomfort. 'Did you ever know a woman named Blanche Hardy or Hazel Lacey?'

'No.' There was no hesitation in Cavanaugh's reply.

'Was Mrs Cheney a moneyed woman, would you say, Mr Cavanaugh?' asked Hardcastle.

'She seemed to be. There was always plenty to eat and drink at her parties.'

'One last thing. Do you know the names of any other men who were at these parties of Mrs Cheney's?'

'No, I don't. Leo Etherington and Guy Slater went there a few times, but I don't know of anyone else, Inspector.'

'Very well, Mr Cavanaugh, you may go,' said Hardcastle.

Cavanaugh put on his cap, saluted Major Corrigan, and left the room, mystified as to why the police had wished to talk to him.

'Have your interviews helped you at all, Inspector?' asked Corrigan.

'Not in the slightest, Major, but one has to try. Thank you for your assistance, and perhaps you'd thank Major Lawford for me. I don't wish to disturb him again.'

Hardcastle was in a foul mood when he and Marriott returned to the police station at Cannon Row.

'That was a complete waste of time, Marriott.'

'But at least we learned that Etherington was having an affair with Hannah Clarke, sir,' said Marriott.

'An affair?' scoffed Hardcastle. 'He'd screwed her once and then took her to see Charlie Chaplin in the hope of getting his leg over once more. And went back to Sutton's Farm disappointed.'

'If he did, sir.'

'What d'you mean by that?' Hardcastle sat down at his desk and took out his pipe.

'We've only Etherington's word for it that he didn't enter Mrs Cheney's house that night, sir. For all we know, he might've murdered her. He was very reluctant to tell us what he'd been up to until you threatened to nick him.'

'You're right, Marriott,' said Hardcastle, in a rare admission that his sergeant may have a point. 'We'll go and talk to young Miss Clarke again.'

'Now, sir?'

'Yes, now.' Hardcastle picked up his hat and umbrella and made for the door. 'Come, Marriott.'

It was six o'clock by the time that Hardcastle and Marriott arrived at the Whilber Street address. When Hannah Clarke answered the door it was apparent that she had abandoned all pretence of dressing like a housekeeper. She was wearing a peach silk one-piece frock, cut rather low at the neckline, and with a hem a good twelve inches from the floor. Her blonde hair was swept up in a style that was fast becoming unfashionable.

'Hello, Inspector.' Hannah beamed at the two policemen. 'Please come in.'

'That's a nice frock,' observed Hardcastle, as the three of them sat down in the drawing room.

'It was one of Mrs Cheney's,' said Hannah. 'The commander said that I could help myself to anything of the mistress's that I wanted, and to get rid of the rest.'

'On the night of Mrs Cheney's murder, Hannah,' Hardcastle began, 'you went to the Bioscope to see Charlie Chaplin.'

'That's right,' said Hannah, 'but I told you that before.'

'And then you said that you went for a walk along Vauxhall Bridge Road looking at the shops with a footman from one of the houses down the road.'

'Yes,' said Hannah, but now she appeared a little less confident of herself than when the two detectives had arrived.

'Are you sure about that, Hannah?' asked Marriott.

'Of course.' But the girl avoided Marriott's questioning gaze.

'What was the footman's name?'

'Oh, er, I can't remember.'

'You can't remember because there was no such footman, was there, Hannah?' said Hardcastle.

Hannah Clarke suddenly burst into tears and the DDI suspected that they were forced in order to avoid answering further questions. But it had no effect on him and he waited until she had recovered herself.

'Well?' demanded Hardcastle.

'Leo took me to see the movie.'

'Leo who?'

'Leo Etherington. He's one of the flyers from Hornchurch.'

'Tell me exactly what happened, Hannah.'

'I didn't know he was coming,' said the girl, dabbing at her eyes with a handkerchief. 'He just knocked at the door and asked me if I'd like to go out. I asked the mistress if it would be all right and she said yes, and she gave me half a crown in case I had to get a cab back.'

'Yes, go on.'

'But I didn't need it because Leo took me to the Bioscope in a taxi, and he paid for my ticket at the cinema.'

'What happened afterwards?'

'He took me for supper at a little restaurant in Victoria Street, and then he took me back to Whilber Street in a taxi.'

'And then what happened? And you'd better tell me the truth, girl. You lied to me on both the occasions that I previously spoke to you and that could get you into serious trouble. It's called obstructing the police in the execution of their duty, and you could go to prison.'

'I didn't mean to, sir.' Hannah started to cry again and this time it was genuine, the tears falling on to the silk dress and making little stains, but she seemed not to notice.

'Mr Etherington brought you back here in a taxi. What time was that?' asked Marriott.

'It must've been about ten o'clock, perhaps a little later.'

'And you took him straight up to your bedroom,' said Hardcastle, as though he knew that that is what had happened. 'What time did he leave the house?'

'About two o'clock, sir,' said Hannah in little more than a whisper. She looked down, staring at an emerald ring that adorned the little finger of her left hand, presumably another of the late Georgina Cheney's possessions.

'And what did Mrs Cheney have to say about that?'

'She never worried about me entertaining a young gentleman, sir. She did it often enough herself,' Hannah added defiantly.

'And was she entertaining that particular evening?'

'Yes,' said Hannah. 'I heard her talking to someone in the drawing room, but the door was closed and I don't know who it was. But like I said she often entertained.'

Marriott glanced at Hardcastle and could see that he was becoming increasingly annoyed at the way in which Hannah had misled him. He knew that if the DDI were to lose his temper any chance of getting more information out of the young girl would be lost, and he decided to intervene.

'Where is your bedroom in relation to Mrs Cheney's, Hannah?' asked Marriott.

'It's on the top floor.'

'And Mrs Cheney's room was on the floor below?'

'Yes, sir.'

'Did you hear anything coming from your mistress's room?'

'No, but I wouldn't have. The mistress's bedroom was at the front and mine used to be at the back.'

'What d'you mean, your bedroom *used* to be at the back?'

'Well, I've moved into the mistress's old bedroom now. It was the commander what suggested it. He said I'd be more comfortable there.'

'And you heard nothing at all? You didn't hear raised voices and you didn't hear Mrs Cheney's companion leaving?'

'No, sir, I never heard nothing.'

'How many nights did Commander Cheney stay here when he came home, Hannah?' asked Hardcastle.

'Just the one, sir.'

'And of course he slept with you that night.' Hardcastle made the statement as though he knew this to be the case. Nevertheless, he was surprised at Hannah's answer.

'Oh, he told you that, did he?' Hannah assumed an air of embarrassment. 'He said it was supposed to be a secret and I wasn't to tell anyone.'

But Hannah was not to know that Hardcastle had not seen Commander Cheney again after their first meeting.

'That girl's nothing but a common tart,' said Hardcastle angrily, when he and Marriott returned to their police station.

'I think she's doing all right in her present billet, though, sir,' observed Marriott. 'She seems to have fallen on her feet.'

'Only when she's not on her back with her legs in the air,' commented Hardcastle drily.

'What do we do next, sir?'

'Hannah Clarke and Sub-Lieutenant Etherington are both lying to us, Marriott. For a start I'll arrest Etherington on suspicion of murder.'

'D'you intend to go to Sutton's Farm now, sir?' Marriott was not surprised at the DDI's announcement, and glanced surreptitiously at the clock above Hardcastle's head. He could see another evening slipping away.

'I'm not going at all, Marriott. Some time tomorrow we'll see

Colonel Frobisher and arrange for Etherington to be nicked by that there Major Corrigan and brought up to London. That'll give those military policemen a chance to show us what they're made of. Anyway, we've got a funeral to attend in the morning. Did Miss Clarke tell you where it's to be held, by the way?'

'Brompton Cemetery, sir. It's in Old Brompton Road.' Marriott forbore from saying that the DDI had been present when Hannah Clarke had told them the details.

'Yes, it would be, I suppose. What time?'

'Ten o'clock, sir.'

'Ah, yes, so it is. Don't forget your black tie, Marriott. In the meantime, get yourself off home, and give my regards to Mrs Marriott.'

'Thank you, sir,' said a relieved Marriott. 'And mine to Mrs H.'

However, although not immediately apparent, a further task assigned to Hardcastle by Detective Chief Inspector Frederick Wensley would delay the arrest of Flight Sub-Lieutenant Leo Etherington.

Charles Marriott put a padlock and chain on his bicycle and left it outside his police quarter in Regency Street. Opening his front door he walked through to the kitchen.

'You're home early, love.' Lorna Marriott had become accustomed to her husband working late hours, particularly when he was involved in a murder investigation. And seven o'clock was early by CID standards.

'Make the most of it, pet,' said Marriott. 'We've been given two more murders to deal with along with the Cheney one.'

'I think you're being taken advantage of, love,' said Lorna, as she darted back and forth across the kitchen preparing supper. 'Your Mr Hardcastle can't have a home life of his own.'

'Oh, but he does.' Marriott took off his jacket and placed it on the back of a kitchen chair. 'He asked me a funny question the other day. He asked me if I'd started saving for Doreen's wedding.'

Lorna laughed. 'Did you tell him how old she was?'

'I did, but he said I couldn't start too soon. Apparently his youngest, Maud, is getting wed next year, whether the war's over or not. Between you and me, I think he's worried about how he's going to pay for it.'

'It doesn't have to be that expensive, surely?' Lorna turned from the cooker, a wooden spoon in her hand.

'It seems that young Maud's going to marry an army officer, and the army expects something special.'

'Well, I hope he doesn't get killed before the wedding,' said Lorna matter-of-factly. Her brother, Frank Dobson, was a company sergeant-major serving with the Middlesex Regiment in France, and she worried constantly that one day she would hear that he had been killed in action. 'Anyway, so long as Doreen doesn't marry a policeman she'll be all right.'

'Talking of which, pet, are the children asleep?' Marriott knew that the two children, James and Doreen, nine and seven respectively, would both be in bed.

'Of course. They see so little of you that one day they'll start asking if they've really got a father.'

Hardcastle let himself into his house in Kennington. He hung up his hat and umbrella and took out his hunter, comparing the time it showed with the hall clock. Opening the glass front of the clock, he moved the minute hand slightly so that it showed the correct time.

'Is that you, Ernie?' Alice called from the kitchen.

'Yes, it's me, love.'

'You're home nice and early. Supper's ready, but you've time for a whisky.'

Hardcastle walked through to the kitchen and kissed his wife on the cheek.

'Now don't go getting under my feet, Ernie.' Alice flicked a stray lock of hair out of her eyes. 'Just go and sit down.'

'"Ace" Wensley's given me two more murders to deal with, love,' said Hardcastle, as he retreated to the door. 'Glass of sherry?'

'Yes please.' Alice Hardcastle turned to look at her husband. 'I sometimes think they take rotten advantage of you, Ernie,' she said, echoing what Lorna Marriott had said to her husband.

TEN

'Why does it always rain at funerals, Marriott?' asked Hardcastle, as a cab set them down in Old Brompton Road.

'I must say it seems to be the case, sir.' Marriott could think of no other way to reply to one of the DDI's unanswerable questions.

'Ah, it seems we're just in time.' Hardcastle raised his umbrella slightly so that he could see the cortège as it entered the cemetery gates. A glass-sided hearse, the coachman of which had rain running off his top hat and drenching his caped shoulders, was led by a solitary horse accompanied by six walking pall-bearers. The hearse was followed by one carriage, the sole occupant of which was a veiled Hannah Clarke. 'Good God Almighty!' exclaimed the DDI, as he doffed his hat. 'If that's a Harrods funeral, Kaiser Bill's me uncle. That's a planting that's been done on the cheap. I'm sure it's not what the commander ordered.'

'But he didn't, sir,' said Marriott. 'Young Hannah said the commander left all the arrangements to her.'

'No, Marriott,' said Hardcastle. 'She told us that the commander *had* made arrangements with Harrods. Anyway, that's what the carney little bitch said, but I've got to the point where I don't believe a word she utters. Which begs the question why was he so uninterested in burying his wife.'

The two detectives followed the small procession at a distance, but in time to see the pall-bearers carry the coffin into the chapel. Once Hannah Clarke had followed it inside, Hardcastle and Marriott moved to the entrance and were able to observe that Commander Cheney's housekeeper was the only mourner.

'We've wasted our bloody time, Marriott,' said Hardcastle. 'I was hoping that we'd see some stranger who we might be able to connect to Mrs Cheney's murder.'

Furious, Hardcastle swept out of the cemetery and hailed a cab. 'Scotland Yard, cabbie,' he said, but he was so incensed that for once he omitted to tell Marriott of the perils of asking to go to Cannon Row.

It was nearing midday. Hardcastle was seated in his office mulling over the implications of the cheap funeral he had witnessed that morning when there was a knock at his door.

'Yes?'

A constable entered the office. 'PC 107 Barnes, sir.'

'What d'you want, lad?'

'I was patrolling my beat this morning, sir, and found myself in Whilber Street at approximately five and twenty minutes to twelve—' Barnes began.

'For pity's sake, lad, I don't have the time to listen to a description of your perambulations. Get to the bloody point. If there is one.'

'Yes, sir. Well, sir, as I was passing the house of the late Mrs Cheney, a lady emerged from the house opposite: that's number twenty-eight Whilber Street, sir.' Barnes paused to refer to his pocketbook. 'She gave her name as Mrs Winifred Curtis.'

'Are you eventually going to tell me what this is all about, lad?' demanded Hardcastle, fast becoming exasperated with Barnes' continuing prevarication.

'Sorry, sir. She said as how she thought we might be interested in the fact that a young woman, who Mrs Curtis believed to be the late Mrs Cheney's maid, had quit the premises. She had two suitcases with her and a valise. Mrs Curtis said the young woman entered a cab and left the area.'

'Ye gods!' exclaimed Hardcastle. 'The cunning little vixen. Did Mrs Curtis say what time this young woman left, lad?'

'No, sir.'

'And you didn't think to ask, I suppose.'

'No, sir, sorry, sir.'

'All right, lad, get round your beat, and on your way out ask Sergeant Marriott to see me.'

'Hannah Clarke's done a shift,' said Hardcastle, when Marriott appeared in the DDI's doorway. 'Our eagle-eyed Mrs Curtis saw her loading suitcases into a cab. Even without her binoculars.'

'No wonder the funeral was at ten o'clock, sir. Hannah must've arranged this some time ago.'

'We'll see if we can find out more about the little trollop from Mrs Curtis. Get your hat, Marriott.'

Hardcastle stopped at the door to the detectives' office. 'Wood!'

'Yes, sir.' Detective Sergeant Herbert Wood rose from his place at the long table and hurriedly stubbed out his cigarette.

'Send someone up to Somerset House a bit jildi and see what they can find out about Hannah Clarke. She's nineteen years of age, so she told us. But I'm beginning to have doubts about everything she said. I want you to find out from Brompton Cemetery who the undertakers were that dealt with Mrs Cheney's funeral at ten o'clock this morning. I'll put money on it not being Harrods. It must be some company damn near next door to the cemetery because I can't see the pall-bearers walking all the way from Harrods' undertaking department. And while you're at it, get the name and address of the person who made the arrangements. When you've done that ask Harrods if Commander Cheney ever made arrangements for the funeral and if so who cancelled 'em.'

'Very good, sir.' Wood grabbed his jacket from the back of his chair and dashed for the door, seizing his hat as he went. When the DDI wanted something done, he wanted it done immediately.

'Inspector, how nice to see you again,' said Winifred Curtis, as Lottie the maid showed Hardcastle and Marriott into the drawing room.

'I hope we're not disturbing your lunch, Mrs Curtis, but this is rather urgent.'

'Not at all, Inspector. I usually take luncheon at one o'clock. Please come in and sit down. I'm sure you'd like a cup of tea.'

'Very kind, madam, but we don't really have time for tea,' said Hardcastle. 'You told one of my officers that you saw a young woman leaving the Cheney house earlier today,' he continued, determined to get straight to the reason for his visit.

'That's right. I thought it was important, so I ran out when I saw a constable and told him all about it. He was such a nice young man and very good at his job, I should think. He wrote down everything I told him.'

'I'm sure he did, Mrs Curtis.' Hardcastle was growing tired of hearing about PC Barnes' efficiency. 'Perhaps you wouldn't mind telling me what you told the constable.'

'Well, of course. But I'm sure you've time for tea. Lottie's just made a pot.'

'Oh, very well,' said Hardcastle, finally deciding that he would get little out of Mrs Curtis unless he accepted her offer of tea. 'Thank you.'

Winifred Curtis rang the small brass tea bell and moments later, Lottie appeared bearing a large tray that held, apart from the tea things, a plate of ginger snaps.

'You see, Inspector, I remembered to get some of your favourite biscuits. I had a feeling I'd be seeing you again.'

'Most commendable,' said Hardcastle, only just managing to restrain his irritation at the woman's constant prattling. 'Did you know if this young woman was the Cheneys' maid?' He decided not to confuse Mrs Curtis by mentioning that Hannah Clarke had recently been elevated to the status of housekeeper.

'Oh, yes, it was definitely her. A flighty young woman if you ask me. Anyway, I just happened to be glancing out of my sitting room window . . .' Mrs Curtis pointed at the window, presumably, Hardcastle imagined, so that he should be under no illusion as to which window she was talking about. 'A cab drew up and the next minute out trotted the maid. Dressed all in black, she was. Very peculiar, I thought.'

'She'd been to Mrs Cheney's funeral, madam,' said Marriott.

'Oh dear. I wish I'd known. I'd've liked to have gone. Just to pay my respects. Not that I knew her that well, of course. Anyway, the cab driver went into the house and came out with two suitcases and a valise. But I told the constable all that.'

'What time was this, Mrs Curtis?' asked Marriott.

Winifred Curtis glanced at an ormolu clock on the mantel. 'About a quarter past eleven, I think. Yes, it was. I'm certain that was the time.'

'She must've come straight back here from the Brompton Cemetery and left almost immediately, sir,' said Marriott.

'And doubtless had her bags packed already to go,' commented Hardcastle. 'I suppose you didn't happen to note the number of this cab, Mrs Curtis.'

'Oh dear me, no.' Winifred Curtis put a hand to her mouth. 'I realized afterwards that that was the sort of question you policemen ask. I'm ever so sorry.'

'No matter, Mrs Curtis,' said Marriott. 'You've been very helpful.'

* * *

The deception that Hannah Clarke had perpetrated on Hardcastle had left him in a bad mood that still persisted after his return to the police station.

'Get someone in here, Marriott.'

Seconds later Henry Catto edged nervously around Hardcastle's office door. 'You wanted me, sir?'

'Are you the only one in the office, Catto?' barked Hardcastle.

'Yes, sir.' As ever, Catto was showing signs of nervousness at being summoned by the DDI.

'You'll have to do, I suppose. Now listen carefully. A cab picked up Hannah Clarke from the Cheneys' place at twenty-nine Whilber Street at about eleven-fifteen this morning. Find it, and find out where the driver took her. Got it?'

'Yes, sir.'

'Well, don't stand there, Catto. Get on with it.'

Alarmed at the enormity of the task he had been given, Catto returned to the detectives' office with a glum expression on his face.

'What's the matter with you, Catto?' asked Marriott. 'You look as though you've lost half a crown and found a sixpence.'

Catto explained about the job the DDI had just given him. 'I don't know where to start, Sergeant,' he complained.

Marriott laughed. 'Come with me, Catto, and I'll show you how the job's done.' He picked up his hat and strode from the room.

Followed by Catto, Marriott turned out of the police station and made for Victoria Embankment.

'There's a cab shelter near the Embankment Gardens,' Marriott explained. 'I've done this before, Catto, so watch and learn.'

Despite it being a hot June day, the windows of the cab shelter were all tightly closed. The stench of frying sausages and bacon, combined with a thick pall of cigarette and tobacco smoke, had generated a fug in the small hut.

Silence fell as the two detectives entered, the assembled cab drivers knowing instinctively that the police had come among them.

'I'm investigating a case of murder.' It was a statement that produced a brief hubbub of conversation, but which was stilled by Marriott's upraised hand. 'At about a quarter past eleven this morning a cab picked up a young woman from twenty-nine Whilber Street. She was dressed all in black, had blonde hair and had two suitcases and a valise with her. I need to speak to this cab driver sooner rather than later. And that means today. Tell him to call at Cannon Row police station and ask for Detective Sergeant Marriott.'

'D'you think it'll work, Sergeant?' asked Catto as he and Marriott walked back to the police station.

'It'll work all right, Catto. I'd bet my pension on it.'

Within thirty minutes of the detectives' visit to the cab shelter, a constable escorted a scruffily dressed man into their office. Bow-legged and stooped, he had a red face, bushy eyebrows and a walrus moustache. His right hand held a battered peaked cap.

'This here is Joshua Figgins, Sergeant, a cab driver,' said the PC. 'He says as how you wanted a word with him.'

'Did you pick up a young lady from twenty-nine Whilber Street at about eleven-fifteen this morning, Figgins?' asked Marriott.

'That's me, guv'nor.' Figgins sniffed loudly and wiped his nose with the sleeve of his ragged coat. 'I ain't done nuffink wrong, 'ave I?'

'Not that I can think of at the moment,' said Marriott, a comment that did little to reassure the cabbie. 'Where did you take her?'

'Victoria Station, guv'nor.'

'Where exactly did you drop her off?'

'Outside on the rank. An' I never hung about because them railway rozzers—' Figgins stopped abruptly, suddenly remembering that he was talking to a policeman.

'Did she take her luggage with her?'

'No, guv. There was a porter 'anging abaht, an' she got him to grab her bags.'

'Did she mention where she was going?'

'When she got in the cab she said something abaht visiting her folks dahn Sussex, but she never said where in Sussex.'

'All right, Figgins, you can go,' said Marriott and, turning to the constable, added, 'See this gentleman off the premises.'

'Right, Sergeant.'

'There you are, Catto,' said Marriott, once Figgins and the PC had departed. 'Now you can go and tell the DDI what a clever detective you are.'

'Thanks very much, Sergeant,' said Catto.

'You needn't tell him how I helped you out, and next time

you'll know how to do it.' Marriott had a soft spot for Catto and could not understand why Hardcastle had such a low opinion of him. In the sergeant's view Catto was good at his job, but suffered a loss of confidence whenever he came into contact with the DDI.

'Well?' Hardcastle looked up as Catto appeared.

'The cab driver who collected Miss Clarke from Whilber Street goes by the name of Figgins, sir, and he dropped her at Victoria Station. During the journey she told him she was visiting her folks in Sussex, but didn't say exactly where.'

'Did this here Figgins say which train she got on, Catto?'

'No, sir. He set her down at the station entrance, and a porter took her bags.'

'Then you'd better get down to Victoria and ask around. See if you can find this porter. He might know which train she caught.'

'Very good, sir.' Catto, delighted that the DDI had apparently found no fault with the manner in which he had conducted the enquiry, turned to leave.

'You're coming on a treat, Catto,' said Hardcastle. 'We might make a detective out of you yet.'

'Yes, sir, thank you, sir,' said Catto, realizing that that was as near as the DDI would ever get to paying him a compliment.

'What d'you propose to do next, sir?' Marriott tapped lightly on Hardcastle's open door and stepped into his office.

'And I suppose you helped Catto with that cab enquiry, Marriott,' said Hardcastle, a man not easily deceived. And certainly not by his detectives.

'That's what a first-class sergeant's for, sir, to teach these young lads the trade,' said Marriott, risking a grin.

Hardcastle grunted. 'We'll have to wait and see what Catto turns up, Marriott. In the meantime, we'd better make a start on these other murders that Mr Wensley's given us. First of all, we'll pay a visit to the Lacey address, and see what we can find out about the murder of Mrs Hazel Lacey. Where is it?'

'Ovington Square, sir.'

'Ah yes, so it is,' said Hardcastle, who was thoroughly conversant with the docket that been handed over by DDI Sullivan at Vine Street.

*   *   *

It was almost four o'clock that same afternoon when a trim young housemaid answered the door of the four-storey dwelling in Ovington Square.

'Yes, sir?' The maid looked nervously at the two detectives.

'We're police officers, lass,' said Hardcastle.

'There's no one here, sir. Just me.' The maid paused, a hand to her mouth. 'Oh dear! It's not about the colonel, sir, is it?'

'He's quite safe, as far as I know,' said Hardcastle, 'but it's you I wanted to talk to. We're investigating the murder of Mrs Hazel Lacey.'

'I don't know nothing about that, sir. And I told them other policemen that came here.'

'When was that?'

'Just after it happened, sir. The end of March. But I wasn't able to tell them anything about the mistress.'

'You might know more than you think. Can we come in?'

'I s'pose it'll be all right, sir.' The maid hesitated briefly and then led the way into the drawing room at the front of the house.

'Sit yourself down, lass,' said Hardcastle, 'and tell me your name.'

'It's Millie, sir. Millie Roberts.'

'And how long have you been employed here, Millie?' asked Marriott.

Millie looked at Marriott and smiled. 'About a year, sir.'

'And I presume the colonel is still away.'

'Yes, sir. He come home for the funeral, but then he said he had to go straight back to France, to a place called Amy something.'

'That would be Amiens,' said Marriott.

'And you've been by yourself ever since, have you, Millie?'

'Yes, sir. The colonel said as how I was to stay on for when he got leave.'

'Tell me about the night Mrs Lacey was murdered, Millie,' said Hardcastle.

'It was awful, sir.' Millie gave a convulsive sob. 'The mistress said she was going out—'

'What time was that?' asked Marriott.

'It must've been about six o'clock. I remember that because cook asked her if she'd be in for dinner, but the mistress said she was going out. Then she looked at me, after cook had gone back downstairs, and gave me a funny little smile, and said that she wouldn't be back till the morning.'

'Did she tell you where she was going?'

'Sort of. She said she was going to a ball and it'd go on till late and so she'd put up at a hotel.'

'Did she say where this hotel was?' asked Marriott.

'No, she never, but I thought it must be up the West End somewhere.'

'Did she say where this ball was being held or anything at all about it?'

'No, sir,' said Millie. 'And then next morning this policeman come to the door and told me the awful news. He wanted to know how he could get in touch with the colonel.'

'What did you say to that?'

'I told him I didn't know 'cept to say I thought he was in France. So the policeman said he'd get in touch with the War Office. Then the colonel come home about two days later and took care of the funeral.'

'This cook you mentioned, Millie,' said Hardcastle. 'Does she still work here?'

'No, sir, she left just after it happened. The master said that there was no need for her to stay on any more.'

'D'you happen to know where she went?'

'She got a position at one of the houses in Yeoman's Row straight off, sir. A house belonging to a Mrs Buckley, I believe. I don't know the number, but it's not far from here.'

'And the cook's name?' asked Marriott.

'Mrs Pollard. Mabel Pollard.'

'Did Mrs Lacey have any gentlemen callers, Millie?' asked Hardcastle.

'Not that I know of, unless they came when it was my evening off, sir.'

'Did Mrs Lacey mention who she was going with to this ball? On the night she was murdered.'

'No, sir, she never said.'

'Well, thank you, Millie,' said Hardcastle. 'Have you any idea when Colonel Lacey is coming on leave again?'

'No, sir. We never knew in advance. He'd just arrive, if you know what I mean.'

'If he should come home in the near future perhaps you'd ask him to get in touch with Divisional Detective Inspector Hardcastle at Cannon Row police station.'

'Are we going to speak to this Mrs Pollard while we're in the area, sir?' asked Marriott, as he and Hardcastle left the Laceys' Ovington Square house.

'We don't know which house it is, Marriott, and I'm not traipsing up and down Yeoman's Row knocking on doors. No, get someone to find out which house this here Mrs Buckley lives in and we'll call there tomorrow.'

ELEVEN

Detective Sergeant Wood was waiting for Hardcastle when the DDI returned to the police station.

'Have you got some answers for me, Wood?'

'Yes, sir. I've sent Keeler up to Somerset House to see what can be found about Hannah Clarke, but he's not back yet.'

'What about the funeral? Find out anything about that, did you?'

'Yes, sir.' Wood referred to his pocketbook. 'It was a firm of undertakers called Crosby and Sons with offices in the Old Brompton Road right next door to the cemetery. The arrangements were made by a young woman who gave the name of Kitty Gordon.'

'Who the hell's she?'

'I've no idea, sir, but I got a description. Mr Crosby – he's the boss – said that she was tall and slender with long blonde hair, and aged about twenty-one.'

'That sounds very much like Hannah Clarke to me,' said Hardcastle. 'But why did she give a false name, I wonder? If it is her.'

Wood had no answer for that. 'I spoke to Messrs Harrods on the telephone, sir, and—'

'That was very adventurous of you, Wood,' commented the DDI, to whom the telephone was anathema. 'What did they say?'

'Apparently they received a telephone call from Commander Cheney asking them to make the necessary arrangements for the funeral of Mrs Georgina Cheney, sir. He explained that he was a serving naval officer and about to return to duty. They undertook to collect Mrs Cheney's body from the mortuary and deal with it all.'

'What the hell happened, then?' demanded Hardcastle.

'Harrods then received a letter from Commander Cheney cancelling all the arrangements without explanation. I took the liberty of obtaining the letter, sir.' Wood handed over the document.

'God damn it!' exclaimed Hardcastle. 'What's that little bitch playing at? I'm sure that this young woman who said she was Kitty Gordon is our Hannah Clarke. I think we'll need to get in touch with Commander Cheney again, and see if he can shed any light on it. Mind you,' he added dolefully, 'he's probably at sea somewhere. Anyway, that's for me to worry about. But now I've got another job for you, Wood.'

'Sir?'

'Yesterday Sergeant Marriott and me called at Ovington Square and spoke to the housemaid.' Seeing Wood's puzzled expression, Hardcastle explained, 'That's where Hazel Lacey lived.'

'Oh yes. She was the woman murdered at the Wardour Hotel in Wardour Street back in March, sir.'

'Correct. The housemaid at Ovington Square said that Mrs Pollard, the Laceys' cook, left their employment shortly after the murder and took a post with a Mrs Buckley in Yeoman's Row. Get someone to find out which house it is.'

'Very good, sir. D'you want me to make enquiries of this Mrs Pollard?'

'No, I'll do that, Wood. Is Catto back yet?'

'Yes, sir. He came in shortly before you returned.'

'Send him in.'

'I found the porter who carried Miss Clarke's bags into Victoria Station, sir,' said Catto, hovering uncertainly in the DDI's doorway.

'Are you going to let me in on the secret, then, Catto?' asked Hardcastle impatiently.

'She caught a train to West Worthing, sir,' said Catto triumphantly.

'Did she now? I wonder where she went from there. I suppose we could ask the Worthing police to check with the cab companies, but I don't hold out much hope.'

'No, sir,' said Catto.

'*No, sir*, Catto?' repeated Hardcastle, and glared at the DC. 'You're not supposed to agree with me, Catto. You're a detective and you ought to come up with a bright idea.'

'I could go to Worthing and make the enquiries myself, sir,' Catto suggested tentatively.

'Good idea, Catto. Do it. But let the Worthing police know you're there. I don't want them complaining that you're clodhopping about on their patch without their say-so.'

'Yes, sir.' Pleasantly surprised, Catto left the office before the DDI could change his mind.

Hardcastle picked up his pipe from the ashtray and crossed to the detectives' office.

'I was just coming to see you, sir,' said DC Basil Keeler. 'I'm afraid I drew a blank at Somerset House. There are dozens of Hannah Clarkes, but there wasn't one who could necessarily be the one who was Mrs Cheney's housemaid.'

'All right, Keeler,' said Hardcastle. 'I'd guessed that might be the case. It seems that she's in the habit of changing her name if what Sergeant Wood found out is anything to go by.' He glanced at the first-class sergeant. 'Marriott, a moment of your time.'

'Sir.' Marriott donned his jacket and followed the DDI into his office.

'A thought has crossed my mind, Marriott.'

'It has, sir?' Marriott was always apprehensive at such an announcement.

'D'you remember when we talked to Beatrice Groves, Mrs Hardy's cleaning lady?'

'Yes, sir.'

'She told us that a housemaid had been employed by the Hardys, but that she'd left before Mrs Groves arrived on the scene.'

'She did, sir, but she said she didn't know the girl's name.'

'But Major Hardy might know.'

'He's in France, sir.' Marriott was horrified that the DDI was about to suggest a trip to the war zone. He was not so worried for himself, but rather what his wife Lorna might have to say about it. Furthermore, he could not understand why Hardcastle was taking an interest in the Hardys' former housemaid.

Hardcastle laughed. 'Don't look so concerned, Marriott,' he said, guessing what was going through his sergeant's mind. 'I might be a dedicated detective, but I'm not that dedicated. No, we'll ask Colonel Frobisher to get a message to him. See to it, will you?'

'Yes, sir.'

*   *   *

'Are you on your own, Charlie?' Sergeant Glover, the APM's chief clerk, was surprised that for once Marriott was not accompanied by Hardcastle.

'He sometimes lets me out by myself, Cyril. I've got a favour to ask, but I don't think it's necessary to bother the colonel with it.'

'Fire away,' said Glover, moving a pad across his desk.

Marriott explained about the murder of Blanche Hardy and the problem of identifying the Cheneys' former housemaid. 'Would it be possible to get a message to Major Hardy asking him if he knew the girl's name, Cyril?'

'Shouldn't be too difficult, Charlie.' Glover made no comment about what he thought was a rather bizarre request. 'Once we find out where Major Hardy is.'

'All I can tell you is that he's with the Tank Corps, Cyril.'

'Well, that's something, I suppose, but there are a lot of them. Last time I looked there were at least twenty-five battalions of the Tank Corps, but I'll see what I can do. It's something that they're all in France. Well, I think they are.'

Only ten minutes had elapsed before Detective Sergeant Wood returned to the DDI's office and placed a slip of paper on the desk.

'Mrs Buckley's address in Yeoman's Row, sir.'

Hardcastle stared at Wood. 'How on earth did you find that out so quickly, Wood?' he asked.

'I telephoned the sorting office, sir, and the head postmaster told me.'

'Good God!' exclaimed Hardcastle, and in a rare admission added, 'There are times, Wood, when I think this job is passing me by.'

'Yes, sir,' said Wood.

'You're not supposed to agree with me, Wood,' growled the DDI. 'Ask Sergeant Marriott to come in when he gets back from seeing the APM.'

Detective Constable Henry Catto was more of a detective than Hardcastle gave him credit for. He had checked that West Worthing railway station was closer to the police station in Ann Street than was the main railway station. It was less than a mile and he could easily walk that short distance. He knew that the DDI would disallow the cost of a cab fare, and Catto could not afford to pay for it out of his own pocket; certainly not on his pay.

'And what can I do for you, young man?' enquired an elderly sergeant, as Catto approached the counter of the police station.

'I'm Detective Constable Catto of the Metropolitan Police, Whitehall Division, Sergeant.'

'Are you now? Come down to help us with our suspicious death, have you?'

'I don't know anything about a suspicious death, Sergeant, at least not down here. My DDI's dealing with three murders in London, though.'

'My word, you are busy chaps up there in the Smoke. Well, what can I do for you?'

Catto explained about the mysterious departure of Hannah Clarke and told the sergeant briefly about her connection with the murder of Georgina Cheney.

'I'm wondering if you can tell me the names of any cab companies that might have picked her up at West Worthing station. I reckon she must've arrived at just after one o'clock yesterday.' Catto had already examined train timetables and had concluded, given what he had learned at Victoria station, that that was the most likely time of Hannah Clarke's arrival.

'There's only the one company licensed to operate from West Worthing station, Mr Catto,' said the sergeant, 'and that's Star Cabs. Here, I'll jot down the address for you. It's not far from here. I'd send one of my chaps with you, but like I said when you got here, they're all tied up with this suspicious death. A young woman was found washed up on the beach early this morning. Been swimming, so they say, but must've got into difficulties.'

'Thanks, Sergeant.' Catto could not immediately understand why a drowned woman should take up so much of the Worthing police's time. 'It's a bit of a long shot, but my guv'nor's a stickler for detail.'

'Aren't they all,' said the sergeant with feeling.

A butler, wearing the traditional tailcoat of his calling, answered the door of Mrs Buckley's residence in Yeoman's Row.

'Good morning, sir.'

'We're police officers, and we'd like a word with Mrs Buckley.

You can tell her I'm Divisional Detective Inspector Hardcastle of Scotland Yard,' said the DDI.

'Has something happened to Brigadier General Buckley, sir?' The butler's face took on a grave expression.

'Not as far as I know,' said Hardcastle. 'I'm making enquiries into a murder.'

'Oh, I see. That's all right, then.' It seemed as though the butler did not regard a murder to be of great importance. 'I'll enquire if the mistress is at home, sir, if you'd care to step inside.'

'We're moving up in the world, Marriott,' said Hardcastle, as the two officers waited in the tiled hall. 'We've gone from a sub-lieutenant all the way to a general.'

'If you'd care to come this way, gentlemen,' said the butler, reappearing from a door at the rear of the hall, 'the mistress is in the drawing room.'

'Hobbs tells me you're from Scotland Yard.' Mrs Buckley, an elegant woman probably approaching forty years of age, was seated in a low bergère armchair. 'He said something about a murder.'

Hardcastle introduced himself and Marriott, and explained about the murder of Hazel Lacey in the Wardour Hotel.

'I read about it in *The Times*, Inspector. An awful thing to have happened, especially as her husband was on active service,' said Mrs Buckley. 'Curiously enough my cook, Mrs Pollard, worked for her.'

'I know, madam,' said Hardcastle. 'That's why I'm here. I'd like to have a word with her, if I may.'

'Of course. D'you think she might be able to help?'

'I shan't know until I speak to her, madam.'

'No, of course not. Silly me,' said Mrs Buckley, with a gay laugh. 'I'll send for her.'

'I'm quite happy to talk to her in the kitchen, madam,' said Hardcastle, aware that domestic servants were more likely to be open when they were not in the presence of their employers.

'Well, if you're sure, I'll get Hobbs to show you the way.' Mrs Buckley stood up and crossed to the bell-pull.

'Madam?' The butler appeared almost instantly.

'Hobbs, perhaps you'd show these gentlemen to the kitchen. They'd like a word with Mrs Pollard.'

'Certainly, madam,' said the butler. He led the way into the hall and down the stairs to the kitchen. 'An inspector from

Scotland Yard's here to see you, Mrs Pollard. What have you been up to, eh?'

'I really don't know what you're on about, Mr Hobbs.' Mrs Pollard, a buxom, rosy-faced woman, wiped her hands on her apron. 'Come into the servants' hall and take a seat, gents. I dare say you'd like a cup of tea.' She glanced at the butler. 'I'll bring you a cup in your pantry, Mr Hobbs,' she said, by way of implied dismissal.

'I'm enquiring into the murder of Mrs Hazel Lacey, Mrs Pollard,' said Hardcastle, once he and Marriott were seated at the kitchen table with cups of tea in front of them.

'Dreadful, quite dreadful,' said Mrs Pollard, 'but not surprising.'

'Why aren't you surprised?'

Mrs Pollard placed her plump arms on the table, linking her hands together. 'Between you and me, Inspector, Mrs Lacey was a bit of a good-time girl.'

'What makes you say that, Mrs Pollard?' asked Marriott.

'There was always some young man calling at the house and taking her off to the theatre or to supper. And her poor husband away at the Front fighting for King and Country. Disgraceful, I calls it. You wouldn't see the general's wife getting up to such shenanigans, I can tell you.'

'We've been told that on the night she was murdered, she was at the Wardour Hotel with a gentleman called Kenneth Reeves,' continued Marriott. 'Does that name mean anything to you?'

'I'm afraid not, no. I was in the kitchen most of the time, but even down here you get to hear things.'

'Did she often go out?' asked Hardcastle, accepting Mrs Pollard's offer of a second cup of tea and a slice of plum cake.

'According to the maid, she was out most evenings.'

'We spoke to Millie, the maid there now, Mrs Pollard,' said Marriott, 'but she was only taken on after the last maid left. D'you happen to know her name?'

'Yes I do,' said Mrs Pollard firmly. 'I had more than one run-in with her. A saucy blonde baggage, she was, with ideas above her station. More than once I had to remind her that she was only a housemaid. But she upped sticks and left the very morning that we heard poor Mrs Lacey had been killed.'

'But what was her name?' asked Hardcastle.

'Kitty Gordon,' said Mrs Pollard, 'and she was only part-time.'

*   *   *

Catto's enquiry of the cab company was much easier than he had dared hope.

'Yeah, I took the lady, Officer. Not likely to forget a pretty bit of fluff like that one,' said a cab driver who was waiting in the office for a fare.

'Where did you take her?' asked Catto.

'A nice little private hotel, Officer. It's called Sea View.'

'How do I get there?' asked Catto.

'I'll run you up there,' said the driver. 'It ain't far from here.'

'My guv'nor won't let me charge for a cab,' said Catto. 'I'll have to walk or maybe catch a bus.'

'That's all right, Officer. I won't charge you, seeing as you're the law on official business,' said the cabbie. 'Always willing to help the police.'

To Catto's surprise the Sea View Hotel on Marine Parade did indeed have a sea view. He ascended the steps, entered the reception area and struck a bell on the small counter. Moments later a middle-aged woman appeared.

'I'm afraid we shan't have any vacancies until tomorrow,' said the woman. 'Didn't you see the sign in the window?'

'I'm not here for a room, madam, I'm a police officer,' said Catto, and produced his warrant card.

'Oh, that's different, then. I'm Mrs Croft, and my husband and I own this hotel. How can I help you, Constable?'

'I'm making enquiries about a young lady who booked in here yesterday. At about half past one, I should think. Her name is Hannah Clarke.'

Mrs Croft shook her head. 'I can tell you for certain that no one of that name arrived yesterday,' she said. 'Only one young lady booked in and she said her name was Kitty Gordon. She had two suitcases and a valise with her, and said that she'd be staying for a week. She paid in advance.'

The name meant nothing to Catto, who had not been privy to Hardcastle's conversation with Detective Sergeant Wood.

'What did she look like, Mrs Croft?'

'Tall with long blonde hair,' said Mrs Croft thoughtfully. 'Oh, and she was dressed all in black complete with a veil, as though she'd been to a funeral. I thought it was rather a strange outfit to wear to the seaside.'

'Is she here now, madam?' asked Catto.

'No, she's not, and that's the funny thing. She went out last evening at about six o'clock saying that she was going for a walk along the front. Then she was meeting someone for supper and that she'd be back at about half past ten. She seemed a respectable young woman and I gave her a key so's she could let herself in. It's not something I do for all my paying guests.' Mrs Croft paused. 'But she never returned.'

'You're sure of that, Mrs Croft?'

'Yes, I am. Her bed hadn't been slept in.'

'When she went out was she still wearing the black clothing she'd arrived in?'

'No. She'd changed into a rather smart white frock with a panama hat and an umbrella. Oh, and she had one of those little bead handbags. I shouldn't think she'd've got more than one of those new powder compacts into it, and she looked the sort of girl who might've owned one.' Mrs Croft accompanied the last comment with a disdainful lift of her head.

'Thank you very much, Mrs Croft,' said Catto, pleased that he had spoken to the lady of the establishment. He doubted that the woman's husband would have been able to furnish such a detailed description of what the mysterious Kitty Gordon had been wearing.

As he left the hotel, Catto began wondering about the missing woman and the story that the Worthing sergeant had told him about the body that had been found on the beach that morning. He determined that he would return to Ann Street police station and pass on the information he had just gleaned.

'Ah, you're back again, Mr Catto,' said the sergeant. 'Did you find what you were looking for?'

'Yes, thank you, Sergeant, but I picked up a bit of information that might help you.'

'Oh, we're always glad of assistance from you London chaps,' said the sergeant airily, but Catto sensed that there was a tinge of sarcasm in the comment. 'Solved our dead body for us, have you?'

'Maybe,' said Catto, and related what he had learned from Mrs Croft.

'I think you'd better have a word with Superintendent Potts. He's the divisional commander and he's taken charge of the investigation.'

'Don't you have any CID officers, then?' asked Catto.

'No, we don't, Mr Catto,' said the sergeant sharply, as though his force was being criticized. He lifted the flap in the counter. 'Come through and I'll show you to Mr Potts' office.'

The sergeant led Catto up a flight of stairs and knocked deferentially on a door.

'This is Detective Constable Catto of the Metropolitan Police, sir. He thinks he might have some information in connection with the body found on the beach his morning.'

'Come in, boy,' said Potts, and glanced at the Worthing officer. 'That'll be all, Sergeant, thank you,' he said curtly. Once the station officer had left the room, Potts said, 'It doesn't do to let the lower ranks know too much about what's going on. They have this habit of gossiping. Now then, I don't know how you think you can help, because it's obviously an accidental drowning, but I'll tell you what I know. A young woman, as yet unidentified, was found on the beach at about six o'clock this morning. She was attired in a bathing dress and it looks as though she'd drowned. The current here can be a bit tricky at times, especially for the unwary.'

'It might just be a coincidence, sir,' said Catto, 'but I was making some enquiries at the Sea View Hotel earlier today.' He went on to tell Superintendent Potts what he had learned from Mrs Croft about the absence of her guest. 'This young lady told Mrs Croft at the Sea View that her name was Kitty Gordon, but she fits the description of a Miss Hannah Clarke. My DDI is anxious to have a word with her in connection with the murders he's investigating.'

Potts emitted a humourless laugh. 'Well, if it is her, he's too late, isn't he?' He opened a large daybook and took out a fountain pen. 'What's the name of your inspector, Mr Catto?'

'Divisional Detective Inspector Hardcastle of the Whitehall Division, sir. He's at Cannon Row police station.'

'It might just be that you've identified our young woman for us,' said Potts. 'I'll speak to your Mr Hardcastle on the telephone and see what he wants to do about it. If it is the woman he's interested in. It might be that he'll want you to stay here to make further enquiries. On the other hand, he might want to come down here.'

Without further ado, Potts removed the earpiece from his 'candle-stick' telephone, jiggled the rest and asked to be connected to Cannon Row police station in London.

It took some time for the connection to be made, and a little longer for Hardcastle to be located. Even so the conversation lasted only a short time. Potts turned to Catto as he replaced the earpiece. 'I got the impression that your inspector doesn't like telephones too much, Mr Catto. Anyway he's coming down and he'll be arriving at West Worthing railway station at twenty minutes to three. He said you're to meet him there. Incidentally, he said that he believed Kitty Gordon to be a name used by this Hannah Clarke he's interested in.'

TWELVE

C atto made sure that he was at West Worthing railway station in Oxford Road well in time to meet the DDI's train.

'Well, Catto,' said Hardcastle, as he and Marriott passed through the ticket barrier, 'according to the superintendent down here it seems you've been doing some detective work.'

'Yes, sir.' As they walked towards the cab rank, Catto explained what he had learned during his time in Worthing.

'You'll be interested to know, Catto, that the woman who made the arrangements for Mrs Cheney's funeral gave the name of Kitty Gordon. So, it looks very much like this here body the locals have found is Hannah Clarke. However, we'll know for sure when I cast my eye over her body in the mortuary.'

But when the three detectives reached Ann Street police station there were further revelations.

Once introductions had been effected, Superintendent Potts pulled a docket across his desk.

'It gets interesting, Mr Hardcastle. A member of the pier-master's staff doing the daily check on lifebelts found a quantity of clothing and an umbrella in a lifebelt locker at the end of the pier.' Potts looked up. 'They match exactly the clothes that your Mr Catto was told by the landlady of the Sea View Hotel that our victim was wearing when she left there yesterday.' He stared at Hardcastle. 'We do know how to go about enquiries of this sort down here, Mr Hardcastle.'

'I'm sure you do, Mr Potts,' said Hardcastle, mildly irritated by the superintendent's attitude. 'Was there by any chance a handbag?' he asked.

'Yes, there was.' Potts retrieved a reticule from his in-tray. 'A bead handbag containing a single key, a handkerchief and a National Registration identity card in the name of Queenie Rogers. Her date of birth was shown to be the third of March 1893. There is also a reference dated March 1917 written by a Mrs Blanche Hardy for a housemaid in the name of Kitty Gordon.' He handed the documents to Hardcastle. 'There's a photograph in the identity card, of course.'

'Well I'll be buggered!' exclaimed Hardcastle, as he studied the photograph. 'That's Hannah Clarke, or at least the name she gave us when we first interviewed her.'

'In view of the circumstances, Mr Hardcastle,' said Potts, 'I've asked for Dr Bernard Spilsbury to attend from London to examine the body. I think we might have a murder on our hands.'

'Where is the body, Mr Potts?' asked Hardcastle.

'At Worthing Hospital in Lyndhurst Road, Mr Hardcastle. I've asked Dr Spilsbury to go straight there and he assured me that he'll arrive by six o'clock.'

'It seems a bit of a strange thing to do, sir,' said Marriott, addressing the Worthing superintendent, 'but is it possible that Miss Clarke, or whatever her real name was, decided to have a swim and left her clothes in the locker?'

'I doubt it, Sergeant,' said Potts. 'While I was waiting for you and Mr Hardcastle to arrive, I sent an officer to the Sea View Hotel to interview Mrs Croft. We do like to be sure of our facts. I'll not tolerate any sloppiness on my division. Mrs Croft confirmed what she'd told your constable: that when the young woman she knew as Kitty Gordon left the hotel she was only carrying an umbrella and this handbag.' He picked it up and flourished it. 'And I defy anyone to secrete a bathing dress in that.'

Hardcastle took out his hunter and glanced at it. 'I dare say we could fill in the time while we're waiting for the good doctor. Allow me to buy you a pint, Mr Potts. I take it you know of a decent alehouse hereabouts.'

'Of course I do, Mr Hardcastle, I'm in charge of the Worthing

Division. But I have work to do. By the way, I've spoken to the Chief Constable and he'd be grateful if you could assist us in our enquiries.'

'That's not possible, Mr Potts,' said Hardcastle, mildly irritated at Potts' refusal to join him for a drink. 'Sir Edward Henry, the Commissioner, is adamant that Metropolitan Police officers will only assist county forces if an official request is made by your Chief Constable *and* that the deputed Scotland Yard officer is put *in charge* of the investigation. Furthermore,' he added, 'the county force would have to pay all the expenses involved.'

'Very well,' said Potts, his face expressing annoyance at Hardcastle's response. 'I'll see you at the mortuary.'

When Hardcastle and Marriott, along with Superintendent Potts, arrived at the mortuary, Dr Bernard Spilsbury was still at work on the cadaver of Kitty Gordon.

'I caught an earlier train and made a start,' he said. Looking up, he saw Hardcastle, stopped work immediately and peeled off his rubber gloves. 'My dear Hardcastle,' he said warmly as he shook hands, 'what on earth are you doing here? Aren't there enough murders in London for you to solve? You told me that you'd already got three on your plate.'

'I don't know if this is a murder until you tell me, sir,' said Hardcastle. 'But this young lady was housemaid to Georgina Cheney. Hence my interest.'

'Was she indeed? But I was given to understand that this woman's name was Kitty Gordon.'

'I identified her as the woman I knew as Hannah Clarke, sir. And it's been established by the local police that she was also known as Queenie Rogers.'

'What an intriguing puzzle, my dear Hardcastle,' said Spilsbury. 'I think that what I have to tell you will confirm that she was murdered.'

Superintendent Potts emitted an affected cough.

'By the way, Doctor,' said Hardcastle casually, 'this is Superintendent Potts of the local force. He's looking into this suspicious death.'

Spilsbury nodded in the superintendent's direction. 'Potts,' he murmured.

'I'm actually in *charge* of the investigation, sir,' said Potts, tugging at his walrus moustache, 'and in charge of the Worthing Division.'

'You're very lucky to have Inspector Hardcastle here, then, Potts,' said Spilsbury. 'He's very good at this sort of thing.' It was a comment that did not please the superintendent. 'However,' he continued, rubbing his hands together, 'I've already finished carving up this young lady and I'm about to sew her up again. Come and have a look.' He gestured at the body on the slab. Where the pathologist had examined the victim, large flaps of flesh from the chest and stomach lay open like the petals of a huge flower.

'I think I'll wait outside, sir,' said a white-faced Potts, and promptly left the room.

'What can you tell me, sir?' asked Hardcastle, turning back from having observed, with a wry smile, the hurried exit of the superintendent.

'There was an absence of water in the lungs, Hardcastle, so you can rule out drowning,' said Spilsbury. 'This young woman had been strangled.'

'So it is murder,' said Hardcastle.

'I would say so, unless she strangled herself prior to throwing herself into the sea,' said Spilsbury, with a chuckle. 'But, joking aside, you know as well as I that one cannot strangle oneself. Unconsciousness supervenes and the hands will relax. However, I gather from what the bold superintendent said that it's not your problem.'

'Only indirectly, sir,' said Hardcastle. 'As I said just now, she was Mrs Cheney's housemaid, but I gather from what was found among her belongings that she was also employed in that capacity by Mrs Hardy, another of the murder victims whose death I'm investigating. You did the post-mortem.'

'I remember. It looks as though you'll be kept busy, my dear fellow.'

'I'll let you get on with your needlework then, Doctor,' said Hardcastle. 'I've a few leads to follow up in London.' Leaving Dr Spilsbury to stitch up his cadaver, Marriott and Hardcastle left the dissecting room and went in search of the Worthing superintendent.

'Well, Mr Hardcastle?' Potts stood up, pinched the tip of his cigarette to extinguish it, and dropped the butt into an ashtray on the wall. 'What's the result?'

'The result, Mr Potts, is that you've got a murder on your hands,' said Hardcastle, with undisguised relish, and repeated the pathologist's findings. 'However, me and my sergeant are off back to London.'

'But can't you stay and give me a hand?' implored Potts, all trace of his earlier bombast now gone.

'As I made clear earlier, Mr Potts, that will only happen if your Chief Constable makes an official request to the Commissioner of Police of the Metropolis for assistance. Good day to you.' But secretly, Hardcastle hoped that he would be required to assist. He was now convinced that the murder of Hannah Clarke, alias Kitty Gordon, whose real name it appeared was Queenie Rogers, was inextricably involved with the three London murders he was already investigating.

'D'you think the Chief Constable will ask the Yard for assistance, sir?' asked Marriott, as he and Hardcastle left Worthing Hospital in search of a cab to take them to the railway station.

'It would be useful, Marriott. I've got a feeling that whoever topped Hannah Clarke, or whatever her bloody name really is, has got to be tied up in the murders of all three of our victims. By the way, where's Catto gone?'

'I took the liberty of sending him back to London, sir.'

'Very wise, Marriott, very wise.'

The following morning, a Saturday, Hardcastle was at his desk by half past eight. At nine o'clock, just as he had got his pipe satisfactorily alight, Detective Sergeant Marriott appeared in the DDI's office.

'Yes, what is it, Marriott?'

'I've just taken a call from Mr Wensley's clerk, sir. You're to see Mr Wensley immediately.'

'I bet I know what that's about, Marriott.' Hardcastle stood up, took his hat and umbrella from the hatstand and hurried across the narrow road that separated Cannon Row police station from Commissioner's Office.

'Come in, Ernie,' said 'Ace' Wensley. 'I expect you know why I've sent for you.'

'Worthing, sir?'

'Exactly. The Chief Constable of West Sussex Constabulary has made an official request for the services of the Metropolitan Police to investigate the murder of Queenie Rogers, alias Kitty Gordon and, I believe, Hannah Clarke. As it's obviously connected with at least two of the three murders you're already investigating, I'm assigning you. I know you've already got a lot to deal with, but I have a feeling that if you solve this one, you'll have cleared up the others.'

'Very good, sir. I'll get back down there straight away.'

'I've told the West Sussex chief that you will be in charge of the enquiry and I've made it a condition that one of his CID officers will be attached to your enquiry. He wasn't too taken with that idea and prevaricated a little. He said that the divisional superintendent, a man called Potts, was quite capable. But I insisted.'

'Thank you for that, sir. From my brief dealings with Potts I think he and I would fall out sooner rather than later.'

'Really? I can't imagine an easy-going chap like you falling out with anyone, Ernie.' But Wensley smiled as he said it. 'Who are you taking as your bag carrier?'

'Marriott, sir. He's very good on a murder enquiry.' Hardcastle paused. 'But don't tell him I said so.'

'By the way,' said Wensley, 'until these four murders are cleared up you will be attached to New Scotland Yard. I've cleared it with the assistant commissioner and he's informed Superintendent Hudson of A Division that you're not available for any enquiries there.'

When Hardcastle returned to his office, he shouted for Marriott and Catto as he passed the open door of the detectives' office, but only Marriott came in.

'Where's Catto, Marriott?'

'He's rest day, sir.'

'Not any more he's not. Where's he live?'

'The section house in Ambrosden Avenue, sir.'

'Send a PC to fetch him here. Now.'

'I can telephone the section house, sir. We've got a direct line from here.'

'Have we really, now?' Hardcastle leaned back in his chair and blew pipe smoke gently towards his nicotine-stained ceiling. 'D'you know, Marriott, if this telephone novelty catches on, policemen will become very lazy. There's already talk of 'em driving about in motor cars.'

'I'm told it's the coming thing, sir.'

'Well, I hope it doesn't come before I've retired, Marriott. Now, about this Worthing job. The chief down there has asked for assistance. We'll catch an afternoon train and start on the enquiry straight away. No doubt the idea of working all through Saturday night and Sunday will come as a nasty shock to them.'

Marriott was not greatly taken with the prospect of losing yet another weekend, but long ago had become resigned to the fact that that sort of disruption was the lot of a CID officer.

'I think Catto did a good job down at Worthing, sir.'

'Mmm! It was only basic detective work, Marriott, but I suppose I ought to give him a pat on the back.'

'I think he deserves to be encouraged, sir.' Marriott was amazed that for once Hardcastle was on the point of paying a junior officer a compliment, especially when that officer was Henry Catto.

'Tell him to see me when he arrives, Marriott.'

'You wanted to see me, sir?' asked Catto.

'Have you thought about studying for the promotion examination yet, Catto?'

'No, sir.' The reason was simple: Catto did not think that the DDI would recommend him.

'Well, it's time you did.'

And that, Catto realized, was the closest he would ever get to receiving praise from the DDI.

'Me and Sergeant Marriott are going to Worthing this afternoon, Catto,' continued Hardcastle, 'to sort out this murder of theirs. I want you here to deal with any enquiries I might have at the London end. Got that?'

'Yes, sir.'

'Good. And don't make a Mons of it, Catto.'

Hardcastle and Marriott had returned briefly to their respective homes to gather what they would need for a prolonged stay out of town. Consequently, it was six o'clock that evening before they arrived, once again, at Ann Street police station in Worthing.

'Can I help you, sir?' asked the sergeant on duty.

'DDI Hardcastle, Metropolitan. I've come to see Superintendent Potts in connection with this murder on your patch.'

The sergeant looked surprised and then glanced at the clock. 'Mr Potts is off duty, sir. It being a Saturday evening.'

'Good God!' exclaimed Hardcastle. 'Well who is here who's got something to do with it?' It was apparent, now that the enquiry had been handed over to the Metropolitan Police, that the West Sussex force was to have nothing further to do with it.

'Only the inspector is here, sir. That's Mr Weaver.'

'You'd better show me to his office, then,' said Hardcastle, getting more irritated by the moment.

The two detectives followed the Worthing sergeant to a room at the rear of the police station.

'That's it, sir,' said the sergeant, pointing to a door marked 'Inspector'.

Hardcastle pushed open the door without knocking.

The uniformed occupant looked up from the papers on which he was working, and frowned at the interruption. 'Who the hell are you, and don't you ever knock?' he demanded.

'Divisional Detective Inspector Hardcastle of New Scotland Yard, and this is Detective Sergeant Marriott.'

'Oh, I beg your pardon, sir,' said the inspector, rising to his feet. 'I'm Tom Weaver. We weren't expecting you until Monday.'

'Well, I'm here, Mr Weaver. And now I want to get on with the job. The sooner I get back to London, the sooner I can get on with my three other murders.'

'You mean you want to start immediately, sir?' Weaver raised his eyebrows in surprise. 'But it's Saturday.'

'I know it's Saturday, Mr Weaver, and surprising though it might seem I do work on a Saturday – and even a Sunday – where murder's involved. The longer I leave it from the time of a topping, the harder it gets to solve it. I'm starting work now and I'll carry on for as long as it takes. Now then, my guv'nor asked for me to be given the services of a local CID officer. Where is he?'

'I'm afraid we don't have any CID officers in the West Sussex Constabulary, Mr Hardcastle,' said Weaver, almost apologetically. 'And I don't know anything about any such arrangement.'

'Ye gods!' exclaimed Hardcastle. 'Just as well I brought a CID officer with me. Detective Sergeant Marriott here is highly experienced in dealing with murders. However, I want a local officer assigned to me full-time. Is that understood, Mr Weaver?'

'I'm afraid I don't have the authority to detach an officer for special duties, sir. It'll be necessary for me to speak to Superintendent Potts, and he'll probably have to talk to the Chief Constable. And that can't be done until Monday.'

'In that case, Mr Weaver, perhaps you'd be so good as to give me the home address of the Chief Constable, and I shall go to see him,' said Hardcastle, fast becoming annoyed at the apparent indifference of the Worthing police. 'This is an urgent matter and unless I have a local officer right now, I shall have no alternative but to communicate with my Commissioner and inform him of your constabulary's distinct lack of cooperation. And no doubt Sir Edward Henry will make his displeasure known to your Chief Constable.'

Weaver dithered. His own senior officers were bad enough, but he had never met anyone quite like this acerbic officer from the Yard.

'If you'll excuse me for a minute or two, sir, I'll see what I can do.'

'I don't know, Marriott,' thundered Hardcastle. 'What on earth's going on down here? They've got a tricky murder to deal with, but no one seems to be doing anything. And that Inspector Weaver doesn't seem to appreciate the urgency of the situation.' Although the DDI would never criticize a Metropolitan Police senior officer to a junior rank, he had no qualms about expressing his opinion of provincial officers.

'I think he's in a rather difficult situation, sir,' ventured Marriott, who had frequently been on the receiving end of Hardcastle's uncompromising demands.

Ten minutes later, Inspector Weaver returned. 'I've arranged for Sergeant Burgess to be attached to you, sir. He's on patrol at the moment, but I've sent the station sergeant out to relieve him. That means that I'll have to man the front office desk.'

'It's a hard life, Mr Weaver,' said Hardcastle unsympathetically. 'Where is this here Burgess, then?'

'I've told him to change into civilian clothes, sir. I hope he'll suit your purposes, but he's very young for his rank.'

'How young?' asked Hardcastle.

'He's twenty-eight, sir, but the Chief Constable thinks highly of him.'

'We shall see,' admitted Hardcastle grudgingly. 'But I suppose he'll have to do. And now, Mr Weaver, I'll need an office here where I can set up shop, so to speak.'

'Oh!' Once again Weaver had been presented with a dilemma. 'Well, I suppose you'd better use this one until the superintendent can make a decision about it.'

Hardcastle had doubts about Superintendent Potts' ability to make a decision; he thought that he would probably have to consult the Chief Constable about any matter concerning police station accommodation. Giving Weaver no chance to resume his seat, the DDI sat down at the inspector's desk. 'Thank you, Mr Weaver. Be so good as to send this here Burgess to me when he turns up. And leave the door open.'

'What's first, sir?' asked Marriott, once Weaver had disappeared to take charge of the front office of the police station.

'We find ourselves somewhere to stay, Marriott.'

'How about the Sea View Hotel, sir? It's where Kitty Gordon stayed.'

'Good idea. And before we go any further, we'll refer to this here corpse of ours as Hannah Clarke. We'll only confuse ourselves if we keep calling her by one of her three names. And by the time we've finished, we'll probably find out she's got a few more monikers to add to the list.'

Hardcastle had been studying the documents that he had brought with him from London for half an hour when a man appeared in the doorway. He was dressed in a light suit and carried a straw boater in his right hand.

'Excuse me, sir. Are you Mr Hardcastle?'

'I am.'

'Sergeant Burgess, sir. Inspector Weaver said you wanted to see me.'

'Come in, Burgess, and close the door. How well d'you know Worthing?'

'I know it very well, sir. I was born here, and I spent some time as a beat-duty constable before being made sergeant.'

'Well, that's something, I suppose. This here is Detective Sergeant Marriott. He's solved more murders than you've had hot dinners and you'll learn a lot from him if you keep your ears open.'

Burgess shook hands with Marriott. 'How d'you do, Sergeant?'

'The name's Charlie,' said Marriott. 'What's yours?'

'Edward. Known as Ted.'

'I've got an important job for you straight away, Burgess,' said Hardcastle.

'Yes, sir?' responded Burgess keenly.

'Find two chairs and bring 'em in here.'

Burgess, believing he was about to be given an important task, looked momentarily stunned by this instruction. 'Yes, sir,' he said eventually.

'That should test his detective skills,' said Hardcastle, chuckling as Burgess hurried away to do his bidding.

Minutes later, Burgess struggled through the door with two upright chairs.

'Right, sit down, both of you,' said Hardcastle, 'and you, Burgess, are to listen to what I've got to say. Now, then, I take it you know all about this here murder I've been sent to Worthing to solve for you West Sussex fellows.'

'Yes, sir. The victim was a young woman called Kitty Gordon who was staying at the Sea View Hotel. But wasn't she drowned?'

'Kitty Gordon was only one of the names she used, Burgess, but she didn't drown; she was strangled and her body was then thrown into the sea. It was made to look like a drowning because she was attired in a bathing dress. It might've looked as though she was going for a midnight swim, but that wasn't the case. My view is that her murderer dressed her in a bathing dress after he'd topped her to mislead us. Her clothes were found in a lifebelt locker by one of the pier-master's chaps when he was doing some checking up. Her handbag and an umbrella were there, too. But it takes more than that to deceive me.'

'So, what exactly d'you want me to do, sir?'

'You've been assigned to me to assist in the investigation and your local knowledge will come in handy.'

'But Inspector Weaver said it was only for today, sir, until he's had time to talk to Mr Potts and get someone permanent.'

'Well, Burgess, you're with me permanent and if anyone tries to take you away there'll be one hell of a row. And I'll start with the Chief Constable.'

Burgess's mouth opened in surprise. He had never heard any of his own officers say that he was prepared to have a row with the Chief Constable.

'If anyone tries to put you on other duties you're to let me know immediately. Is that clear?'

'Yes, sir,' said Burgess.

'Good. The first thing we'll do, Marriott, is get up to the Sea View Hotel and find ourselves a couple of rooms. Then we'll see what more the landlady can tell us that she hasn't told Catto. What was her name?'

'That's Mrs Croft, sir,' volunteered Burgess. 'I know her.'

'There you are, Marriott, I told you that it'd be handy to have a local officer with us.'

'There's a bus that we can catch at the end of Ann Street, sir, that'll take us straight there.'

Hardcastle studied the young sergeant sternly. 'Get one thing clear, Burgess. Officers from Scotland Yard do not take buses to go about their enquiries in a murder investigation. They use cabs and your Chief Constable picks up the tab.'

'Yes, sir,' said Burgess, becoming increasingly surprised at each of Hardcastle's utterances. He had never, in all his service, taken a taxi in the course of police duty.

Hardcastle picked up his bowler hat and umbrella. 'Come along, then,' he said, and led the way through to the front office. 'Ah, Mr Weaver.'

'Sir?' said Weaver, standing up.

'D'you have a telephone here?'

'Yes, sir.'

'Good. Be so good as to call me a cab.'

THIRTEEN

It was close to five o'clock when Hardcastle, Marriott and Burgess arrived at the Sea View Hotel. Hardcastle and Marriott were carrying the small suitcases they had brought with them from London.

'Hello, Mr Burgess. What are you doing here on a Saturday evening?' Mrs Croft appeared surprised as the three men entered the reception area of the hotel, and glanced at the London detectives' suitcases.

'I've been attached to the enquiry into the death of your guest Miss Gordon, Mrs Croft,' said Burgess. 'And these gentlemen are from New Scotland Yard,' he added. 'Divisional Detective Inspector Hardcastle and his assistant Detective Sergeant Marriott.'

'Good afternoon, ma'am,' said Hardcastle, raising his hat.

Mrs Croft frowned as she acknowledged each of the two London officers in turn. 'I don't understand,' she said. 'The policeman who was here yesterday said that the unfortunate Miss Gordon had been drowned. Why should Scotland Yard be interested?'

'I'm afraid that Miss Gordon wasn't drowned, ma'am,' said Hardcastle. 'She was murdered.'

'Oh, the poor dear girl,' exclaimed Mrs Croft, her face blanching as she put a hand to her mouth, and promptly sat down on the only chair in the reception area. 'Who would do such a thing?'

'That's why we've come to Worthing, ma'am,' said Marriott. 'To find her killer.'

'You mean he's here somewhere?' asked Mrs Croft, looking quite anguished at the prospect of a murderer being in the vicinity.

'I'm afraid we don't know where he is at the moment, ma'am,' said Hardcastle. 'But I'll soon have him dancing on the hangman's trap, be assured of that.'

'Oh my goodness.' Mrs Croft appeared even more distressed by Hardcastle's uncompromising statement.

'My sergeant and I would like to take rooms here for a few days, Mrs Croft,' said Hardcastle. 'Can that be arranged?'

'By all means, Inspector,' said Mrs Croft warmly. She recovered instantly, believing that some prestige would attach to her hotel as a result of having as guests Scotland Yard officers who were investigating a murder. 'I have empty rooms because Saturday is changeover day at hotels like this one. I must say, though, that since the war started people aren't so keen to have holidays at the seaside, what with so many men being away at the Front. Or dead,' she added mournfully. 'Women aren't willing to come away by themselves, you see. It makes it a bit difficult for my hubby and me to make ends meet. Mind you, the fact that Miss Gordon was murdered might help trade.' She stood up, suddenly taking a perverse pride in the fact that her hotel had accommodated a murder victim. 'However, you don't want to hear any more of my complaining, Inspector. I'll show you the rooms.'

'Thank you, Mrs Croft,' said Hardcastle, 'but that will have to wait. Me and my colleagues would like to inspect the room that Miss Gordon occupied. I take it that you haven't let it out to anyone else?'

'Certainly not, Inspector. She paid for a week in advance and all her things are still there. I asked the policeman who came yesterday what I should do with them, but he said that I'd have to wait for the superintendent at Worthing to decide what's to be done.'

'I see.' Hardcastle smiled at the thought that a superintendent would be required to make such a decision. 'I think we'll be able to take care of that for you, Mrs Croft.'

'I'll show you up, Inspector, and then I'll make sure your rooms are ready for you.'

Kitty Gordon's room was on the first floor with a view of the seafront and the pier which, Hardcastle noted, was only a short distance away from the hotel. But contrary to Mrs Croft's complaint that trade had suffered as a result of the war, the beach was crowded with holidaymakers. Women in large hats were seated in deckchairs watching children playing in the surf, and there seemed to be no shortage of men. Although a few were in army or navy uniform, the other men were in civilian attire. Despite the warmth of the evening many were wearing jackets, collars and ties and straw boaters. Several intrepid souls had ventured into the sea, the women holding up their skirts, the men with their trousers rolled up. Somewhere in the distance a band could be heard playing.

Hardcastle stood in the centre of the room and gazed around. It was typical of seaside accommodation; similar, in fact, to one in which he had stayed when forced to take a week's holiday in Southend-on-Sea before the war. A single iron bedstead, a wardrobe, a chair, a dressing table, and a washstand on which were a bowl and a ewer comprised the furnishings. Brown curtains, brown paintwork and cheap wallpaper depicting roses, all combined to give the room a depressing air.

One of the two suitcases that Hannah Clarke had taken with her when she had left Whilber Street rested on a folding luggage rack. The other stood beside it, along with her valise.

'She seems to have brought a lot of baggage with her for a trip to the seaside, sir,' commented Marriott.

'Unless she planned to go further afield, Marriott,' said Hardcastle. 'Take a look in the wardrobe.'

Marriott pulled open the door of the wardrobe. 'There are only the black mourning weeds she arrived in, sir,' he said, 'and a pair of shoes.'

'Try the suitcase, Burgess. Start with the one on the rack,' said Hardcastle.

Burgess opened it up. 'More clothing, sir.'

'Is that all?'

'Not quite, sir.' From the pouch at the back of the suitcase, Burgess extracted a cheque book and handed it to the DDI. 'That looks interesting, sir,' he said, and switched his attention to the valise.

'Interesting indeed.' Hardcastle flicked open the cover. 'I suppose it belongs to our victim,' he said, 'unless she pinched it. It was issued by Williams Deacon's Bank in Victoria Street, London, Marriott. We'll have to make a few enquiries there when we get back.'

'We could ask Catto to do it, sir,' suggested Marriott.

'I don't think so,' said Hardcastle. 'Catto has his limitations, and making enquiries at a bank is one of them.'

'There's a ration book in the name of Queenie Rogers in the valise, sir,' said Burgess. 'And an address book.'

'There should be an address on that ration book.'

'There is, sir. Disraeli Road, Wandsworth, London S.W.'

'I can see you're coming on a treat, Burgess. We'll make a detective of you yet,' said Hardcastle, taking hold of the slim leather-bound address book and flicking through it. 'There are quite a few names in here, Marriott. We'll need to go through it and trace these people.'

'Yes, sir,' said Marriott, groaning inwardly. He knew who would be doing the work.

'And we'll pay a visit to this Disraeli Road address. I think we might find something interesting there.'

The search continued, but there was little more to interest the detectives. Apart from the documents that Burgess had discovered in the suitcase and the valise, the luggage contained only clothing. Hardcastle noted that the frocks were of good value, but decided that they had probably belonged to the late Georgina Cheney. Or even Blanche Hardy.

'It strikes me that Hannah Clarke was planning on staying here for a while, but I somehow doubt that she intended to live in this hotel permanently,' said Hardcastle.

'Mrs Croft said she'd paid for a week's stay, sir,' said Burgess.

'Quite so, but I wonder where she was going from here.'

'Perhaps to one of the people listed in the address book, sir,' suggested Marriott. 'Or maybe back to the Disraeli Road address that Ted Burgess found on the ration book. Perhaps she really was here just for a holiday.'

'Maybe, but Catto said she told the cab driver that she was visiting her folks in Sussex,' said Hardcastle. 'Well, I think that's all we can do for the moment. We'll see if our rooms are ready and then we'll take Burgess here out for a pint. I dare say you know of a decent pub hereabouts, Burgess, being as you're a local, so to speak.'

'Yes, sir. There's one not far from here.' Burgess continued to be surprised by the attitude of the London DDI. He had never once been taken out for a drink by an inspector. In fact, the senior officers of the West Sussex Constabulary were at pains to keep themselves aloof from the lower ranks.

The public house that Burgess had recommended was a decent enough hostelry, and Hardcastle amazed Marriott by paying for the first round.

Hardcastle took out his watch, glanced at it, briefly wound it and dropped it back into his waistcoat pocket.

'See you at the police station at nine o'clock tomorrow morning, Burgess.'

'Tomorrow's Sunday, sir,' said Burgess.

'I know,' said Hardcastle.

Hardcastle and Marriott had been at work for half an hour when Sergeant Burgess arrived.

'I hope I'm not late, sir.'

'No, you're right on time, Burgess,' said Hardcastle. 'Sergeant Marriott and me have been going over what we know so far, and what needs to be done tomorrow.'

'Have you got a job for me, sir?' asked Burgess keenly.

'Yes, I have, Burgess. I want you to get yourself back up to the Sea View Hotel and take a written statement from Mrs Croft. Make sure you include what Kitty Gordon said to her when she arrived.

And that means everything, no matter how unimportant it might seem. What she said exactly about how long she'd be staying. What she was doing there; a holiday or what. What she said about going out and did she say where she was going? Did she mention who she was meeting or did she talk about going to a restaurant for supper, if so which one? Were there any callers asking for her, before she arrived, while she was there, or after she'd left? Have you got all that?'

'Yes, sir.' Burgess had been rapidly taking notes while the DDI was talking. In the last twenty-four hours he had learned more about the investigation of murder than in the whole of his service.

'Where's the bathing dress the girl was wearing?' asked Hardcastle, suddenly changing the subject.

'Er, I don't know, sir.'

'Well, find it, Burgess. Tomorrow morning I want to visit every shop that sells such garments. We'll take it with us and show it around. I'll want to know who, if anyone, purchased it. Whether it was Miss Gordon or whether it was a man. If it was a man we'll get any identifying details and take a description. And we'll make a note of the time the purchase was made.'

'Yes, sir.' Burgess was staggered at the pace and the thoroughness of the London DDI's instructions, and that he had issued them without any reference to notes.

'Make me a list of those shops nearest to the Sea View Hotel and the pier; I noticed that they're close to each other. Once that's done get copies made of the photograph in the girl's identity card so that we can show it around. I'm particularly interested in anyone who saw Miss Gordon in the company of a man.'

'We don't have any facilities for photography here at Worthing police station, sir.'

Hardcastle stared at the young Sussex sergeant. 'You don't have the facilities? Good grief! In that case get hold of a reliable local photographer and tell him to do it. And I don't want to hear that he said they'd be ready next week. I want them within the hour. In fact there ought to be someone about on a Sunday, seeing as how the beach will probably be crowded with people who want their pictures taken.'

'Who's going to pay for them, sir?'

'The West Sussex Constabulary, of course.' Hardcastle saw the look of concern on Burgess's face. 'Don't worry, Burgess, I'll be the one telling Mr Potts to put his hand in his pocket.'

'Very good, sir.' Burgess was extremely glad that he was not the one who would have to approach the superintendent for reimbursement.

'Very well,' said Hardcastle. 'We'll meet here again at two o'clock and you can tell me how you've got on.'

'Shouldn't I give him a hand, sir?' asked Marriott, once Burgess had departed.

'It'll be quicker for him to do it, Marriott.' Hardcastle took out his pipe and began slowly to fill it with tobacco. 'He's a local lad and we wouldn't know where to start. Anyway, it's Worthing's murder.'

Sergeant Burgess was looking extremely pleased with himself when he returned to Worthing police station at two o'clock.

'Have you got some answers, Burgess?' demanded Hardcastle.

'I've got the statement from Mrs Croft, sir. She said that Miss Gordon went out last evening at about six o'clock saying that she was going for a walk along the front. She also said that she was meeting someone for supper and that she'd be back at about half past ten. Miss Gordon didn't mention to Mrs Croft who she'd be meeting or where she'd be going for supper. And when she left the hotel that's the last Mrs Croft saw of her.'

Marriott sifted through the papers that he and Hardcastle had brought from London. 'That's exactly what she told Catto, sir,' he said, proffering the statement that Catto had made about his enquiries in Worthing.

Hardcastle waved it aside. 'I know that, Marriott.'

'Miss Gordon told Mrs Croft that she'd be staying a week and paid in advance, sir.' Burgess continued to read from the statement he had taken. 'She also volunteered the information that she was taking a short holiday.'

'Well, that don't add much to the pile.'

'But that is what she said, sir,' said Burgess, fearing that he was being criticized by the DDI.

'I've no doubt, Burgess. Much as we'd like to, we can't get witnesses to tell us more than they know. Now, what about the photos?'

'I contacted a photographer I know, sir. He's a reliable chap and has done jobs for us before.' Burgess opened his briefcase and extracted a handful of copies of the photograph in the identity card that bore the name of Queenie Rogers.

'Good. They'll be useful for tomorrow's enquiries.' Hardcastle lit his pipe. 'Don't you smoke, Burgess?' he asked.

'Yes, sir, but never in the presence of a senior officer.'

'Well, you're working with London coppers now, so light up.'

'Thank you, sir.' Burgess took out a pipe and filled it.

'I'm glad to see you don't smoke cigarettes, Burgess. Marriott here does, and I keep telling him they'll do him no good.'

'They're more convenient than all the paraphernalia that goes with pipe-smoking, Ted,' said Marriott, 'but I hope you don't wear a wristwatch. That'd really upset the guv'nor.'

Burgess stared at Marriott open-mouthed, but remained silent. He could never visualize this sort of casual conversation taking place between an inspector and a sergeant in his force.

'Quite right, Marriott,' said Hardcastle. 'I'm surprised you haven't knocked the thing off on something.'

'I haven't done so yet, sir.' But even Marriott was surprised at how Hardcastle's usually acerbic mood had softened since their arrival in Worthing. He could only assume that it had something to do with the sea air.

'I think that'll do for today,' said Hardcastle. 'Enjoy your weekend, Burgess.'

'Thank you, sir.' Burgess was starting to learn a lot about London detectives in general and Hardcastle in particular. Half a Sunday would not be regarded as a weekend in the West Sussex Constabulary. In addition, he would have to see the young lady he was courting and explain why he had failed to meet her the previous evening.

On Monday morning Hardcastle and Marriott enjoyed an excellent breakfast at the Sea View Hotel. Hardcastle suspected that it was far superior to that served to the other guests and attributed it to the fact that he and Marriott were investigating the murder. Mrs Croft had also supplied each of the two detectives with a copy of the *Argus*, the local newspaper. Banner headlines proclaimed: LONDON WOMAN MURDERED ON WORTHING PIER – YARD CALLED IN.

'I wonder who leaked that to the press,' said Hardcastle, but was resigned to the fact that it would have been difficult to keep it secret.

At Hardcastle's behest, Mrs Croft had called a cab, and he and Marriott arrived at Ann Street police station only to walk into a storm.

The sergeant on duty looked up as the two London detectives entered. Behind him stood Inspector Weaver. Both appeared somewhat apprehensive.

'Good morning, sir,' said Weaver. 'Superintendent Potts would like to see you, sir. I think he's somewhat upset.'

'Is that so?' said Hardcastle. 'In that case, you may tell him that I'm in your office should he wish to talk to me.'

'But, sir . . .' Weaver was not looking forward to acting as a go-between, especially where these two particular officers were concerned.

'Is Sergeant Burgess here, Mr Weaver?' Hardcastle dismissed the inspector's concerns; he was in no mood for petty squabbles.

'He looked in earlier, sir, but he said that you'd given him several enquiries to make.'

'Quite right. I did.' Hardcastle, followed by Marriott, made his way to the office that he had commandeered and slammed the door.

But only minutes later that door was flung open and Superintendent Potts stood on the threshold.

'I left a message for you to see me, Mr Hardcastle.'

'I believe you did, Mr Potts. Well, I'm here,' said Hardcastle. 'Was it something important in connection with the murder I'm investigating for you?'

'Perhaps your sergeant could leave us for a moment,' said Potts.

'My sergeant is assisting me in this investigation, Mr Potts, and as you've presumably come here to impart some new information about this murder, he stays.'

'I haven't,' snapped Potts. 'I wish you to know that I'm extremely annoyed that you have taken one of my officers for your enquiries without so much as a by-your-leave.' The superintendent was red in the face and appeared to be having great difficulty in controlling his temper.

Hardcastle took out his pipe and slowly filled it. 'My Commissioner specifically asked for a CID officer to be assigned to this enquiry, Mr Potts,' he said mildly. 'But when I arrived on Saturday afternoon I found that that request had been completely ignored. What's more I subsequently learned that you don't have any CID officers. As there was no time to waste, I therefore directed Inspector Weaver to select a suitable uniformed officer. As a result, Sergeant Burgess has been assigned to me and I find that he's most satisfactory.'

'Now look here . . .' Potts had never been spoken to like this before, even by the Chief.

'But as there seems to be a problem,' continued Hardcastle in level tones, 'I shall now go to Horsham and speak to the Chief Constable about the lack of cooperation I'm receiving from the superintendent of the Worthing Division.' Before Potts could reply to this blatant threat, Hardcastle turned to Marriott. 'See if you can find a cab to take us to Horsham, Marriott. I understand that it's about twenty miles from here, but as the Chief Constable will be paying for it, I don't mind how much it will cost.'

'I don't think there's any need to disturb the Chief, Mr Hardcastle,' said Potts, hurriedly backing down. 'You can keep Sergeant Burgess. Not that he's much good,' he added churlishly. 'It's just that you've caused me a great deal of inconvenience in having to rearrange my duty rosters.' And with that final complaint, the superintendent swept from the office. As a final show of pique, he slammed the door.

'Now, perhaps, we can get on, Marriott,' said Hardcastle.

FOURTEEN

Sergeant Edward Burgess returned to the police station at ten o'clock.

'Good morning, sir.'

'You're up and about bright and early, Burgess,' said Hardcastle. 'By the way, Superintendent Potts has agreed that you're assigned to me for as long as I need you.'

'Thank you, sir.'

'Well, what have you been doing?'

'I've drawn up a list of three likely shops nearest to the Sea View Hotel that sell bathing dresses, sir. And I've identified a number of restaurants that might've been visited by the dead woman. I haven't made any enquiries because you said you'd wish to make them yourself.'

'Quite right. Come, Marriott, we'll make a start.'

'D'you want me to come with you, sir?' asked Burgess.

'Of course.' Hardcastle picked up his bowler hat, paused and then took hold of his umbrella.

'It's not raining, sir,' observed Burgess hesitantly.

'But it might,' said Hardcastle. 'In fact, Burgess, one does not even have to leave this police station to run into a squall,' he added. It was a comment that, unsurprisingly, meant nothing to Burgess. 'Be so good as to call a taxi. You can use the police station telephone.'

'But the superintendent—'

'Never mind what the superintendent says about it, Burgess. I'm in charge of this enquiry.'

'This is the last shop on your list of three, Burgess,' said Hardcastle. 'Let's hope we fare better with this one than we did with the last two.'

'So do I, sir.' Burgess feared that Hardcastle would think that he had not been thorough.

The three officers had stopped outside an establishment that dealt solely in ladies' fashions, and had the appearance of being at the upper end of the market. The garments in the window display were tastefully arranged and exhibited what, even to Hardcastle's unpractised eye, were expensive gowns.

A young woman looked askance at the three men as they entered the shop, assuming briefly that they had come to the wrong place.

'May I help you, sir?' she asked, directing her request to Hardcastle. 'I'm Miss Kersh. Rebecca Kersh, the manageress.'

'I hope so, Miss Kersh,' said Hardcastle, raising his hat. 'I'm Divisional Detective Inspector Hardcastle of Scotland Yard and I'm enquiring into the murder of the woman on Thursday evening,' he added.

'I read about that in the *Argus*, Inspector. One doesn't expect such a terrible thing to happen here in Worthing.'

'Show the young lady the bathing dress, Burgess.'

The Worthing sergeant opened his briefcase and placed the garment on the counter.

'This is the bathing dress in which the victim was found, Miss Kersh,' said Hardcastle. 'Did you sell it to a customer on Thursday?' he asked.

Miss Kersh fingered the costume and examined the maker's label. 'Yes, Inspector, quite definitely,' she said. 'We're the only establishment that sells that particular line. It's an import from America.' She crossed to a cabinet and took an identical costume from a drawer. 'It's very avant-garde and not to everyone's taste,' she said, holding it up. 'A little too revealing, if you see what I mean, and likely to raise a few eyebrows if worn on the beach here.' The costume would have left the wearer's arms and shoulders bare, apart from supporting straps, and the frilled skirt would have reached no lower than the middle of the thighs.

'How many did you sell on Thursday?'

'Only the one. We bought six and in fact we've only sold that one.' Rebecca Kersh pointed at the bathing suit the police had brought with them.

'Show Miss Kersh the photograph, Burgess.'

'Was this the young woman who made the purchase, miss?' asked Burgess, handing the manageress a copy of the photograph.

'It wasn't me who sold it,' said Rebecca Kersh. She glanced across the shop. 'Miss Craig, are you free?'

'Yes, Miss Kersh,' said the assistant as she joined the little group.

'I believe you sold this bathing dress on Thursday.' The manageress indicated the costume spread out on the counter.

'Yes, Miss Kersh, I did.'

'Was this the lady to whom you sold it?' Rebecca Kersh handed the assistant the photograph.

'It wasn't a lady,' said Miss Craig. 'It was a gentleman.'

'I'm not surprised,' said Hardcastle, thinking that such a flimsy garment would be easier for a man to put on a dead woman than one of the more fashionable and all-embracing bathing outfits usually seen on English beaches. If, indeed, that is what had occurred. 'Can you describe this man, Miss Craig?'

'He was tall, sir,' said Miss Craig thoughtfully, 'and his hair was wavy. But I particularly noticed his suit: very well cut and from Savile Row, I'd imagine.'

'How old would you say he was, Miss Craig?' asked Marriott.

'Difficult to say, sir. I couldn't be sure.'

'Did he ask for this specific bathing dress?'

'Not exactly.'

'I think you'd better explain, Miss Craig,' said the manageress. 'These officers are investigating the murder of the young woman on Thursday. They told me that this is the bathing dress she was wearing.'

'Oh, how awful!' exclaimed Miss Craig. 'And to think I sold it.' But quickly recovering, she continued. 'The gentleman said he was buying it for his fiancée as a surprise. I asked him what size the young lady was and he said that she was about my build.'

'Would you mind turning around, Miss Craig?' said Hardcastle, making a circling movement with his forefinger. 'What d'you think, Marriott?'

'This young lady is certainly similar to Hannah Clarke, sir,' said Marriott, once Miss Craig was facing them again.

'I suppose this man didn't pay for the purchase with a cheque, did he?' asked Hardcastle hopefully.

'No, he paid cash,' said Miss Craig promptly.

'What time did you make this sale?' asked Marriott.

'At about a quarter to six,' said Miss Craig. 'I remember because we close at six o'clock and that was the time when the gentleman left. In fact he was our last customer.'

'I suppose he didn't happen to ask if you knew of a restaurant where he could take his fiancée for supper, did he?' asked Marriott. He knew it was a vain hope, but a question like that often provided an answer that would save the detectives time.

'No, he didn't,' said Miss Craig, frowning slightly at what she thought was an irrelevant query.

'Thank you for your assistance, Miss Kersh, and you too, Miss Craig,' said Hardcastle. 'You've both been most helpful. Sergeant Burgess here will now take written statements from you. If you have the time, that is. If not, you could perhaps come to the police station at a time that is more convenient to you both.'

'No, Inspector,' said Rebecca Kersh, 'we'll make the time now. This is obviously a very important matter.'

'All we have to do now is find the restaurant where this man took Miss Clarke,' said Hardcastle, as the trio of police officers left the shop. 'Where's the first restaurant on your list, Burgess?'

'It's very close to the pier, sir. I thought that as the young lady was probably killed there, the murderer might've taken her for a meal somewhere close by.'

'I don't know why he wasted money buying the girl a meal if he intended murdering her,' said Hardcastle.

'They may have squabbled over dinner, sir, and that led to his murdering her for some reason. Or perhaps he was waiting until there weren't too many people on the pier to witness the murder, sir,' suggested Burgess.

Hardcastle stopped and looked closely at the Worthing sergeant. 'Have you ever thought about transferring to the Metropolitan Police, Burgess? I think your talents are wasted down here.'

Marriott was astonished at the DDI's comment. It was, in a sense, a compliment the like of which he had never heard Hardcastle paying one of his own officers.

'Well, no, sir.' Burgess was just as surprised as Marriott. None of his own senior officers had ever complimented him on the way in which he carried out his duties. 'As a matter of fact, I'm getting married later this year, so things are a bit unsettled.'

'Who's the lucky lady, Ted?' asked Marriott.

'She's called Nancy Forster, Charlie. She's a nurse at Worthing Hospital and we've been walking out for a year now.'

'Well, congratulations and good luck to you,' said Marriott.

'Hail a cab next time you see one, Burgess,' said Hardcastle, cutting across the conversation about Burgess's forthcoming nuptials, 'and tell the driver which restaurant he's to take us to.'

It was midday and the restaurant was beginning to fill up. A fussy little man bustled towards the three policemen.

'A table for three, sir?'

'We're not here for lunch,' said Hardcastle.

'I'm afraid we don't serve coffee at this hour, sir. All our tables are required for luncheon guests between twelve and two.'

Marriott took a deep breath; this was just the sort of pettiness that was guaranteed to rile the DDI. And that could be counter-productive.

'We don't want coffee,' snapped Hardcastle. 'We're police officers enquiring into the murder that took place on Thursday evening.'

'Oh, I do beg your pardon, sir. A terrible thing, terrible.' The

flunkey immediately became nauseatingly subservient and half
bowed. 'I'm the manager, sir. How may I be of assistance to you?'

'What's your name?' asked Hardcastle.

'Morrison, sir. George Morrison.' The manager glanced at a
passing waiter. 'Luigi, take over for me.'

'Yes, Mr Morrison,' said Luigi.

Without waiting to be asked, Burgess produced the photograph
of the murder victim. 'Was this young woman in here on Thursday
evening last, Mr Morrison?'

'Yes, sir, most definitely. I remember her, such a beautiful young
lady. And the gentleman was very generous.'

'What did this man look like?' asked Hardcastle.

'Very smart. A dark suit, very well tailored.'

'But what did he look like, Mr Morrison?' asked Marriott. 'Apart
from what he was wearing.'

'Tall, sir. About your height I should think.'

'How old d'you think he was?'

'I couldn't really say, sir,' said Morrison. 'The lighting in here
is rather discreet at that time of the evening.'

'What time would that have been?' asked Hardcastle.

'One moment, please, sir.' Morrison crossed to the cash register and
thumbed through a bundle of bills. 'Table seven arrived at eight o'clock
on Thursday. They enjoyed a three-course dinner and a bottle of the
Nuits-Saint-Georges 1904; that's eighteen shillings a bottle. We still
have some left over from before the war,' he explained. 'And coffee
and cognac to follow.'

'And what time did they leave?' asked Marriott.

'I suppose at about half past nine or thereabouts.'

'Thank you, Mr Morrison,' said Hardcastle. 'Sergeant Burgess
here will take a statement from you setting out what you've just
told us.'

'We are very busy at the moment, sir.' Morrison glanced around
the restaurant. Most of the tables were now occupied.

'This is an extremely serious and important matter, Mr Morrison,'
said Hardcastle sternly. 'I'm sure that Luigi can take care of things
for twenty minutes or so.'

'Yes, I suppose so. Very well. Perhaps if we were to go into my
office, sir, that would be more convenient.'

* * *

The three police officers adjourned to a nearby pub and lunched on meat pies and several pints of bitter.

'Well, Burgess, you certainly selected the right places for our enquiries,' said Hardcastle.

'D'you think it'll be any help, sir?' asked Burgess, delighted that Hardcastle was pleased.

'The description of the man who was with Kitty Gordon, as she called herself down here, was too vague for us to do anything with,' said Hardcastle. 'But it's no more than I expected. Witnesses usually come up with different descriptions of what they think people look like. The only thing about the descriptions given us by Miss Kersh and Morrison at the restaurant is that they didn't differ. Even so, it's not much help. The man they described could've been any one of a hundred men. Have a look round this pub, Burgess. At least four of the men in here would fit that description.'

'What are you going to do next, then, sir?'

'Go back to London,' said Hardcastle.

'Does that mean you're finished down here, sir?' asked Burgess. He was enjoying the sort of freedom that his present assignment was affording him and had hoped that it would last longer.

'Not necessarily. We've enquiries to make at the Wandsworth address you found on the ration book and that may lead us back here again. However, I shall have a word with Superintendent Potts and remind him that you're assigned to this here murder enquiry until I tell him otherwise. There may be things for you to do, in which event Marriott here will get in touch with you with the details.'

'Is it any good circulating a description of the man seen with the victim, sir?'

Hardcastle scoffed. 'Not unless you want to be swamped with false sightings, Burgess. Personally, I think our murderer's long gone. He'll be back in the Smoke by now, if I'm any judge. I think a man wearing a Savile Row suit, if that's what he was wearing, is more likely to belong in London than down here.'

'What about Miss Gordon's property, sir?' asked Burgess.

'Ah yes, the property.' Hardcastle thought about for a moment. 'Have it removed to the property store at your police station, Burgess, and secured as evidence in a murder enquiry. And if anyone argues the toss, tell 'em to get in touch with me.'

*   *   *

Despite what he had told Sergeant Burgess, Hardcastle did not intend to return to Worthing unless it was absolutely essential.

Leaving Burgess outside the public house, Hardcastle hailed a cab and he and Marriott returned to the Sea View Hotel. There they settled their bill, collected their bags and told Mrs Croft that they may be returning at some time.

'What about Miss Gordon's luggage and clothing, Inspector?' asked Mrs Croft.

'All in hand, Mrs Croft,' said Hardcastle airily. 'I've instructed Sergeant Burgess to collect it.'

From the hotel the two detectives went straight to West Worthing railway station and caught the London train.

Charles Marriott had hoped that once back in London, Hardcastle would have decided that he had done enough for one day.

'We'll visit this Disraeli Road address in Wandsworth, Marriott. I'm sure we'll find some answers there.'

'When d'you propose to do that, sir?'

'Now of course, Marriott.' Hardcastle raised his eyebrows in surprise. 'But first we'll pay a call on Mr Fitnam.'

'Will he be there, sir?'

For a moment or two, Hardcastle studied his sergeant. 'Of course he'll be there, Marriott. He's a CID officer.'

Hardcastle's imminent departure was, however, interrupted by the arrival of Detective Sergeant Herbert Wood in the DDI's office.

'What is it, Wood?'

'A message from Sergeant Glover at the APM's office, sir. He said to tell you that contact has been made with Major Hardy of the Tank Corps. Major Hardy's maid was called Kitty Gordon, sir.' Wood expressed no surprise at receiving such a curious message, and knew better than to make comment on it.

'Thought as much, Wood,' said Hardcastle.

'Well, well, Ernie, and what brings you out to a working division?' Arthur Fitnam, the DDI of V Division, stepped across his office, shook hands with Hardcastle and nodded at Marriott.

'Working division be damned,' said Hardcastle. 'I've got three murders on my books, two of which were handed me by the Elephant. How many have you got?'

'It's obvious that Mr Wensley thinks you're a great detective, Ernie.' Fitnam laughed. 'You must be worn out. You'd better sit down, and you, Skipper,' he said to Marriott, 'and tell me how I can solve these jobs for you.'

'That's not all, Arthur. I've now got one down at Worthing, but there's a connection with a house on your toby.'

'Oh?' Fitnam took a sudden interest.

'Disraeli Road, Arthur. Marriott here'll give you the exact address.'

Fitnam took Marriott's pocket book. 'Don't mean anything to me, Ernie, but hold on a minute.' He crossed to his office door. 'Grimes,' he shouted.

'Yes, sir?' Detective Sergeant Daniel Grimes stepped into his DDI's office.

'Does this address mean anything to you, Grimes?' said Fitnam, handing Marriott's pocketbook to his sergeant.

Grimes cast an eye over the entry. 'No, sir, nothing.'

'Have a look on the voters' list and tell me who lives there.'

Grimes returned a few minutes later. 'There's no one registered for that address, sir. Probably means that only women live there, if anyone.'

'What are you going to do about it, Ernie?' asked Fitnam, once Grimes had departed.

'Go and knock on the door, I suppose, Arthur,' said Hardcastle. 'But tomorrow morning will do for that.'

FIFTEEN

I t was nine o'clock on Tuesday morning when Hardcastle and Marriott arrived at the Disraeli Road address in Putney. The house outside which their cab stopped was a three-storey terraced property, but the small front garden was overgrown with weeds and long grass, and the doorstep had not been whitened in a very long time.

'It looks a bit run down, Marriott,' said Hardcastle, stating the obvious. 'I don't reckon it's occupied. Either that or the occupants don't care what it looks like.'

It took the DDI a mere three strides to reach the front door, and he beat loudly on the tarnished lion's head knocker. But there was no reply, at least not from that house. However, the adjacent front door opened and a grey-haired woman in a pinafore apron emerged and stood on her step with arms akimbo.

'There ain't no one there, love,' said the woman. 'Ain't been for ages.'

'We're police officers, madam,' said Hardcastle, as he raised his hat.

'Ah!' exclaimed the woman, as though the arrival of the police came as no surprise.

'Who are you, madam?'

'Mrs Forbes. Bessie Forbes. And I'll tell you this much: their front garden's a bleedin' disgrace. The back one's the same an' all. Time something was done about it.'

'D'you know who lives here, Mrs Forbes?'

'Dunno, mister. There was some flighty bit of a girl what used to come and go, but it must've been at least a month since I saw her last. That don't mean she ain't been, o' course.'

'What did this girl look like, madam?' asked Marriott.

'Ah, now you're asking.' Mrs Forbes adopted a thoughtful expression. 'Tall slim girl she was, with long blonde hair,' she said eventually. 'Never spoke to no one. I passed the time of day with her once, but she ignored me. So I never bothered after that. Proper stuck-up madam she was,' she added as a final condemnation.

'Did you ever see a man calling here, Mrs Forbes?' asked Hardcastle.

'I did see a man once or twice, love.'

'What did he look like?'

'He was tall an' all. 'Bout the same as my late husband Bert an' he was close on six foot. Got hisself drowned off of Jutland two year back.'

'What age was this man you saw?'

'Ah, now you're asking.' Mrs Forbes sneezed, withdrew a colourful handkerchief from her apron pocket and blew her nose noisily. 'It's the weather,' she explained. 'It always makes me nose run like a bleedin' Derby winner.'

'The man's age?' persisted Hardcastle.

'Can't say really. He could've been anything.'

'Did the man and the woman arrive here together?' asked Marriott.

'Sometimes, but sometimes they come separate. The man usually come at night, though. On his tod an' all.'

'Thank you for your help, Mrs Forbes. If either the man or the woman should return, I'd be obliged if you didn't mention that I've been looking for them.'

'Aha! Been up to no good, I'll be bound. Well, I can't say as how I'm surprised. I always thought there was something a bit dodgy about the pair of 'em.'

Leaving Mrs Forbes impatient to disseminate this latest piece of neighbourhood gossip, Hardcastle and Marriott stopped at the gate of the house.

'Now here's someone who might be of assistance, Marriott,' suggested Hardcastle, as he sighted a postwoman. 'Excuse me, miss. We're police officers,' he said, raising his hat. He produced his warrant card, knowing that an officer of the Royal Mail would be unlikely to impart information unless she was sure of his identity. 'Divisional Detective Inspector Hardcastle of Scotland Yard.'

'How can I help you, sir?'

'This house here,' continued Hardcastle, pointing. 'Have you ever delivered letters there?'

'Quite a few times. But the last occasion must've been a week back, I suppose. I can't recall making another delivery since then. I s'pose they must've moved.'

'D'you happen to remember the name on the letters, miss?' asked Marriott.

'Half a mo'. The postwoman took out a notebook and flicked through its pages. 'I keep a list, you see,' she explained. 'I do it in case there's ever an air raid and people are killed or injured. You'd be surprised how useful that can be if the police are trying to find out who lived where. Now then, ah, here we are. A Miss Queenie Rogers is the only person I've got down, and that was the name on the letter I delivered.'

'Thank you, miss,' said Hardcastle. 'You've been very helpful.' That information came as no surprise; it was, after all, the name that was on the ration book found in Kitty Gordon's possessions.

'There was a letter for a man a few weeks ago,' said the postwoman, 'but I can't remember the name. I certainly don't have a man listed in my book.'

'Right,' said Hardcastle, as he and Marriott turned towards Putney High Street. 'I think we'll get a warrant and see what's inside that there drum.'

Once Hardcastle had attested to his reasons for requiring a search warrant, the stipendiary magistrate at South-Western police court did not quibble.

An hour later, Hardcastle and Marriott were back at the Disraeli Road address, together with two constables from Wandsworth police station.

'Right, lad, get that door open,' said Hardcastle.

Using his truncheon to good effect, one of the constables broke the glass panel in the front door. Putting his hand through the hole he had made, he released the latch and stood back.

'There you are, sir.'

Hardcastle entered the hall and turned right into the parlour. For a moment or two he surveyed the room. It was sparsely furnished and tidy, but appeared not to have been cleaned for some time. Followed by Marriott, he went from room to room, floor by floor.

On the first floor, the main bedroom contained only a bed, but it had been stripped down to the mattress. The other rooms on that floor, and all the rooms on the top floor, were empty.

'There's nothing here, Marriott,' said Hardcastle, with mounting frustration. 'It looks as though we've wasted our bloody time. We'll get back to the office.' And he led the way back downstairs to the hall.

'There's something we missed, sir,' said Marriott, pointing. Secured to the back of the front door and covering the letter box was a wire cage. Inside was a single letter. 'It's padlocked, sir.'

'It won't be for long.' Hardcastle opened the front door. 'Come in here, lad,' he said, addressing one of the two constables. 'See if you can get into that cage and get that letter out for me.'

'Yes, sir.' The PC launched a kick at the wire cage with such force that it broke away from the door and fell to the floor. 'There we are, sir,' he said, with a grin.

'Good shot, lad,' said Hardcastle, stooping to retrieve the letter. 'You ought to play football for your division.'

'I do, sir,' said the PC.

'This can't be the letter that that postwoman was talking about,

Marriott; it's got no stamp on it and it's just addressed to someone called Chester.' Hardcastle opened the letter. 'There's no sender's address on here and all it says is "It all worked out all right. The police don't suspect me. I'll meet you at Worthing as arranged."' He handed the letter to Marriott. 'And it's signed Queenie. She must've delivered it by hand, but Chester never picked it up. What d'you make of it?'

'If the postwoman delivered a letter to Queenie Rogers a week ago, sir,' said Marriott, 'it means that she must've returned here sometime in the last week to pick it up and to leave the one we just found. And that was probably the letter that told Queenie to go to Worthing.'

'I think they're using this address just to exchange information, Marriott. It's looks as though our Hannah Clarke, alias Queenie Rogers, and this Chester, whoever he is, are in some sort of fiddle together. But just what they're up to remains to be seen. What's more, if Queenie had arranged to meet this here Chester at Worthing, he's likely our murderer. We've collected two address books so far. One at Whilber Street and the other one with Hannah's possessions in Worthing.'

'When we get back to the nick, sir, I'll speak to Bert Wood. I gave him the two address books to check. Maybe he found a Chester in one of them.'

'I doubt if we'll have that much luck, Marriott,' said Hardcastle gloomily. Turning to the footballing PC, he said, 'One of you is to stand watch on this house while the other one goes back to the nick to arrange for the property to be made secure again.'

'Very good, sir.' Not wishing to spend a few hours standing outside an empty house, the PC made a decision. Going outside, he said to his colleague, 'That DDI says you're to hang on here, Alf, while I make arrangements to get that door mended.'

'Just my bloody luck,' said Alf.

'Fetch Wood in here, Marriott,' said Hardcastle when he and Marriott arrived back at Cannon Row police station.

'You wanted me, sir?'

'Sergeant Marriott tells me you've been checking those two address books we found, Wood.'

'Yes, sir. Not too much success, I'm afraid. The one found at Whilber Street had the pages A to C torn out and—'

'I know that, Wood, but I'm more interested in the one we found at Worthing, the one that was in Hannah Clarke's luggage. Was there a Chester someone in it?'

'I believe there was, sir. I'll fetch the book.' Wood returned a few moments later. 'There's a telephone number listed against the name Chester, sir, but I don't know whether that's a surname or a Christian name.'

'I think you can take it that it's a Christian name, Wood. What was the address?'

'There wasn't an address, sir. Just a telephone number.'

'Well, don't keep me in suspense, Wood, spit it out.'

'It was a Chiswick number, sir. I checked with the GPO and they said that the subscriber lived at an address in Rosemont Road, Acton.'

'All right, Wood. That'll do for the time being, but don't go anywhere. I might need you later.'

'Search warrant, sir?' queried Marriott.

'I don't think so,' said Hardcastle. 'What was it that General Baden-Powell said? Softly, softly, catchee monkey, wasn't it?'

'I believe so, sir,' said Marriott, having difficulty in making a connection between their murder enquiries and the World Chief Scout.

'Exactly,' said Hardcastle. 'If we go blundering into that address and Chester ain't there, someone is bound to hear about it and warn him. And if that happens he won't return. No, Marriott, we'll mount an observation.'

'D'you have anyone in mind, sir?'

Once again Hardcastle surprised his sergeant. 'Catto and Carter, Marriott. Fetch 'em in.' Lighting his pipe, he sat back and waited for the two DCs to appear.

'You wanted to see us, sir?' Gordon Carter, the senior of the two, assumed the role of spokesman.

'I've got an observation job for you two at Acton. In Rosemont Road.' Hardcastle explained exactly what the two detectives were to do. 'But before you go, I'll speak to Mr Buxton, the DDI on T Division. He might know of a suitable house opposite the one I'm interested in. Then you can hole up there and keep watch. So, wait until I send for you.'

'Yes, sir.' Carter was not happy about what could turn out to be a lengthy observation, and neither was Catto.

'What d'you want us to do if we spot this Chester man, sir?' Catto asked.

'You get a message to me as fast as you can and sit tight, Catto. I'll be down there straight away.'

'See if you can get Mr Buxton on that telephone thing, Marriott,' said Hardcastle, once the two detectives had returned to their office.

With an inaudible sigh, Marriott took hold of Hardcastle's telephone and asked to be connected to the DDI on T Division.

'Mr Buxton, sir.' Marriott handed the earpiece to Hardcastle and moved the 'candlestick' apparatus nearer to the DDI.

'Bert? It's Ernie Hardcastle on A.' Having explained to DDI Buxton what he wanted and why he wanted it, Hardcastle replaced the earpiece on its rest. 'He said he'll ring us back, Marriott, whatever that means.'

'D'you want me to stay until he does, sir?' asked Marriott, aware that if anything was to put Hardcastle in a bad mood it was having to contend with a telephone.

'Certainly not, Marriott. I know how to deal with that thing.' Hardcastle pointed at the offending instrument before leaning back and lighting his pipe. It was half an hour before he shouted for his sergeant.

'Sir?'

Hardcastle handed Marriott a slip of paper. 'Mr Buxton's given me this address. The man who lives there is a Conservative town councillor called Victor Newton, and he's a member of Mr Buxton's lodge. Apparently that makes him trustworthy.' He stared briefly at Marriott, a cynical expression on his face. 'Tell Carter and Catto that he's willing to accommodate them so they can keep watch from his front bedroom window.'

'They're on their way, sir,' said Marriott, when he returned from giving Carter and Catto their instructions.

Hardcastle took out his hunter, glanced at it and briefly rewound it. 'Just time to have a word with the manager of Williams Deacon's Bank about that there cheque book we found among Hannah Clarke's possessions in Worthing, Marriott.'

'I'd like to speak to the manager,' said Hardcastle, addressing the young cashier in the Victoria Street branch of Williams Deacon's Bank.

'I'm afraid he's a bit tied up at the moment, sir.'

'Oh? Victim of a robbery, was he?' asked Hardcastle jocularly.

'I'm sorry, sir, I don't quite understand.'

'I'm a police officer and I wish to see him on urgent business, young man. Perhaps you can tell him that Divisional Detective Inspector Hardcastle is here.'

'One moment, sir.' The cashier slammed the cash drawer beneath the counter, took out the keys and disappeared through a door at the rear.

'I wonder why he ain't in the army, Marriott,' said Hardcastle, while they awaited the cashier's return.

'This way, gentlemen.' The cashier opened a door at the end of the long mahogany counter and ushered the two detectives into the manager's office.

'Roland Peachey, gentlemen.' The bank manager crossed the room and shook hands with each of the detectives.

'Divisional Detective Inspector Hardcastle of New Scotland Yard, Mr Peachey, and this is Detective Sergeant Marriott.'

'Take a seat, Inspector, and tell me how I may be of service. You wish to open an account, perhaps?'

'I already have an account, Mr Peachey,' said Hardcastle. 'With Barclays.'

'Oh!' said Peachey, a slight frown settling on his forehead. 'How can I be of assistance, then?'

Marriott produced the cheque book that had been found among Hannah Clarke's possessions in Worthing, and handed it to the manager.

'I wondered if you could tell me anything about this cheque book, Mr Peachey,' said Hardcastle.

Peachey put on his spectacles, sucked through his teeth and closely examined the cheque book.

'It's certainly one of ours, Inspector, but I'm sure you're aware that I can't divulge any information about this account without a warrant issued under the Bankers' Book Evidence Act of 1879.'

'Yes, I did know that,' said Hardcastle somewhat tersely. He did not much care for being lectured about the criminal law. 'However, I'm dealing with the murder of a young woman in Worthing last Thursday, and I have reason to believe that she was the holder of the account to which this cheque book applies.'

'Oh, that puts a rather different complexion on it,' said Peachey. 'What was the young woman's name?'

'Hannah Clarke, Kitty Gordon or Queenie Rogers, Mr Peachey,' said Hardcastle, rather smugly. 'She's been known to use all three names. And maybe more.'

'Good gracious!' exclaimed Peachey, suddenly very concerned. 'I hope this doesn't mean that some fraud has been perpetrated on the bank,' he said, and pressed a bell push on his desk.

'It's a possibility, I suppose,' said Hardcastle, with a measure of satisfaction.

A slightly built woman entered the office. Her hair was dressed into a severe bun and she wore gold-rimmed spectacles with circular lenses.

'Yes, sir?'

'Be so good as to find out to which of our clients this cheque book was issued, Miss Carmichael.'

It took only five minutes before Miss Carmichael returned and handed the manager a slip of paper.

'All I can tell you, Inspector, is that this cheque book was *not* issued in any one of the three names you gave me.'

'Can you tell me who the account holder is, then, Mr Peachey?'

'Not without the warrant I mentioned earlier, Inspector.' Peachey placed the slip of paper in the centre of his blotter. 'Excuse me one moment,' he said, and walked from the room.

Hardcastle leaned over the desk and read the name. 'Well, I'll be buggered!' he exclaimed.

'If there's nothing else I can help you with, Inspector,' said Peachey, returning to his office, 'I am rather busy. Unless you have something to tell me.'

'Not at present, Mr Peachey, thank you. I'll let you know of anything I discover that concerns your bank. And I'd be obliged if you didn't mention my interest to the account holder. Whoever that is.'

'Of course not,' murmured Peachey, and shook hands with the two policemen once again. 'If you should wish to transfer your account here, I'm more than willing to accommodate you. Or you, Sergeant Marriott,' he added.

'Sergeants don't need bank accounts,' said Hardcastle. 'They don't get paid enough.'

SIXTEEN

The house occupied by Councillor Victor Newton was immediately opposite the one in which Hardcastle had taken an interest.

The middle-aged man who answered the door in response to Gordon Carter's knock was of medium height and somewhat rotund in build. He held a bundle of papers in one hand, had a pencil tucked under the arm of his spectacles and gazed quizzically at the two men on his doorstep.

'Mr Newton?'

'Councillor Newton actually,' murmured the man. 'You must be the police officers that Bert Buxton mentioned when he telephoned me.'

'Yes, sir. I'm Detective Constable Carter and this is Detective Constable Catto.'

As Newton shook hands with Carter and Catto, he tucked the third finger of his right hand into the palm. Carter recognized the sign, but was not of the craft, as Freemasons are wont to call their fraternity.

'Come in, gentlemen. I understand that you have an interest in the house opposite.'

'That's correct, sir,' said Carter. 'If it's not an inconvenience, we'd like to keep observation on it.'

'Yes, Bert mentioned that,' said Newton. 'I've arranged a couple of chairs close to the window in the front bedroom. I think that would be a suitable place for you to keep watch.'

'That's very helpful, sir,' said Catto. 'As a matter of interest do you know anything about the people who live in that house?'

'I've only ever seen a man going in and out of there, perhaps three times in all,' said Newton, as he ushered the two detectives into his sitting room. 'But I rather got the impression that no one lives there. Not all the time.'

'Can you describe this man you saw, Councillor?' asked Carter.

'Difficult to say, really.' Newton gave Carter's question some thought. 'I'd say he was a professional man by the way he was dressed, or perhaps a service officer in plain clothes.'

'What age d'you think he was, sir?' asked Catto.

'I couldn't really say, Constable. I only noticed him a couple of times, and then I only got a view of his back. At a guess anything between twenty and forty, I suppose. Not that that's much help to you.'

'It's something for us to build on, sir,' said Catto, not wishing to offend the councillor by saying that it was of no use whatsoever.

'I'll show you to the upstairs room, then,' said Newton, 'and I'll get the maid to bring you chaps a cup of tea.'

Carter and Catto settled themselves on the chairs in the window, satisfied that they had a good view of the house opposite. The maid, an attractive young girl, brought cups of tea and slices of cake. She seemed particularly taken with Catto.

'What's your name?' asked Catto, smiling at the girl.

'It's Abigail, sir.' The maid blushed.

'You don't have to call me "sir",' said Catto. 'My name's Henry and this is Gordon.'

Abigail giggled and almost ran from the room.

At lunchtime, she reappeared with a pile of sandwiches and two bottles of beer.

'The master thought you might be hungry . . . Henry.' Abigail added Catto's Christian name diffidently and blushed again.

'This could turn out to be quite an enjoyable stint, Gordon,' said Catto, when Abigail had departed.

'Depends on how long we're likely to be stuck here,' said Carter, no great lover of prolonged observation duty. 'And what are we supposed to do if this bloke turns up?'

'The guv'nor said we weren't to do anything, but to let him know,' said Catto. 'But I shouldn't worry too much, Gordon. Beer and sandwiches on tap, and a pretty housemaid at our beck and call. I'm happy to stick it out for a few days.'

But their period of duty was destined to come to an abrupt end. At four o'clock, Carter spotted a policeman approaching the door of the house from which they were watching.

'I wonder what the hell he wants,' said Carter.

Moments later, the PC entered the room. 'Are you two Carter and Catto from Cannon Row?' he asked.

'That's us. What's up?'

'I've got a message from your DDI. He says as how you're to break off the observation and return to the nick.'

'Did he say why?' asked Carter.

'No, mate. I'm only a humble PC. DDIs don't tell me what's going on.'

Carter thanked Councillor Newton for his assistance and hospitality, and explained that there had been a change of plan.

It was close to five o'clock by the time Carter and Catto got back to Cannon Row.

'What's happening, Sergeant?' Carter asked when the two of them entered the detectives' office.

'There's been a change of plan, Carter,' said Marriott, 'and a development that means there's no need to keep watch on the Rosemont Road house.'

'That's a pity,' said Catto.

'A pity?' queried Marriott. 'Don't tell me you've suddenly taken a liking to observation jobs, Catto.'

'No, Sergeant,' said Carter, 'he's suddenly taken a liking to Councillor Newton's comely young housemaid.'

Marriott laughed. 'Well, you can forget all about her, Catto. The guv'nor wants to see both of you. Now.'

'Learn anything?' barked Hardcastle, when the two DCs presented themselves.

'Councillor Newton wasn't a great help, sir,' said Carter, and related the sparse description of the male caller that Newton had given them.

'Well, it don't matter because I think I know who he is. Right, carry on, and ask Sergeant Marriott to come in.'

'Bert Wood's checked the voters' register for the Rosemont Road address, sir,' said Marriott.

'Nothing,' said Hardcastle.

'Exactly, sir. There's no one registered at that address as a voter. Wood also checked with the rates department at Acton town hall.'

'And the ratepayer was our Martins Deacon's bank account holder.'

'Yes, sir. And Wandsworth town hall confirmed that the same person's the ratepayer at the Disraeli Road address.'

'Got him,' exclaimed Hardcastle, with a measure of satisfaction.

'Arrest him, sir?' asked Marriott.

'Not until we've got enough evidence to make sure we can hang him with it, Marriott,' said Hardcastle.

'Where d'you propose to start, sir?'

'With the three widowers of our murder victims.'

'But they're all serving abroad, sir, apart from Commander Cheney and he's at sea.'

'Ways and means, Marriott,' said Hardcastle mysteriously. 'Ways and means.'

'I didn't expect to see you again, Inspector,' said Lieutenant Commander Hugo de Courcy, as he limped across his office and shook hands. 'What can I do for you?' He waved a hand towards a couple of chairs.

'I realize that this might be difficult, Commander de Courcy,' said Hardcastle, 'but I need to get in touch with Commander Cheney again.'

'It so happens you're in luck there, Inspector. Bob Cheney has been posted to the Royal Naval College at Greenwich as an instructor. By the time he got back to Scapa Flow he found that his ship had sailed earlier than scheduled. In the circumstances, given that he'd lost his wife and had two young sons, it was decided that a shore-based appointment would be a compassionate sort of posting for him. It so happened that there was a vacancy for a commander at Greenwich.'

'Excellent,' said Hardcastle.

'Is there likely to be a problem in us seeing him, Commander?' asked Marriott.

'None at all, Sergeant. I'll send him a signal warning him that you're coming.' De Courcy paused. 'Unless you want to surprise him,' he added with a chuckle. 'When would you propose going to Greenwich?'

Hardcastle took out his hunter and glanced at it. 'This afternoon, Commander.'

'Very well.' De Courcy scribbled a short message on a pad, and sent for his clerk. 'Send this signal to Greenwich immediately, Rawlings,' he said, when the clerk appeared,

'Aye, aye, sir,' said Rawlings, and hurried to the wireless room.

*　　*　　*

The vast complex of the Royal Naval College dominated the south side of the Thames at Greenwich. Hardcastle eventually found an ageing naval pensioner now acting as a custodian.

'I've got an appointment with Commander Cheney,' said Hardcastle, having first identified himself.

'The trouble, sir,' said the custodian, having searched a directory in vain, 'is that they don't always keep these 'ere books up to date.' He shouted across the hall to another attendant. 'Any idea where Commander Cheney's cabin is, cully?'

'Yes, I do.' The attendant joined the little group. 'Follow me, gents, and I'll show you up.'

Commander Robert Cheney looked considerably smarter than the last time Hardcastle and Marriott had spoken to him. His uniform was clearly new; the gold lace rings of rank sparkling and fresh medal ribbons adorned his jacket.

'Inspector, good to see you again. Do take a seat and tell me how I can help you.'

'This seems to be a splendid place to work, Commander,' commented Hardcastle, gazing around Cheney's opulent office.

'Given that the war's nearly over my job here is pretty much a waste of time, Inspector. Half this lot will be on the beach by this time next year, I shouldn't wonder. Me included, very likely. However, I'm sure you haven't come here to discuss my career prospects.'

'No, Commander, it's about your housekeeper.'

Cheney raised his eyes in surprise. 'My housekeeper? But I don't have a housekeeper.'

'Hannah Clarke, sir,' said Marriott.

'She was my late wife's maid, Sergeant,' said Cheney. 'And I gave her notice immediately. There was no point in keeping her on when there was no one in the house.'

'Hannah Clarke told us that you'd appointed her housekeeper and increased her pay by twenty pounds a year.'

'Absolute rubbish,' exclaimed Cheney. 'I told her to pack her bags and go that same day. I also told her to leave the keys with Cutty Curtis. He lives opposite our house in Whilber Street.'

'She certainly left, Commander,' said Marriott, 'but not until nine days after your wife had been murdered.'

'I don't understand,' said Cheney. 'Why would she stay there that long?'

'But then she herself was murdered that same evening, Thursday the twentieth of this month, in Worthing,' said Hardcastle.

'There was nothing about that in the newspapers, Inspector. And murders always make the front page.'

'As a matter of fact there was, Commander, but the reports stated that her name was Kitty Gordon.'

'Oh, I did read about that, but I didn't make a connection. Well, I wouldn't, would I? The name Kitty Gordon didn't mean anything to me.'

'I have reason to believe that Hannah Clarke, whose real name was Queenie Rogers, was also implicated in two other murders I'm investigating, Commander,' continued Hardcastle.

'Are you suggesting that Hannah murdered my wife?' Cheney was clearly having difficulty in grasping the DDI's revelations.

'I don't think so, but I do believe that she had an accomplice, and it was that accomplice who did commit the murders.' Hardcastle removed a slip of paper from his waistcoat pocket. 'Does that name mean anything to you, Commander?'

Cheney glanced at the piece of paper and returned it. 'Not a thing, Inspector,' he said.

'Show Commander Cheney the letter received by Harrods, Marriott.' Hardcastle waited until Cheney had scanned the missive. 'The funeral director at Harrods assured one of my officers that they received this letter from you, Commander.'

'But that's not my writing and most certainly is not my signature. Are you telling me that this damned woman countermanded my orders, Inspector? I hope to god that Georgina wasn't buried in a pauper's grave.'

'No, she wasn't,' said Marriott. 'We were at the funeral and your late wife was properly interred at Brompton Cemetery.'

'Well, at least the bitch got that right,' said Cheney.

'What about this half-finished letter, Commander?' asked Hardcastle, signalling to Marriott to produce the threatening letter found in the escritoire at Whilber Street. 'Is that your late wife's handwriting?'

Cheney afforded the letter but a brief glance. 'Certainly not. I've no idea who wrote that. It's a threat. Georgina would never have written anything like that, apart from which the grammar is appalling. D'you know who did write it?'

'I suspect it was your late housemaid, Commander,' said Hardcastle. 'There is one other thing. I ask this because there are similarities between all three murders. Did your wife have money of her own?'

'Yes, she did. Her father was a diplomat, but he was a wealthy man in his own right. When he died he left Georgina a considerable sum.'

'Is her estate still intact, Commander?' asked Marriott.

'Oh my God!' exclaimed Cheney. 'It was about seven hundred or so pounds less than I thought it should be. I left the matter with my solicitor to see if he could discover where it had gone.'

'I think I know,' said Hardcastle. 'I'll keep you informed of anything I learn.'

'What made you ask that question about Mrs Cheney's money, sir?' asked Marriott, when he and Hardcastle were on their way back to Westminster.

'Beatrice Groves, who was in Mrs Blanche Hardy's employ, told us that Mrs Hardy was quite well off. She told Mrs Groves that her father had owned a factory in Middlesbrough, and had left her a tidy sum when he died. That's why I want to get in touch with Major Hardy. He might know if any of his wife's money has gone astray, so to speak.'

'And I suppose you'll want to ask Colonel Lacey the same question, sir.'

'You got a better idea, then, Marriott?' Hardcastle leaned forward and tapped the end of his umbrella on the screen separating him from the cab driver. 'Take me to Horse Guards Arch instead, cabbie.'

'Ah, I'm glad you called in, Inspector,' said Lieutenant Colonel Ralph Frobisher. 'Sergeant Glover's received a reply from Major Hardy about his housemaid.'

'Yes, he telephoned me with the answer, thank you, Colonel,' said Marriott.

'But now I've another favour to ask, Colonel,' said Hardcastle. 'It concerns Major Hardy of the Tank Corps and Lieutenant Colonel Gerard Lacey of The Buffs.' He explained about the money missing from Georgina Cheney's estate and went on to air his suspicions that a similar shortfall might be apparent in the estates of Blanche

Hardy and Hazel Lacey. 'Is it possible for the two officers to be
asked if they know anything of this?'

Frobisher pursed his lips, leaned back in his chair and steepled
his fingers. 'I think it would be better if a military police officer
were to interview them rather than sending a signal to BEF HQ,
Inspector. In that way, our officer can elicit the necessary details.'
He moved forward and placed his arms on his desk. 'Despite what
you may think, Mr Hardcastle, our chaps are quite good at inter-
viewing people.'

'I'm sure they are.' Hardcastle's reply was diplomatic, and
disguised what he really thought.

'All I have to do now is find out where these officers are serving,
and that could be a problem.' Frobisher scribbled a few lines on a
pad. 'There are over twenty-five battalions of the Tank Corps and
at least ten of The Buffs. It may take some time, Inspector.'

'I wonder how long it will take, sir,' said Marriott, as he and his
sergeant left the APM's office at Horse Guards.

'It might not matter, Marriott,' said Hardcastle, 'because I'm
going to prepare an information so's we can get a warrant to have
a look at the bank account that is connected to the cheque book
that was found among Hannah Clarke's belongings at Worthing.
And another to search the house where he lives.'

'But we don't know where he lives, sir.'

'We will do by the time we've copped a gander at his bank account.'

At nine-thirty promptly the following morning, Hardcastle and
Marriott were at Bow Street police court.

'I need to see the beak in his chambers before he sits in open
court, Sergeant,' said Hardcastle to the warrant officer.

'Very good, sir,' said the warrant officer. 'The chief's sitting in
Court One this morning. If you'll come this way I'll show you to
his chambers.'

'Good morning, Your Worship,' said Hardcastle, as he and
Marriott entered the chambers of the Chief Metropolitan Magistrate.
'I have an information and I respectfully ask for a warrant to inspect
the bank account named in that information.'

'Don't get too many of these,' murmured the magistrate, as he
donned his spectacles and perused Hardcastle's information closely.
'What exactly is your interest, Inspector?'

'I am investigating four murders, Your Worship. As a result of my enquiries so far, I think that this bank account will provide evidence to support my belief that the holder is responsible for those murders.'

'Very well.' The magistrate took out his fountain pen and scribbled his signature at the bottom of the warrant.

Armed with the document, Hardcastle hailed a cab in Bow Street and instructed the driver to take him and Marriott to Williams Deacon's Bank in Victoria.

SEVENTEEN

I t was just after ten-thirty when Hardcastle and Marriott arrived at the bank in Victoria Street.

'I somehow thought that you'd return with one of these, Inspector,' said Roland Peachey, when Hardcastle handed him the warrant. He donned his spectacles and examined the document closely. 'That all seems to be in order.'

'It would be, Mr Peachey,' said Hardcastle sharply. 'It was issued by the Chief Magistrate.'

'Quite so. As a matter of fact, I've already had the necessary documents put to one side.' Peachey pressed a bell push on his desk. 'Be so good as to bring in those documents I set aside for Inspector Hardcastle, Miss Carmichael,' he said when his secretary appeared.

Miss Carmichael returned with a docket and a small pile of paper, and placed them on the table at one end of the office. Casting a disdainful glance at the two detectives who were about to violate the privacy of a client's account, she left the office and closed the door.

'Well, those are the documents you wanted, Inspector,' said Peachey, waving a hand at the table. 'I'll remain here so that if there's anything you wish to have explained I'll be happy to do so.'

But Hardcastle did not need any assistance; he knew what he was looking for. He put on his spectacles and began to go through the paperwork.

'It's all here, Marriott, and it fits. On Monday the fourteenth of

January, he paid in two thousand pounds; four-fifty on Tuesday the second of April; and seven hundred and fifty pounds on Thursday the twelfth of June.'

'Each of those deposits was made within days of the murders of Blanche Hardy, Hazel Lacey and Georgina Cheney, sir,' said Marriott.

'And that's exactly what I expected to find, Marriott. But there's more. The day following each of those deposits, he issued cheques for five hundred pounds, a hundred and fifty pounds and two hundred and fifty pounds respectively.' Hardcastle looked up and rubbed his hands together. 'All payable to Queenie Rogers. I do believe we've got 'im, Marriott,' he said triumphantly.

Roland Peachey had been seated behind his desk, a slightly bemused expression on his face, while this exchange had been going on. 'Is there something in what you've found that's detrimental to the bank, Inspector?' he asked apprehensively.

'Not unless counting a murderer among your customers is considered detrimental to its reputation, Mr Peachey.'

'Where to now, sir?' asked Marriott.

'Take a note of that address, Marriott, and we'll go and arrest the bugger.'

'But he's unlikely to be there at this hour of the day, sir.'

'I know that, Marriott. We'll leave it until later.' Hardcastle turned to the bank manager. 'Thank you for your assistance, Mr Peachey. But before we go, I must ask you to keep these documents in a safe place. I've no doubt that counsel for the Crown will call you to give evidence and he'll most likely require you to produce them.'

Outside the bank, Hardcastle hailed a cab, and he and Marriott returned to Cannon Row police station. Once there, he summoned Detective Sergeant Wood.

'I've got a following job for you, Wood, and you're to take a couple of DCs with you. And I don't want any foul-ups with this.'

'Right, sir,' said Wood. 'I'll take Carter and Keeler.'

'Good choice.' Hardcastle scribbled a few details on a slip of paper. 'That's most likely where he is now,' he said, indicating an address, 'and the other one is where he'll finish up. When he's there telephone me from the local nick. And you're to keep a discreet observation until Sergeant Marriott and I arrive. Once you see my cab pulling up, you're to join us. Got that?'

'Yes, sir,' said Wood.

It was not until six o'clock that evening that Hardcastle received a call from Wood telephoning from Brockley police station to say that their suspect had arrived.

'Come, Marriott,' said Hardcastle, seizing his hat and umbrella.

Once in Parliament Street, the DDI hailed a cab. 'Manwood Road, Brockley, driver. D'you know where that is?'

'Of course I do, guv'nor.' The driver gave the impression of being mildly offended that he might not know his job. 'Don't live far from there meself.'

'This is it,' said Hardcastle, as the cab drew to a standstill outside an immaculate double-fronted house in Manwood Road, Brockley, in south-east London. It was two storeys high, and the railings and gate had been freshly painted in green.

When Hardcastle and Marriott alighted from the cab, DS Wood and DCs Carter and Keeler appeared as if from nowhere.

'He's there, sir,' said Wood.

'I should hope so,' said Hardcastle. 'Tell that cab to wait and you're to join me when I send for you.'

A housemaid answered the door and gazed quizzically at the two men on the step.

'We're police officers, miss. Is your master at home?'

'I'll enquire, sir,' said the maid, bobbing briefly.

'Don't bother, lass. I'll enquire myself,' said Hardcastle, and he and Marriott brushed past the maid and entered the drawing room.

'Inspector Hardcastle. What on earth are you doing here?'

'Rollo Henson, I am arresting you on a charge of murdering Georgina Cheney on or about the eleventh of June 1918. Anything you say will be put in evidence.'

'The hell you are, Detective.' The woman who rose from an armchair was about thirty years of age and spoke with a strong American accent. To Hardcastle's surprise, the bottom of her red silk day dress was at least fourteen inches from the ground, revealing a trimly turned ankle and glacé kid shoes. But the greatest surprise of all was that her hair was cut quite short and coiffed into what Hardcastle's eldest daughter would have told him was a 'bob'.

'Are you Mrs Henson?'

'Yes, I'm Lydia Henson. What's this about my husband murdering someone? It's preposterous.'

'I'm Divisional Detective Inspector Hardcastle of Scotland Yard, madam, and this is Detective Sergeant Marriott. I can assure you that I have adequate evidence to support the charge.'

'You know I'm a barrister, Inspector,' said Henson, 'and I seem to recall telling you that on the night of that terrible incident I was at a bar mess dinner.'

'So you said.' Hardcastle smiled. 'But I've no doubt that will be disproved when I question the other lawyers who were there.' He turned to Marriott. 'Get the others in.'

Marriott returned to the front door and ordered Wood, Carter and Keeler to join him and the DDI.

'Who are these people?' demanded Mrs Henson, when the three officers entered the drawing room.

'They're police officers, madam,' said Hardcastle, 'and they are about to search these premises.'

'Do you have a warrant, Inspector?' enquired Henson mildly.

'As a lawyer, Henson, you'll know perfectly well that I don't require one,' said Hardcastle. 'I am empowered by common law to search the premises of someone I've just arrested.'

'This is outrageous,' protested Lydia Henson. 'My husband is a distinguished barrister. How can you possibly imagine that he's committed a murder?'

Ignoring Lydia Henson's outburst, Hardcastle turned to Wood. 'Take Carter and Keeler with you, Wood, and search this house thoroughly. I want you to seize all the papers you can find, especially anything relating to a bank account.'

'Yes, sir,' said Wood. 'Right, Carter, you start on the top floor. Keeler, come with me.'

'Are you just going to stand there, Rollo, and let these people violate my house?' Lydia Henson's accent became even stronger.

'Just sit down and keep quiet, Lydia,' said Henson irritably. 'This whole ridiculous business will be sorted out very soon.' He glanced at Hardcastle. 'You should know that I shall lodge a strong complaint with the Commissioner of Police about your high-handed and completely unwarranted behaviour, Inspector.'

'That is your right, Henson,' said Hardcastle mildly.

Henson and his wife resumed their seats, but did not invite either of the CID officers to sit down. For the next thirty minutes, the little group maintained an uncomfortable silence.

'We've finished, sir,' said Wood, returning to the drawing room. 'We've seized a quantity of bank papers and other correspondence. Carter has taken possession of them.'

'All right, Wood, escort Mr Henson here out to the cab.'

Henson smiled at his wife. 'I'll see you later this evening, honey.' But that was to prove an overconfident promise.

Leaving Wood and his colleagues to make their own way, Hardcastle and Marriott accompanied Henson in the cab on the way back to Cannon Row police station. Henson remained silent during the journey, only too well aware that anything he said would be recorded by Hardcastle.

It was not until he was in the charge room that Henson spoke. 'If you're going to question me, Inspector, I demand to have a solicitor or some other independent person present during the interview.'

'I have nothing to ask you, Henson, or should I call you Chester?' said Hardcastle mildly, a comment that appeared to disconcert Henson. 'Unless you wish to make a confession.'

But Henson remained silent.

'Put the charge, Sergeant,' said Hardcastle, addressing the station officer.

'Rollo Henson, you are charged with the wilful murder of Georgina Cheney on or about the eleventh of June 1918 against the peace. You are not obliged to say anything in answer to the charge, but anything you do say will be taken down in writing and may be given in evidence.'

Henson said nothing, and having been deprived of his personal possessions, his braces and bootlaces, was placed in a cell.

'And now, Marriott,' said Hardcastle, once he and Marriott were back in the DDI's office, 'I want you to go through all the papers that Wood seized from Henson's house and see if we've got anything useful.'

Despite the protests of the prostitutes who thought they had a right to appear first at Bow Street police court, Hardcastle escorted his prisoner into the dock of Number One Court.

'Rollo Henson, charge of murder, Your Worship,' cried the gaoler.

The hacks in the press box immediately started scribbling. Although murder cases appeared at Bow Street from time to time, they were nevertheless rare.

'You have an application, Mr Hardcastle?' asked the Chief Metropolitan Magistrate, as A Division's DDI stepped into the witness box.

'I respectfully request a remand in custody, Your Worship.'

'Remanded until Saturday the sixth of July when I shall take a plea,' said the magistrate, as he made a note in the ledger.

Since returning from court, Charles Marriott had spent all morning examining the papers seized from Henson's house.

'I think it's time for a pint, Marriott,' said Hardcastle, appearing in the doorway of the detectives' office.

'I've just found a couple of interesting things, sir,' said Marriott as he stood up. 'First of all there's a letter addressed to Chester Smith and signed Queenie. It had been through the post and was delivered to Disraeli Road, Putney.'

'What does it say, Marriott?'

'Nothing of value, sir. It merely said that everything was all right. I suppose that was in answer to a query raised by Henson.'

'Fat lot of good that is,' said Hardcastle. 'But if we're going to prove that Rollo Henson and this here Chester Smith are the same person, we'll get Inspector Collins to examine the Disraeli Road address for fingerprints and then compare them with Henson's prints. See to it, Marriott. What else did you find?'

'Henson's cheque book, sir.'

'Another one?' exclaimed Hardcastle. 'But we found his cheque book among Hannah Clarke's possessions at Worthing.'

'I suspect she stole it, sir, intent on forging one of the cheques.'

Hardcastle laughed. 'Oh dear, Marriott. Ain't it wonderful when villains fall out?'

'There's a stub in this one, sir,' said Marriott, flourishing the cheque book taken from Manwood Road, 'that shows he issued a cheque in favour of Warne's Hotel on Friday the twenty-first of June. I've made some enquiries and there is a Warne's Hotel in Worthing.'

'That didn't show up on the accounts we examined at the bank,' said Hardcastle.

'It probably hadn't been cleared by then, sir,' said Marriott.

'Really?' said Hardcastle, who was not too conversant with banking procedure. 'That was the day that Hannah Clarke's body was discovered on the beach.' He rubbed his hands together. 'In that case we'll definitely have a pint, Marriott, and this afternoon we'll go to Worthing. Has that photographer who took Henson's picture when he was nicked come up with the prints yet?'

'Yes, sir. Delivered this morning while we were at court.'

'Bring some copies with you, Marriott.'

Determined to waste as little time as possible, Hardcastle and Marriott arrived at Ann Street police station in Worthing at three o'clock that afternoon.

'Good afternoon, sir.' The station sergeant hurried across and lifted the flap in the counter to admit the London detectives.

'Is the superintendent in his office, Sergeant?'

'Yes, sir. Shall I show you up?'

'I know where it is,' growled Hardcastle, and mounted the stairs.

'Ah, you've returned at last, Mr Hardcastle,' said Superintendent Ronald Potts sarcastically.

'I require the services of Sergeant Burgess again, Mr Potts,' said Hardcastle.

'I'm afraid that Sergeant Burgess is engaged on other duties,' said Potts dismissively, as though that were an end to the matter.

'Nevertheless it's vital that I have him to assist me.'

'Is there any chance that you might catch this murderer of ours, Mr Hardcastle?' asked Potts. 'The Chief Constable has expressed his concern to me about your lack of action.'

'Well, Mr Potts, you can tell your Chief that I have a man in custody who probably committed the murder of the woman you know as Kitty Gordon. Once I have the evidence he'll be appearing at the Old Bailey in due course.'

'*The Old Bailey!*' exclaimed Potts heatedly. 'If he's to appear anywhere it should be the assizes at Lewes.'

'I'm charging him with one other murder and very likely two more,' said Hardcastle mildly, 'all of which occurred in the County of London. There is no chance that the Director of Public Prosecutions will sanction separate trials just so that you can have the glory of chalking that one up in your books.'

'But that's outrageous.'

'And that is why I require Sergeant Burgess to assist me in making sure that the evidence against my prisoner is watertight. I wouldn't like to have to complain to the Chief Constable that you're obstructing me in the execution of my duty, Mr Potts.'

'How dare you speak to me in such an insubordinate manner. I shall make a formal complaint about your attitude.'

'You'll need a witness to support your complaint, Mr Potts,' said Hardcastle, a half smile on his face.

Potts levelled his gaze at Marriott. 'You heard what Mr Hardcastle just said to me, Sergeant, didn't you? It's your bounden duty to—'

'I'm sorry, sir, what did you say? Marriott looked vaguely at the superintendent. 'I wasn't really listening.'

'Damn you, the pair of you. Speak to Inspector Weaver. He'll arrange to get Burgess for you.' And with that capitulation, Potts returned his attention to the file he had been reading when Hardcastle had burst into his office.

'You should really pay more attention to what people are saying, you know, Marriott,' said Hardcastle as he and Marriott descended to the ground floor.

'Yes, sir, of course, sir,' said Marriott, but being behind the DDI, he did not see that Hardcastle was smiling.

'Mr Weaver,' said Hardcastle, as he pushed open the door of the inspector's office.

'Hello, sir. What can I do for you?'

'I've most likely nicked your murderer for you, Mr Weaver,' said Hardcastle, and explained about the arrest he had made. 'And now I need your Sergeant Burgess again. I've spoken to Mr Potts and he's reluctantly agreed to release him. Perhaps you'd arrange it.'

'Of course, sir. He's patrolling at the moment, but I know where he'll be making his next point.'

Ten minutes later, a breathless Sergeant Burgess arrived at the police station. 'Mr Weaver tells me you've made an arrest, sir,' he said.

'Indeed I have, Burgess, and now I need your help to tie up the loose ends. We'll start at Warne's Hotel. Perhaps you'd call a cab.'

'But it's no more than quarter of a mile from here, sir,' said Burgess. 'It's on Marine Parade at the corner of York Street.'

'You worry too much about the cost, Burgess, but a walk in the sea air will do us good. Don't you think so, Marriott?'

'I'll just change into plain clothes, sir,' said Burgess. 'I keep them here, just in case.'

'Very resourceful,' murmured Hardcastle.

EIGHTEEN

'**M**r Burgess, what brings you here? No trouble, I hope.' The manager of Warne's Hotel, immaculately attired in morning dress, crossed the foyer towards the group of police officers.

'These gentlemen are from New Scotland Yard, Mr Quilter.'

'I'm Divisional Detective Inspector Hardcastle, Mr Quilter,' said the DDI, 'and this is Detective Sergeant Marriott.'

'How can I help you, gentlemen?'

'Show Mr Quilter the photograph, Marriott,' said Hardcastle.

'We believe that this man stayed here on the night of Thursday the twentieth of June last, Mr Quilter,' said Marriott, handing the manager the photograph of Rollo Henson.

'I can't say that I recognize him,' said Quilter, having studied the photograph carefully. 'Is he in some kind of trouble?'

'We suspect him of having committed a murder here in Worthing around that date, Mr Quilter,' said Hardcastle.

'Good heavens,' exclaimed Quilter. 'Would that be connected with the girl who was found on the beach near the pier?'

'That's our conclusion,' said Hardcastle.

'The clerk who handled the booking for that day is more likely to be able to assist,' said Quilter, and led the way across the foyer to the reception counter. 'Shaw, these gentlemen are from the police.'

'Yes, sir?' said the clerk, apparently unimpressed by this announcement. For a man who, during the course of his service, had greeted both King Edward the Seventh and King George the Fifth, the arrival of the police was of no great moment.

'Mr Shaw, would you look at this photograph and tell me if you've seen this man before?' said Marriott.

Shaw studied the photograph carefully. 'Yes, sir, I recognize him. He stayed here. If you'll bear with me one moment, I'll tell you when.' He turned to a ledger and thumbed quickly through the pages. 'Ah, here we are. He booked in under the name of Mr R. Henson and he stayed here on the night of the twentieth of June.'

'Are you quite certain about that, Mr Shaw?' asked Hardcastle.

'I'm positive, sir,' said Shaw.

'Is there a particular reason that you remember him?'

'Yes, sir. When he returned to the hotel that evening and asked for his key he was out of breath, sir, and he seemed to be somewhat animated about something.'

'Did he say what?'

'No, sir, and it was hardly my place to enquire.'

'What time was this?'

Shaw gave the question some thought. 'It would've been about eleven o'clock that evening, sir,' he said eventually. 'And the gentleman left early the next morning.'

'Was the booking just for one night, Mr Shaw?' asked Marriott.

'Yes, sir. Just the one night. He'd arrived at about three o'clock the day before.'

'Had he booked in advance?'

Shaw referred to the ledger once more. 'Yes, sir, by telephone on the eighteenth of June.'

Hardcastle turned to the manager. 'Would it be possible to release Mr Shaw from his duties for half an hour or so, Mr Quilter, in order that he can make a written statement?'

'Of course, Inspector.' Quilter turned to the clerk. 'You can use my office, Shaw.'

'It's very likely that Mr Shaw will be called to give evidence at the Old Bailey in due course, Mr Quilter.'

'I quite understand, Inspector,' said the manager. 'A dreadful business. Things like that aren't good for the holiday trade.'

'They weren't too good for the victim either,' said Hardcastle.

Once Marriott had taken a statement from Shaw, the three officers left the hotel.

'What's next, sir?' asked Burgess.

'The shop that sold the bathing dress,' said Hardcastle, this time insisting on taking a cab.

*   *   *

Rebecca Kersh, the manageress of the fashion shop, appeared surprised when the three police officers entered her shop only four days after their last visit.

'Good afternoon, gentlemen.'

'Good afternoon, Miss Kersh,' said Hardcastle. 'We'd like another word with your assistant Miss Craig, if that's possible.'

'Of course. She's having a break at the moment. Come through to the staff room.'

Dorothy Craig had just finished her cup of tea and was about to return to the shop when the policemen entered the room.

'Miss Craig, these officers would like to speak to you again.' Rebecca Kersh turned to Hardcastle. 'I'll leave you here if this is suitable for your purpose,' she said, and addressing the shop assistant again, added, 'There's no need to rush back, Miss Craig. Business is remarkably light this morning.'

Hardcastle did not wish to waste any time. 'Sit down, Miss Craig. I'd like you to look at the photograph that Sergeant Marriott will show you, and tell me if you recognize the man.'

Dorothy Craig looked carefully at the photograph. 'That's the man who purchased the bathing dress the day before that poor girl was found drowned,' she said without hesitation.

'You're quite sure, Miss Craig?' asked Marriott.

'I'm certain,' said Dorothy Craig. 'It's the only one we've ever sold and it's the only time I've ever sold a lady's bathing dress to a man.'

'I'll need you to make a written statement to that effect, Miss Craig,' said Hardcastle.

'But I made one when you were here before, Inspector.'

'Yes, I know, but in this one you will identify the man in the photograph, Miss Craig,' explained Hardcastle gently. 'And you will probably be called to give evidence.'

'Good gracious! Where?'

'Probably at the Old Bailey in the City of London,' said Marriott.

Dorothy Craig looked suitably impressed. 'Gosh!' she exclaimed. 'Isn't that where they try all the famous murderers?'

'Yes,' said Hardcastle, 'and some not so famous ones.'

Once the statement was taken, Hardcastle, Marriott and Burgess moved on to the restaurant where, it was thought, Henson had taken Hannah Clarke for what proved to be her last supper.

Dismissing the restaurant manager's protests that they were 'rather busy' just now, Hardcastle showed him the photograph of Rollo Henson.

'D'you recognize this man, Mr Morrison?'

'Definitely. That's the man who came with the pretty girl on that Thursday night, Inspector. The day before she was found on the beach,' said Morrison. 'I've no doubt about it.'

Once again, a statement was taken to add to the growing pile of evidence against Rollo Henson.

'Ever given evidence at the Old Bailey, Burgess?' asked Hardcastle, as they waited outside the restaurant for a cab to appear.

'No, sir,' said Burgess.

'Well, you will when this case comes up. And just to make sure that you'll be there, I want you to find the pier-master's man who found the murdered girl's clothing in the lifebelt locker and take a statement from him detailing what he found and when he found it.' But Hardcastle's device was to ensure that Burgess would be away from Worthing for at least a week. And was designed more to inconvenience Superintendent Potts than to oblige the young Worthing sergeant.

'Very good, sir,' said Burgess enthusiastically.

'And now Sergeant Marriott and me will make our way back to London, Burgess.'

It was close to nine o'clock by the time that Hardcastle and Marriott returned to London.

'I think we've done enough for one day, Marriott, and a very satisfactory day too.'

'I don't think there's any doubt that we've got the right man, sir.'

'The right man, Marriott?' Hardcastle stared at his sergeant. 'Of course we've got the right man. Now then, as far as tomorrow's concerned, I wonder where Sergeant-Major Cuthbert Curtis, barrister-at-law, will be on a Saturday morning.'

'Either at home or at the recruiting office, I suppose, sir.' Marriott could not understand why Hardcastle needed to see Curtis again.

'Find out, Marriott. I want to talk to him.' Hardcastle glanced at his watch, wound it and dropped it back into his waistcoat pocket. 'I think we'll have an early night. See you at eight tomorrow morning. Get off home now and give my regards to Mrs Marriott.'

'Thank you, sir.' Marriott did not share the DDI's view that nine o'clock constituted an early night. 'And mine to Mrs H.'

Marriott's first job on arriving at the police station on Saturday morning was to telephone the Central London Recruiting Office in Great Scotland Yard. At ten o'clock he tapped on Hardcastle's door.

'Mr Curtis is on duty at the recruiting office this morning, sir.'

'We'll walk down and have a chat with him, then,' said Hardcastle.

Together the two detectives strode down Whitehall towards Trafalgar Square. Hardcastle paused to buy a box of matches from a one-legged ex-soldier, and later he and Marriott stopped to doff their hats to a passing military funeral.

'Will it ever be over, Marriott?' Hardcastle's question was a rhetorical one; the roll of dead from the Great War seemed unending.

'According to the papers things are going well out there, sir.'

They turned into Great Scotland Yard and mounted the steps of the recruiting office.

'Hello, Inspector,' said Curtis, rising from behind his desk. 'What brings you here?'

'Some assistance if you have a moment, Mr Curtis.'

'By all means. Come into the office.'

'You're probably aware that I've arrested a man named Henson for the murder of Georgina Cheney, Mr Curtis,' said Hardcastle, once the three of them were ensconced in Curtis's tiny office.

'I saw a brief piece about it in *The Times*, Inspector,' said Curtis. 'It was also the subject of much gossip up at the Bailey, mainly because Henson is a barrister.'

'Quite so. In that connection I've a favour to ask.'

'Fire away.'

'Rollo Henson claimed that he was at a bar mess dinner the night of Mrs Cheney's murder, but I'm certain that he wasn't. D'you know of a reliable source who I might ask, and who would be willing to give evidence?'

'Which Inn of Court did Henson belong to, Inspector?'

'Inner Temple, Mr Curtis,' said Marriott.

'Ah, you're in luck, then. That's my inn, too. Now, let me see . . .' Curtis spent a few moments thinking and then wrote a name on a slip of paper. 'Mr Justice Cawthorne is the man to see. He's something of a trencherman and never misses one of these dinners. Have a word with him.'

'But I can hardly expect a High Court judge to come to court to give evidence, Mr Curtis.' Hardcastle sounded perturbed at the very thought of seeing a High Court judge in the witness box rather than on the bench.

'You may be right,' said Curtis, with a smile. 'He'll probably make a written statement that will be accepted in evidence by the presiding judge at Henson's trial. I doubt that any defence counsel would have the courage to argue with that. Except perhaps Edward Marshall Hall,' he added wryly.

'Where are we likely to find this judge, Mr Curtis?' asked Marriott.

'He sits in the Probate, Divorce and Admiralty Division. You'll find him at the Law Courts in the Strand. Best thing is to find his clerk and he'll arrange for you to see the judge when he rises for lunch. But you'll have to wait until Monday; I doubt that he'll be sitting on a Saturday. That's the best I can do, Sergeant Marriott. To coin an apt phrase, High Court judges are a law unto themselves.'

'It looks as though that's all we can do until Monday, sir,' said Marriott, as he and Hardcastle walked into Whitehall. He was hoping that the DDI might decide to take the rest of the weekend off, but that hope was immediately dashed.

'D'you remember Etherington telling us that he met Georgina Cheney at some charity function at the Langham Hotel, Marriott, and that she'd arrived with another man?'

'Yes, sir.' Marriott referred to his pocket book. 'Etherington told us that it was on Saturday the eleventh of May.'

'So it was, Marriott, so it was.' Hardcastle hailed a cab. 'Langham Hotel, cabbie.' And turning to Marriott, said, 'We'll see if they know who brought Georgina Cheney to this do when Etherington took her off of him.'

'We're police officers,' said Hardcastle, and identified himself to the Langham Hotel's concierge.

'How may I be of assistance, Inspector?'

'There was some sort of charity affair held here on Saturday the eleventh of May,' said Hardcastle.

'Ah, one of many, sir. In aid of the war wounded, I seem to recall. But then most of them are.'

'I dare say,' said Hardcastle. 'Do you have a guest list for that there function?'

'Indeed I do, Inspector.' The concierge opened a drawer in his desk and rummaged around until eventually he produced a dog-eared document. 'Was there someone in particular you are interested in?'

'Does the name of Rollo Henson appear on your list?'

'Henson, Henson,' muttered the concierge, as he ran his finger down the column of names. 'Yes, he we are: Rollo Henson accompanied by Mrs Georgina Cheney.'

'I bloody thought so, Marriott,' exclaimed Hardcastle. 'So much for his story that he'd not seen her since leaving Malta.'

'Shall I take a statement, sir?'

'Yes,' said Hardcastle, and addressed the concierge. 'I'm seizing that document and my sergeant will take a statement from you saying that the list you've handed him was a true list of those attending that function here on the night in question.'

'I'm not sure the manager would like you to take that, sir,' said the concierge, somewhat disturbed at what he saw as Hardcastle's high-handed action.

'Well, he'll just have to lump it,' said Hardcastle. Turning to Marriott, he asked, 'Have you got that photograph of Henson with you?'

'Yes, sir.'

'Good. In that case we'll go to the Wardour Hotel and see if anyone there can identify Henson as the man who was with Hazel Lacey the night she was topped.'

'Yes, sir.' Marriott could see the rest of Saturday slipping away.

The visit to the Wardour Hotel in London's West End proved to be disappointing. As 'Posh Bill' Sullivan had said, the reservation had been made by telephone the day prior to the murder by a man calling himself Kenneth Reeves. But no one recalled having seen the mysterious Kenneth Reeves. Hardcastle was in no doubt that Reeves was Henson, but mere supposition was not enough.

However, Hardcastle was a more resourceful detective than those who had investigated Mrs Lacey's murder. Leaving the hotel, he stopped and spoke to the linkman. 'Have you worked here long?' he asked.

'For the past two years, sir. Ever since I was invalided out of the Life Guards in '16. Squadron Quartermaster Corporal, I was.'

'I see you were in South Africa,' said Marriott, noting the man's Boer War medal ribbons. 'And Mons.'

'That I was, sir. A bloody rout was that Mons caper an' all.'

'I'm a police officer,' said Hardcastle. 'What's your name?'

'Jethro Walsh, sir.'

'Well, Walsh,' said Hardcastle, 'I'm investigating the murder that took place here on the twenty-seventh of March.'

'Oh, I remember that, sir. A right to-do that was.'

'In that case, have a look at this photograph.'

Jethro Walsh took a pair of glasses from a pocket in his ornate tunic, and looked carefully at the photograph of Henson. 'That's him, sir. Mr Reeves that is. He was definitely here that night.'

'Why d'you remember him so clearly, Mr Walsh?' asked Marriott.

'I never forgets a gent what gives me a handsome tip, sir, and Mr Reeves bunged me a sov,' said Walsh, fingering his waxed moustache.

'Did any of the police officers who were here that day speak to you?' asked Hardcastle.

'No, sir.' Walsh paused. 'No, I tell a lie, sir. There was one: a gent in a bowler hat and sporting a Piccadilly window.'

'What did he ask you?'

'He asked me to call him a cab, sir.'

Once Hardcastle had arranged a relief for the linkman, Marriott took a statement from him.

'I bloody knew it, Marriott,' said Hardcastle as they walked away from the hotel. 'Shoddy police work.'

It was unlikely that a High Court judge would be at court before ten o'clock in the morning. It was, therefore, fifteen minutes before that hour when Hardcastle and Marriott were set down outside the Royal Courts of Justice in the Strand.

'D'you know there are three and a half miles of corridors in this place, Marriott,' said Hardcastle, as they approached the door.

'I hope we don't have to walk along all of them before we find His Lordship, sir.' Marriott was amazed yet again at one of the

DDI's inconsequential pieces of information. Particularly as the police had very little to do with the civil courts.

Hardcastle approached a constable standing at the start of a long, echoing entrance hall that was dominated by high Gothic arches.

'I'm DDI Hardcastle of A, lad.'

'Sir?' The PC saluted.

'I'm looking for the clerk to Mr Justice Cawthorne.'

'Ah yes, I knows where he is, sir. I'll get one of the messengers to show you the way. If you was to get lost we might never find you again.'

Hardcastle fixed the PC with a stony stare, and the PC wiped the smile from his face.

After walking for what seemed an age, the messenger eventually tapped on a door and admitted the two detectives.

The judge's clerk was a man of about sixty, attired in the customary black jacket and striped trousers of his calling.

Hardcastle introduced himself and Marriott and explained why they wished to see the judge.

'His Lordship is just refreshing his memory with today's case papers at the moment, Inspector,' said the clerk. 'He usually goes into court at ten-thirty or just after. I'll let him know you're here. In the meantime, gentlemen, please take a seat. I've no doubt you could do with a cup of tea.'

'Very kind of you, sir,' said Hardcastle.

At twenty minutes to eleven, Hardcastle heard a voice shouting for someone called Monaghan. The clerk rose, tapped on a communicating door and after a brief conversation with the judge ushered the two detectives into his chambers.

'My clerk tells me you wish to see me on an important matter concerning a murder, Inspector.' Mr Justice Cawthorne was a jolly, round-faced man of ample proportions. His girth bore testimony to his love of bar mess dinners, and his rubicund complexion seemed to indicate a liking for port. 'Sit yourselves down.' He waved at a couple of easy chairs and sat down himself.

'I'm investigating the murder of a Mrs Georgina Cheney, My Lord,' began Hardcastle. 'And I've charged a barrister by the name of Rollo Henson with that murder.'

'Yes, I read that he'd been arrested. If he's hanged he'll be disbarred you know.' Cawthorne looked gravely at Hardcastle and then burst into laughter at the DDI's bemused expression. 'Joking aside, Inspector, how can I help you?' The judge took off his spectacles and began polishing the lenses with a pocket handkerchief.

'When I first interviewed Mr Henson he claimed that on the night of the murder he was at a bar mess dinner, My Lord.'

'And you think he's lying, eh?' said Cawthorne. 'What date was this?'

'Tuesday the eleventh of June this year, My Lord.'

'Tell Monaghan to bring the lists, Sergeant,' said Cawthorne. 'He'll know what I mean.'

'Yes, My Lord,' said Marriott, and crossed quickly to the clerk's office.

Monaghan appeared a few seconds later. 'Which one, My Lord?'

'Eleventh of June.'

'This is the one, My Lord,' said Monaghan, handing a list to the judge. 'Incidentally, My Lord, counsel and parties to the action are all assembled in court,' said Monaghan, glancing pointedly at the clock.

'You worry too much, Monaghan. They won't start without me,' said the judge, who then laughed and waved a hand of dismissal. He examined the list and then looked up. 'Henson was not at the dinner that night, Inspector, and now I suppose that you want a statement from me, eh?'

'That would be most helpful, My Lord.'

'Here, give me the form. I'll write it.' Cawthorne took out a fountain pen and quickly wrote a brief statement. 'I think you'll find that this will satisfy whichever judge tries Henson's case, Inspector.'

NINETEEN

A fortnight later, Hardcastle and Marriott were summoned to attend a conference in counsel's chambers at Hare Court in that area of London known as the Temple.

'Dryden Bradley, gentlemen. I'm one of a number of counsel assisting Sir Gordon Hewart, the Solicitor-General, in the matter of the Crown and Henson,' said the barrister, as he shook hands with the two detectives. 'I'll just make some space for you to sit down.' The speaker was a tall man, some forty years of age, with a high forehead, a moustache and beard. He spent a few moments clearing a couple of chairs of briefs and law books, and deposited them on the floor. 'The Solicitor will be appearing for the Crown in this case, but if he finds himself on his feet in another court, Mr Cedric Kitchen KC will be briefed to stand in for him.'

'I've met Mr Kitchen, sir,' said Hardcastle. 'I interviewed his butler, a year or so back, in connection with the case that resulted in the conviction of Hilda, Lady Naylor. And I've appeared at the Bailey in a case Mr Kitchen was prosecuting.'

'Splendid,' said Bradley. 'Then you'll know his methods, should he be appearing.' The lawyer drew a substantial pile of paper across his desk and unfastened the pink ribbon that bound it. 'I have to say, Mr Hardcastle, that your investigation into this matter has been extremely thorough. What d'you think Henson's motive was?'

Hardcastle thought that to be abundantly clear. Nevertheless, he expounded his thoughts on the matter.

'Put simply, sir, murder for profit. I examined the bank account of Rollo Henson and found that substantial sums of money were paid into that account within days of the three murders. It seems to me that he wooed these women with the intention of stealing as much money from them as he could. And then he murdered them when they found out what he had done and threatened to tell their husbands. Of course, there may have been others who did not protest and were not, therefore, murdered.'

'Quite so, but we can't proceed on a supposition.'

'I have obtained a statement from Commander Robert Cheney, sir, and he said—'

'One moment, Inspector.' Bradley raised a staying hand and riffled through the appendix to Hardcastle's report. 'Yes, I have his statement here. He avers that the sum of about seven hundred and fifty pounds was missing from his late wife's estate.' The barrister looked up. 'And that of course equates with the sum paid into Henson's account on the twelfth of June this year.' He paused. 'Within hours of Mrs Cheney's murder.'

'That's correct, sir. However, I'm still awaiting similar confirmation from Major Hardy and Colonel Lacey that sums were missing from their respective wives' savings. Unfortunately, both officers are serving with the BEF and the army is having some difficulty in locating them.'

Bradley waved a hand of dismissal. 'It's of no great consequence, Inspector. I think we have more than enough here to hang Henson,' he said, laying a hand on Hardcastle's report. 'It seems obvious from the enquiries you made in Worthing, and the statements you obtained, that Henson also murdered the woman known variously as Hannah Clarke, Kitty Gordon and Queenie Rogers. What motive do you attribute to that?'

But it was Marriott who replied. 'Again the bank statements of Henson, sir. They show that he paid sums of money to Queenie Rogers that were roughly equal to a quarter of the sums he acquired from the other three murdered women. A handwriting expert has examined the unfinished letter found at Whilber Street, and he will testify that in his expert opinion it was written by Rogers. Reading between the lines, it seems to indicate that she was unhappy with her share of the proceeds and was threatening to expose him. And she stole his cheque book, presumably with a view to forgery.'

'That seems logical, Sergeant Marriott,' said Bradley, 'but in doing so she risked exposing her own part in this conspiracy. I think it's a safe deduction that she also made that threat verbally, and in a sense signed her own death warrant.'

'If Rogers hadn't stolen Henson's cheque book, sir, we wouldn't have found him,' said Hardcastle, and then hurriedly added, 'Well, not so soon anyway.'

The conference lasted for almost three hours, Dryden Bradley checking and double-checking every item in Hardcastle's report.

At one o'clock, he stood up and stretched. 'All we have to do now, Inspector, is to prepare for the preliminary hearing before the Bow Street magistrate, and oversee the wearisome task of depositions.' He glanced at his watch. 'Perhaps you gentlemen will allow me to buy you lunch at the Cheshire Cheese.'

'That's most kind of you, sir,' said Hardcastle.

October was a good month. British troops had captured Cambrai, and there were reports that the civilian population of Germany was starving and ill disposed to continue a war they already saw as lost. Rumours also abounded that the Kaiser's government had accepted

President Wilson's 'Fourteen Points' as a basis for peace. But those hopes were dashed when the Germans began prevaricating, forcing Wilson to declare that peace terms would not be discussed without an unconditional German surrender.

The weather was dull and unsettled, there was very little sun and the temperature consistently fell short of fifty degrees Fahrenheit. And, as it had done for most of the month, it was raining when on Monday the fourteenth of October, over three months after his arrest, Rollo Henson's trial opened at the Sussex Assizes at Lewes.

The venue of the trial surprised Hardcastle, for he had assumed that it would be held at the Old Bailey. But he was not to learn the reason until the day it began.

As Dryden Bradley had predicted, the Solicitor-General was otherwise engaged and Cedric Kitchen KC was appearing for the Crown.

Kitchen swiftly crossed the vast echoing hall with his gown flowing and his wig in his hand. He was well built and at least six foot tall, with a shock of auburn hair, and bushy eyebrows and sideburns. He was followed by the bearded Bradley, juggling a substantial brief under one arm and a law book in his hand.

'M'dear Hardcastle,' said Kitchen, 'how good to see you again. As Hewart is in the Prize Court, I'm for the Crown in this case. You've met Bradley, my junior, of course.' Kitchen shook hands with the DDI and then with Marriott. 'How d'you do, m'dear fellow,' he murmured.

'Excuse me not shaking hands, Inspector,' said Bradley, 'but as you can see my leader's using me as a packhorse.'

Kitchen sank on to one of the benches. Waiting until Hardcastle and Marriott had sat down beside him, he said, 'I think we've got this fellow Henson buttoned up, eh?'

'I'd like to think so, sir,' said Hardcastle.

'There's some young fellow called Burgess from Worthing sculling about here somewhere, along with a pretty girl called Dorothy Craig and a rather stuffy-looking chap called Morrison who runs a cafe of some sort on Worthing seafront. Apparently they're witnesses in this case, but then you'd know that.'

'That's correct, sir,' said Hardcastle, and explained the parts Burgess, Dorothy Craig and Morrison had played in the investigation.

'Yes, of course; thought I'd seen their names somewhere in me brief. He sounds a useful chap, this Sergeant Burgess. Stand up all right in the box, will he?'

'I have every confidence, sir,' said Hardcastle.

'Good, good. By the bye, we've only indicted Henson with the murder of Hannah Clarke. That's why we're here and not at the Bailey. Incidentally, she'll be referred to as Queenie Rogers throughout the trial. Don't want to confuse the jury, eh what?'

'Why only her, sir?' Hardcastle could not conceal his surprise.

'It's probably the easiest to prove, and it's a safety net, m'dear fellow,' said Kitchen. 'If he's found not guilty on that one – although I wouldn't bet on his chances – we'll go ahead with Cheney and the rest, one after another, until we get a conviction, eh what? If he goes down on Rogers, we'll take the others into consideration, if he's prepared to stand for them. After all they can only hang the bugger once, eh what?' He glanced at his watch. 'Well, we'd better be getting inside. Don't want to upset His Lordship before we've even started, eh what?' Planting his wig untidily on his head, he led the way into court.

Hardcastle was always impressed by assize courtrooms with the huge Royal Arms behind the judge's seat, and had often wondered what effect the awesome surroundings had upon prisoners indicted with murder. And quite a few such murderers had stood in the court's high dock.

The red-robed judge appeared, bowed to counsel and took his seat.

Then came the customary cry from a court official that would start the proceedings: '*Oyez! Oyez! Oyez! All persons having business before this court of oyer and terminer and general gaol delivery pray draw near.*'

'Put up the prisoner,' said the judge.

Two prison warders escorted the tall, handsome figure of Rollo Henson into the dock. Despite having been kept in custody for three months, his hair was still of a fashionable length and well cared for. Hardcastle assumed that he had paid an incarcerated barber to care for his appearance.

'Cedric Kitchen for the Crown, My Lord,' said Kitchen, rising to his feet.

'Who appears for the defendant, Mr Kitchen?' The judge made a little parody of peering at counsel's benches as if seeking the defence counsel.

'I understand that he wishes to defend himself, My Lord.'

'Does he indeed.' The judge raised his eyes to the prisoner. 'Is this correct, Henson?'

'It is, My Lord,' said Henson.

'I would remind you of the old adage, Henson, that a lawyer who defends himself has a fool for a client.'

'Nevertheless, My Lord, I wish to defend myself.' Henson returned the judge's gaze with the air of defiance of a man convinced of an acquittal.

'I will not tolerate it. You are facing an indictment for murder, and you *will* appoint counsel.' The judge took out his watch and consulted it. 'I shall adjourn until two o'clock, by which time I expect to see counsel here briefed to defend you.'

'Damn that man Henson,' exclaimed Kitchen, as he marched out of the courtroom.

When the court reconvened at two o'clock a barrister in a silk gown rose.

'Arthur Gould for the defence, My Lord.'

'Are you familiar with the case, Mr Gould?'

'Hardly, My Lord,' said Gould, in apologetic tones. 'I have only spent an hour with my client.'

'In that case, I shall adjourn until Wednesday the sixteenth at ten o'clock in the forenoon.' The judge rose, bowed to counsel and swept angrily from the court.

'That ain't pleased His Lordship, Inspector,' confided Kitchen.

'D'you know of Mr Gould, sir?' asked Hardcastle.

'Arthur Gould KC is a tolerably able counsel on the south-eastern circuit with chambers here in Lewes, Hardcastle. He'll do his best for Henson. Not that it will do that scallywag much good, eh what?'

In accordance with the judge's direction the court reconvened two days later.

The clerk shuffled his papers and looked up.

'Rollo Henson, you are charged in that on or about Thursday the twentieth of June in the year of Our Lord one thousand, nine hundred and eighteen in the Borough of Worthing in the County of West Sussex you did murder a woman known variously as Hannah Clarke, Kitty Gordon and Queenie Rogers, against the peace. How say you upon this indictment?'

'Not guilty, My Lord,' said Henson in a strong voice that echoed around the courtroom.

'Bring in the jury,' said the judge.

It was at that point that Hardcastle and the other witnesses were obliged to leave the court.

It was not until the afternoon that Hardcastle was called to give evidence. Cedric Kitchen took him through all the details of his investigation, an examination that took a total of three hours and ran over to the following day. Arthur Gould spent a further thirty minutes in cross-examination.

Over the ensuing weeks witness followed witness.

With an economy of words, Doctor Bernard Spilsbury described in clinical detail the cause of death of the woman whom he now knew to be Queenie Rogers. Finally, just to make sure that there should be no doubt in the jury's mind, he repeated that she had been strangled and expressed the opinion there was no other way in which her death could have been caused.

Sergeant Burgess spoke confidently when describing how Queenie Rogers' clothing had been found on Worthing pier, and assured counsel that the pier-master's assistant was available to give evidence if required. In fact Burgess gave the appearance of thoroughly enjoying his first sortie into the big world of an assize court. It was a performance that led Kitchen later to comment that the young Worthing sergeant had 'come up to snuff'.

Dorothy Craig refused to be shaken when identifying Rollo Henson as the man to whom she had sold the bathing suit in which the body of Queenie Rogers had been found. She was adamant that Henson was the man, and repeated what she had told the detectives: that it was the only bathing dress of that style that the shop had sold, and was the only time she had ever sold a lady's bathing dress to a man, and that was why she was so certain.

Detective Inspector Charles Stockley Collins testified that Henson's fingerprints, taken after his arrest, matched those found at Disraeli Road, an address also frequented by Queenie Rogers. He went on to give the usual supporting statistic that the likelihood of two different person's fingerprints being identical was in the region of sixty-four thousand million to one, a figure that appeared to impress the jurymen.

Roland Peachey, the manager of Williams Deacon's Bank, gave

details of the payments in and out of Henson's account, laying particular emphasis on the payments made to Queenie Rogers.

Slowly but surely the damning evidence against Henson stacked up, but despite that, such was his arrogance, he insisted on giving evidence on his own behalf, against his counsel's advice. It was a pathetic performance.

Arthur Gould rose to examine his witness. 'Mr Henson, do you admit being on Worthing pier during the late evening of the twentieth of June?'

'I do, sir.' Henson answered the question in a firm voice.

'Please tell My Lord and the jury why you were there.'

'I had met my fiancée, Miss Rogers, earlier in the evening and we had gone for supper together. We then went for a stroll along the pier. It was a fine evening and very warm, so I suggested that we went for a swim. Queenie demurred, however, saying that she had no costume, but I'd bought one for her as a surprise.'

'Where did this conversation occur?' asked Gould.

'On the pier, sir.'

'Yes, go on.'

'By then we were at the far end of the pier. There was no one about and Queenie changed quickly into the bathing dress and put her clothes into a nearby locker.'

'It's been suggested by the prosecution that it was you who undressed Miss Rogers and you who put the bathing dress on her.'

Henson smiled. 'I am not competent to deal with the complexities of a lady's apparel, sir.'

'Quite so. Did you intend to go for a swim yourself?'

'Of course. I wasn't going to let Queenie go in on her own. I knew she was a competent swimmer and she proved it when she dived off the pier.' Henson's face took on an immeasurably sad expression. 'I saw her enter the water, but she didn't surface. I waited for some time, but I could see no sign of her. At first I thought she might've been swimming underwater towards the beach. I didn't know what to do. I ran off the pier and made for the beach, but I couldn't see her anywhere. I imagined that she must've hit her head on some projection beneath the water and had been knocked unconscious. I knew then that she must've drowned.'

'Thank you, Mr Henson. Please wait there. Counsel for the Crown may wish to ask you some questions.'

Cedric Kitchen rose to cross-examine. There was none of the theatrics practised by so many barristers, like adjusting their gown or fiddling with their spectacles. Kitchen's questions were incisive and devastating.

'When you realized that Miss Rogers was missing, did you make any attempt to call someone, the police for example?'

'I didn't see the point, sir,' said Henson lamely.

'What did you do, then, Henson?'

'I returned to my hotel – Warne's in Worthing – and left for London the next day.'

'Let me make sure I've got this right. You thought your fiancée had just drowned, but you did nothing. You just went home.' Kitchen paused to emphasize that telling observation by directing his gaze at the jury. Returning his attention to Henson, he continued. 'You said in your evidence-in-chief that you suggested to Miss Rogers that *both of you* should go for a swim.'

'Yes, sir.'

'Did you have your own swimsuit with you? Or a towel perhaps?' asked Kitchen airily.

'No, sir. It was a spur of the moment idea.'

'A spur of the moment idea, eh?' Kitchen savoured the phrase. 'Although you had had the foresight to purchase a bathing costume for Miss Rogers, but not one for yourself.' He did not wait for a reply. 'You described Queenie Rogers as your fiancée, did you not?'

'Yes, sir.'

'But you are married already, are you not? To a Lydia Henson, and you live with her at Manwood Road, Brockley, London.'

'Yes, but we're getting divorced.'

'Are you really? Does Mrs Henson know about this proposed divorce?' asked Kitchen sarcastically, and once again looked meaningfully at the jury. Waiting until the subdued tittering had subsided, and in the absence of a reply he knew would not be forthcoming, he continued. 'You said that Miss Rogers was a competent swimmer, did you not?'

'Yes, sir.'

'Surely then, she would have appreciated the dangers of diving off a pier in the dark. I suggest to you that she would she have objected and proposed that, if she were to swim at all, it would have been safer to enter the water from the beach.'

'Perhaps,' said Henson reluctantly, 'but there were too many people about, and she couldn't have changed into her bathing dress on the beach.'

'But there are a number of bathing machines on Worthing beach, aren't there?'

'Yes, sir, but I think they were closed. It was late.'

'Even so, one presumes that Miss Rogers was not somehow going to clamber back on to the pier's end from the sea, was she?' Kitchen managed to lard that question with an element of sarcasm.

'I don't know, sir.'

'No, I shouldn't imagine so.' Kitchen paused to peruse his notes again. 'So, she would have emerged from the water on to the beach. Yes?'

'Yes,' said Henson.

'And walked all the way from there back to the end of the pier – a distance of some nine hundred and sixty feet – *in her bathing dress* – in order to recover her clothing?'

'I suppose, sir,' said Henson lamely, suddenly realizing that he had not given sufficient thought to his murderous plan.

'But you knew perfectly well that she would not emerge and that, therefore, the problem would not arise. I put it to you, Henson, that you chose the pier because there was no one about at that hour. No one who would have seen you strangling Miss Rogers, undressing her and attiring her in the bathing suit you had purchased for her earlier that day, and throwing her lifeless body into the sea.'

'I did not, sir,' protested Henson in anguished tones. 'I loved her. I wouldn't have harmed a hair of her head.'

'So you say, Henson, so you say. You claimed that you could not have undressed Miss Rogers because of the complexities of a lady's apparel. But you have heard evidence that the clothing found in the lifebelt locker consisted only of a light summer frock, a chemise, a pair of bloomers, and a pair of art silk stockings. Nothing too complex about that, I'd've thought. What say you to that?'

'I can only protest my innocence, sir.'

Kitchen turned to the judge. 'I have no further questions for the accused, My Lord.'

TWENTY

Three weeks later, the judge began his lengthy summing up, and eventually the jury was sent out to consider its verdict.

'D'you think he'll be found guilty, sir?' asked Hardcastle.

'British juries are fickle bodies, m'dear Hardcastle,' said Kitchen, 'but if he ain't, I'll eat me damned wig. Can't say fairer than that, eh what?'

The jury's deliberations took the rest of that day and half the next, on one occasion during which the foreman sought directions from the judge. But finally the members of the jury all agreed and filed back into the courtroom.

'Has the jury reached a verdict?' enquired the clerk.

'We have,' said the foreman.

'How say you upon the indictment of murder?'

'We find the accused, Rollo Henson, guilty.'

Henson, flanked by two warders, gripped the dock rail until his knuckles showed white. His face was ashen and beads of perspiration broke out on his forehead. Like so many 'gentlemen' murderers before him, he had been convinced that the jury would acquit him. But the jury, as it always did, comprised men of property and professional standing. As such, they were unlikely to be sympathetically disposed in favour of one of their own class who had 'let the side down'. But to Henson, the shock of his conviction at once sapped his self-confidence and destroyed his arrogance.

'Prisoner at the bar, do you have anything to say before sentence of death is passed upon you?' asked the judge.

'As God is my witness, My Lord, I am innocent,' protested Henson, hardly managing to get the words out. 'I loved her.'

The judge donned the black cap. 'Rollo Henson, you have rightly been found guilty of the heinous crime of murder. It is my view, based upon the evidence, that you saw Queenie Rogers as one who had threatened to bring you down. For those reasons, and because of your insatiable greed, you decided to be rid of her and so you decided to dispose of her in the most callous fashion imaginable.

It saddens me that a member of the bar should find himself standing before me. The sentence of this court is that you be taken from this place to the place from whence you came and thence to a place of lawful execution where, after three Sabbath days have elapsed, you shall be hanged by the neck until you are dead. And may the Lord have mercy on your soul.'

The judge's chaplain, an ascetic, skeletal individual of at least sixty summers who appeared never to have smiled in his entire life, intoned the single word 'Amen'.

It was Monday the eleventh of November, and outside the Home Office in Whitehall crowds could be heard singing and dancing to celebrate the end of the Great War, and shouting for Lloyd George, the prime minister.

Seated within this imposing building, the Home Secretary examined the docket containing details of Rollo Henson's conviction and sentence of death. But he saw no reason to interfere with that sentence, particularly as Henson, in the face of overwhelming evidence, had subsequently admitted to murdering Blanche Hardy, Hazel Lacey and Georgina Cheney. Taking out his fountain pen, Sir George Cave wrote the damning words on the docket: *'Let the law take its course.'*

At one minute to eight on the morning of Monday the twenty-fifth of November 1918, two weeks after the Armistice, the two warders who had been Henson's constant companions in the condemned cell moved a cupboard to reveal a door. They pinioned the condemned man's arms and hurried him through the door to the scaffold. Exactly sixty seconds later, John Ellis, the official hangman, consigned Rollo Henson to the hereafter.

The customary black flag was hoisted over Lewes prison, and the black-framed notice of execution was posted on the gate.

Six months later, there being nothing in law to prevent it, Lydia Henson inherited her late husband's estate. With unseemly haste, she withdrew his ill-gotten gains and returned to her native New York where she set up business as a fashion designer.

But there was a strange corollary to the case of Rollo Henson.

Several months after Henson's execution, during which time the population was slowly coming to terms with the reality of the war's crippling legacy, a constable appeared in Hardcastle's doorway.

'Excuse me, sir.'

'What is it, lad?'

'There's a Major Crawford downstairs and he's asking to see you, sir.'

'Did he say what it's about?' asked Hardcastle.

'He said it's in connection with the Henson case, sir.'

'Show him up, lad, and on your way down ask Sergeant Marriott to step in.'

Leaning heavily on a walking stick, Major Crawford, attired in civilian clothing, limped into the DDI's office. His face was badly disfigured on the left side, he wore a black patch over his left eye and the empty left sleeve of his jacket was pinned up.

'I'm Geoffrey Crawford, late of the South Wales Borderers,' announced the visitor.

'Do sit down, Major Crawford,' said Hardcastle, as Marriott hurried to position a chair. 'I didn't realize you were wounded or I'd've come down to see you rather than obliging you to climb the stairs.'

'It's of no matter.' Crawford sank gratefully into the chair.

'I'm Divisional Detective Inspector Hardcastle, and this is Detective Sergeant Marriott. What can I do for you?'

'To begin at the beginning, Inspector, I was badly wounded at the Somme,' Crawford began, 'and I lay out in a shell hole in no-man's-land for what seemed like days. Eventually I was taken prisoner by the Germans and was in one of their hospitals for months before being transferred to a prisoner-of-war camp at Fallingbostel.'

'I'm sorry to hear that, Major.'

'Apart from being wounded, I found that I'd lost my memory. Somehow or other my identity discs had been lost and of course we didn't carry any documents into battle with us; documents that might've identified me. In short I had no idea who I was, and neither had the Germans. As a consequence I was posted missing believed killed – not that I knew that at the time. However, my memory returned at about the time I was repatriated when the Armistice was declared. But when I got home, I found that my wife Amelia was dead, and she'd been buried in Chepstow. Both Amelia and I were born and brought up there, you see.'

'What does this have to do with the case of Rollo Henson, Major?' asked Hardcastle.

'I'm coming to that, Inspector. Before I joined the army, my wife

and I lived on the outskirts of Guildford, but during my absence at
the Front she frequently spent time with her married sister in Chepstow.
At some time in late 1917, it seems that Amelia had promised to
spend a couple of weeks with her sister, but she didn't arrive. Her
sister was concerned that she might've been the victim of an air raid,
and travelled to Guildford to find out what had happened to her.
Amelia's maid told my sister-in-law that Amelia had fallen down the
stairs and broken her neck. Believing me to be dead, my sister-in-law
took Amelia's body back to Chepstow to be buried there.'

'Was the matter enquired into by the Guildford Borough Police,
Major?' asked Marriott.

'I believe so, Sergeant,' said Crawford. 'From what I've gathered
they decided it was a tragic accident and that was the finding of the
coroner's inquest. But the disturbing factor is that when her estate
was put into probate it was found that she'd left all her money – a
substantial amount, I may say – to someone called Rollo Henson.
Until I read the report of the Henson case in *The Times*, the name
had meant nothing to me, and I'd never heard of this Henson.'

'I think I can explain, Major.' Hardcastle went on to give Crawford
details of Henson's catalogue of murders. 'As a matter of interest,
Major,' he asked in conclusion, 'do you happen to know the name
of the housemaid who found your wife's body?'

'I didn't know the girl personally, and neither did I ever meet
her, Inspector, but my sister-in-law told me that the girl's name was
Queenie Rogers.'

Lightning Source UK Ltd.
Milton Keynes UK
UKOW02f1507300115

245401UK00002B/12/P

9 781847 515308